Praise for the works of Maggie Brown

Pursuing ~

Brown writes well   into the
story of a repressed la\   ...nge singer.
Two people almost polar   ...traction absolutely
sparked. What I was mo.   ...u with was the characters.
The whole cast of charact. _ in this book is wonderful. Every
friend, family member, you name it, had an important role to
play. If you are looking for a good romance with a little intrigue,
give this book a shot.

-Lex Kent's Reviews, *goodreads*

This story grabbed me from the beginning and it was
extremely hard to put it down. I liked the secrets, and innuendos,
the harmony between Pandora and Winter. Loved the attraction
from the beginning. This story is really wonderful.

-Kat W., *goodreads*

The lead characters were well developed and the attraction
between them was palpable—you could tell they couldn't help
but gravitate towards one another. The other characters were
equally well written. I particularly enjoyed the fact that the
author didn't build massive angst from minor miscommunication
issues and the leads were fighting to make things work. The
author's writing style was engaging and the Australian setting
was a refreshing change.

-Melina B., *NetGalley*

It was one of the best books I've read in a while and that
is saying a LOT because there are some truly fantastic books
out there in just the last few months alone! I loved Winter so
much! She was so bold but yet so insecure... almost broken in
some respects. Pandora was so much stronger than she let on

yet there is a side of her that longs for things she thinks she can't have. The magic the two of them have is off the charts! They are vibrant, sexy, talented and fascinating. I could not get enough of them. The story is so full of drama and angst, love and lust, jealousy and joy, anger and acceptance and even a bit of danger. It is a definite must read and re-read and then read it again sort of book and you will love it too!

-Ameliah R., *NetGalley*

Reinventing Lindsey

I'm a total sucker for matchmakers falling in love, so I leapt at the chance to review this one. Despite being into the premise, I was still pleasantly surprised by how much I enjoyed it, and I couldn't put it down! I was totally engrossed by Lindsey and Daisy and the slow burn that crackles between them. Everything about the writing style worked for me.

-*The Lesbian Review*

Playing the Spy

The characters in this book were great. It wasn't just the two mains, but the supporting cast was well done too. Everyone was fleshed out and I remembered all of their names even if they didn't play a huge role. Brown definitely writes characters well. This is a book that is easy to recommend to romance fans. I really enjoyed this and expect others will too.

-Lex's Reviews, *Goodreads*

Mackenzie's Beat

A fast-paced, well-done detective story. It is exciting and interesting—a classic page-turner that could easily keep you up all night. The plot uses established crime-drama ploys to keep the story moving along, from the gradual piecing together of clues to the detective herself being threatened—and it accomplishes this very well. The main characters are welldrawn, powerful, independent women and they have a wideranging, and at times, amusing supporting cast...

-Curve Magazine

In the Company of Crocodiles

This book was great from start to finish. Hard to put down, there was always something happening or about to happen, and I genuinely wanted to reach the end and never let it end in equal measure. Maggie Brown did a superb job of keeping everything so twisted and suspenseful that the revelation at the end was exactly what you want in a good thriller—surprising yet believable.

-The Lesbian Review

The Last Time We Met

Other Bella Books by Maggie Brown

I Can't Dance Alone
Mackenzie's Beat
Piping Her Tune
The Flesh Trade
In the Company of Crocodiles
Playing the Spy
Reinventing Lindsey
Pursuing Pandora

About the Authors

Maggie Brown has nine published works, which include three GCLS finalists. She lives in Queensland, Australia, where the weather is warm, the people are laid-back and the lifestyle relaxed. As well as liking a good joke, her favorite way to relax is to chill out with a glass of wine with friends. Most of the time she sits too long at the computer, drinks too much coffee when typing, and becomes a hot mess when struck down with writer's block.

Check out her website. *Maggiebrown-books.com*

The Last Time We Met is Leni Hanson's first co-novel. A voracious reader, she has an impassioned interest in stories with lovable characters who are loyal, funny, epicurean, and assertive.

She's a wife. A romanticist. A traveler. A collector. An anything chocolate and Mexican Coca-Cola lover. A sports enthusiast of epic proportions. She lives by the motto: *Never give up, never surrender.*

The Last Time We Met

Maggie Brown
Leni Hanson

BELLA BOOKS
2021

Bella Books, Inc.
P.O. Box 10543
Tallahassee, FL 32302

Printed in the United States of America on acid-free paper.

First Bella Books Edition 2021

Editor: Cath Walker
Cover Designer: Kayla Mancuso

ISBN: 978-1-64247-191-5

Acknowledgments

Thanks again to Cath Walker for her patience and advice. She's an awesome editor.

Our appreciation to Jessica Hill for her support, and Bella Books, for publishing this novel.

And finally, to Doctors Without Borders, whose humanitarian efforts have helped tens of millions of people and inspired this book.

A Note from Leni Hanson

A million thanks to my mentor and friend, Maggie Brown, who took on the daunting challenge of co-authoring this book with a new writer. I'll always be grateful more than words can express.

Dedication

To our Moms

CHAPTER ONE

Cold sweat prickled across Merritt Harrington's skin at the sight of the ghostly line of mountains in the distance. She turned her back on the view—she never wanted to see that godawful place again. In her time with Médecins Sans Frontières, aka Doctors Without Borders, the assignment in the Andes was up there as her very worst.

Finally on her way out of Peru, her anxiety receded for the first time in weeks. She hitched her backpack onto her shoulders and fondly waved to the five nurses who hung out the windows shouting their farewells. They were the best medicine, efficient and cheery, full of jokes. Laughter always helped in horrific situations—it got you through the toughest, shittiest times.

Once the bus had disappeared into the traffic, she adjusted her crewneck sweater over her shoulders and chest. The air was cool, for though Lima was built on a coastal subtropical desert, the Pacific currents kept the temperatures low. And after the mountain-thin air and cold rain up in the Andes, her body had yet to adjust fully.

At the airport entrance, a cramp hit again in the muscle below her hip. Teeth clenched against the pain, Merritt arched her back and rotated her pelvis until it eased. The high altitude, lack of fresh food and little sleep during the last few weeks had taken their toll. Her body was a mess. And after their ordeal, the journey from Huaraz to Lima had seemed never-ending. The last thing she had wanted to do was sit on a bus for eight hours, but all available air transport had been needed for the injured. The trip had also been mentally draining, the winding curves and sheer drops exacerbating her already stretched nerves.

Inside Jorge Chavez International Terminal, she headed for the check-in counter to join the two other members of her team in the line. When they showed their passports with their DWB special visas, an attendant took them immediately to an airport lounge to wait for their flights.

Noting the comfy chairs and tables laden with drinks and food, Terry Westbrook let out a long sigh. "Now *that's* a sight for sore eyes."

The tightness around Karl Muller's mouth softened. "God, yes. I've been dreaming about this for days."

Merritt shot him a sympathetic glance. With his open grin and blue eyes that twinkled behind cute black-rimmed glasses, it was unusual for the Swiss trauma surgeon to show much stress. One of the nicest guys she'd ever worked with, he was always solid under pressure.

Terry, the third member of their unit, was from Massachusetts. She was easygoing, with short dirty-blond hair, a slightly hawkish nose and coffee-colored eyes. Contrary to Merritt who jogged occasionally for relaxation, she was a yoga fanatic with a supple, sturdy body to show for it. They'd met while working together in Virginia at the Inova Fairfax Hospital's trauma unit as residents, became best friends, and joined DWB together.

Terry was a triage and resuscitation expert, Merritt a trauma and burns specialist, and with Karl as the field surgeon, they made an efficient, respected team.

"Let's get a drink," said Terry as Karl disappeared to find somewhere to charge his phone.

Merritt rubbed her hand wearily through her hair. It felt gritty, ropey, like pieces of string. All she wanted was a long hot shower to scrub away the dirt, and to get rid of the stench of death and suffering. Or try to. "I need to take a decent shower first."

"You go ahead. I need alcohol after that fucking nightmare," Terry said with a longing look toward the bar.

All Merritt could do was nod before she hurried away. Everyone had their own way to de-stress and Terry would no doubt be tipsy by the time they boarded. She didn't blame her. She always took losing a patient hard, especially children.

In the quiet haven of the restroom, Merritt grasped the porcelain counter as she stared into the mirror. There was no doubt the two and a half years full-time with DWB had changed her, though this last mission had taken the greatest toll. Weight loss had accentuated the hollows and cheekbones, and for the first time in her life she could definitely see more than a glimpse of her mother in her reflection. Which was a good thing. Her mother was a real beauty.

Merritt's body had changed as well, much leaner after food rationing and the long grueling hike down the mountain. But the real toll had been on her mentally. She shuddered as her mind flashed back over the past three weeks. The assignment had been appalling. Her nerves had been at screaming point as they worked, always conscious that the next tremor could bring down more of the mountain, on the rescue crews this time.

When the emergency call had come through, they had been attending a briefing session at the DWB's head office in New York. An avalanche in the Andes had buried an entire mountain village of over two thousand people. With only minutes for a brief message home, they were rushed to McGuire Air Force Base to be flown by jet to Lima. From there, they'd been helicoptered up the slopes of Mount Huascaran.

Having never heard of the mountain, she'd managed a quick Internet search on the way to the airfield. Huascaran was Peru's highest peak, twenty-two thousand feet. Although popular with climbers, it had a violent history. In 1962, an avalanche had killed more than four thousand when the edge of a giant glacier broke away and thundered down its slope. Eight years later, in 1970, the great Peruvian earthquake, measuring 7.9 on the Richter scale, had a catastrophic impact on the mountain. It destabilized Huascaran, sending a section hurtling down to the valley below. Over twenty thousand people were killed that time.

The information had sent chills through Merritt. She'd wondered if this one, so many years later, was going to be as bad. If the mountain was now stable, or if another landslide would follow.

When they'd arrived there had been no time to worry about personal safety, for rescue efforts had been already well underway. Teams of emergency service personnel were digging people out from under the pile of rocks, ice, and snow. So as soon as they'd hit the ground, the work had been all-out.

A Peruvian team from Lima had been the first medical responders, followed by five nurses from National Nurses United who'd arrived an hour before their DWB unit. They'd all worked in shifts, rationing sleep time.

Air evacuation of the injured had been interrupted when the rain began. Great wet sheets that sliced ferociously into the mountain. After twelve hours, the deluge abated to constant showers. Visibility had plummeted to nearly zero, which effectively stopped anymore air rescue traffic. Every available tent housed the injured. The rain had continued relentlessly, and low clouds formed a blanket over the alps. The mountain had turned to mud and slush. Occasionally, they'd heard the rumbling of landslides in the distance, the cracking of trees. Terrifying sounds, especially at night.

Of the four hundred and two people dug out alive, only fifty had been airlifted out before the rain. When hope for any more buried survivors had dwindled, a small emergency contingent had remained to continue digging. The rest of the rescue and medical crews, as well as those villagers who could walk, had made the arduous trip down the mountain. They used every stretcher and makeshift hammock to carry non-ambulatory survivors. The landslides had wiped out established tracks, leaving gaping chasms and unstable debris. It had been a frightful slog down slick icy slopes and sometimes seemingly impassable terrain. In some parts they had to crawl around crevices and stitch rock faces with rope ladders to move the wounded. And still the rain continued. Coming down from the roof of the world, she had never experienced anything so arduous or demoralizing. Thirty-seven people had died in the tents before the descent, but they had lost a further twenty-one on the way down. The last, a child, three years old.

Merritt shook the disturbing images out of her mind as she showered. Twenty minutes later, clean and dressed, she went back to the lounge. Terry had a glass of wine in her hand, with another sitting on the table for her. In fresh clothes, Karl looked more relaxed as he tapped away on his phone.

He pulled his eyes from the screen to glance up at her. "You look like a different woman."

"I feel a lot better. It's amazing what a good shower will wash away."

They were silent, the unspoken hanging in the air between them. They all knew what she meant. Karl looked at the floor as if he struggled with the answer, but simply said, "It makes you value what you have. The best thing now is to have a *verdammt* good time with our loved ones and forget about this for a while."

"We're going to have a blast," said Terry.

Merritt raised her glass in salute. "We will." Privately though, she knew Terry was capable of handling the memories, but it was going to be more difficult for her this time. She made a mental note to book a counselor while on her vacation. Since she wasn't going back to the States, she wouldn't be able to access the organization's counseling service.

Although her home was a condominium in the Washington DC area, Merritt was spending the entire five-week break with her parents in Australia, something she wasn't quite sure about. She loved her mother, but her father still had the knack of upsetting her. Representing the US Senate Committee on Foreign Relations, he was in Canberra for ten weeks for special trade and border control talks. His visit coincided with the Asia-

Pacific Trade Summit being held in Australia, and on Friday night, the US Embassy was sponsoring a gala dinner and ball. He'd specifically asked Merritt to be present. She was under no illusion that it wasn't anything more than she was useful politically as a member of the prestigious Médecins Sans Frontières.

Terry was accompanying her for the first week, then flying over to New Zealand to visit her sister, Alice and her husband Ben, a policeman in Auckland.

As was their custom, they'd left "vacation" suitcases in storage at DWB headquarters ready to be shipped. From experience, they'd learned to be prepared, having often been called away at a moment's notice to somewhere halfway across the world. And as Merritt and Terry were both single with no ties, they usually took their long R&Rs together at some resort without going home. She'd thrown in a few extra formal clothes this time, knowing she was going to need them in Canberra.

"When don't you ever *not* have a good time, Terry?" said Karl with a ghost of a smile. "Just make sure you get Merritt out partying."

Terry laughed good-naturedly. "Now *that* sometimes is a challenge."

"Rubbish," exclaimed Merritt, though she knew it was perfectly true. She preferred quieter entertainment than a nightclub. They were getting too old for that scene anyhow.

"I can imagine Terry would be hard to keep—" He paused to listen to the flight announcement over the PA system. "Bern. That's me." He gulped down his beer and picked up his knapsack. "You girls have a great time. I'll see you in five weeks." He gave them both a hug before he disappeared out the door.

They waited another half an hour to board their Qantas flight to Sydney. Merritt didn't relish the twenty-five-hour trip, but business class this time was a bonus. At least they'd be able to get a decent rest. She could never master the knack of sleeping soundly in economy seats. All she ever could do was doze, invariably arriving with a stiff neck and aching back. Terry, on the other hand, was able to crash anywhere. On a rock if she had to.

As soon as the plane was in the air, Terry had her seat down and eyes closed. Figuring it would be better to sleep on the long leg across the Pacific after the Santiago stop, Merritt ordered a snack. In the quiet cabin without distractions, she thought about her future. Though she relished the humanitarian aspect of the service, there were acceptable and unacceptable risks. The Andes' catastrophe could have ended up a disaster for the medical and rescue crews. It was only luck, or the grace of God, they all weren't buried up there in the mountains.

The experience reinforced what she'd already decided. When her contract was up in six months, she wouldn't renew it. It was time she moved on. Her mental well-being was beginning to suffer. Though she'd never regret that she'd joined the organization. It had been the most fulfilling time of her life. What had attracted her most about DWB was the fact it was non-governmental and non-sectarian. She'd had enough of strict rules living with her father, sick of his nanny-state mentality.

She had no idea if Terry wanted to leave the service as well. With her unflagging good humor and laid-back attitude, she was more suited to the life. They'd met at a hospital softball game, spent the night at the after-party swapping stories and found they had a lot in common. From then on, they had become good friends. Merritt had never considered her as a lover. That sort of attraction, for her at least, had never been there. She wasn't too sure about Terry. Sometimes she got the impression she was just waiting for Merritt to say something. But she'd never pushed it.

They'd both had romances over the years. Merritt had dated two women while at Fairfax: a surgeon and an ER nurse. She'd never been able to commit to either of them for long. There hadn't been that special spark.

That *special spark*, thought Merritt bitterly. For eleven years she hadn't been able to forget how it felt. What stupid idiot would want the most humiliating moment of her life back. It was about time she buried *that* memory forever and moved on.

When she walked into Sydney International Airport, Merritt felt like Dorothy—swirling around in a tornado for weeks, finally landing in Oz. Terry had already shrugged off the somber mood from Lima and changed into vacation clothes. With her affinity for bright colors and big jewelry, she looked like she'd stepped out of *Elle* magazine. In jeans, navy blouse, and hair pulled into a ponytail, Merritt felt positively drab beside her. Though she'd managed some sleep, she felt ragged around the edges and could only reply in monosyllables to Terry's happy chatter.

On their way out of the terminal, they found the lobby swarming with the press and an excited crowd of mainly teenaged girls. As they sidled past, they craned their heads to identify the celebrity in the middle of the commotion.

Terry gave a low whistle. "Holy hell," she whispered in her ear. "It's Austen Farleigh."

Merritt froze. Here was the moment she had always dreaded, yet conversely longed for. To see her again.

Terry tugged at her sleeve. "Come on. Let's get closer. I think she's fantastic."

She should have resisted, but she allowed herself to be pulled along by Terry, who had no qualms squeezing through the fans until she stood only a few feet away from the singer.

Merritt sucked in a gulp of air. Austen looked even more breathtaking than she remembered. Her short hair was cut edgily, her body toned and taut and her face now held a striking angular maturity. She was dressed in her customary black—that hadn't changed. She looked powerful and confident, completely at ease as she joked and flirted with her fans. Not even the constant flashing of cameras seemed to faze her. She acted, and looked, the quintessential arrogant superstar.

Merritt suddenly felt jaded, her anger directed mostly at herself. All these years she had wanted someone who wasn't worth the effort. This woman was completely self-absorbed, living in a bubble of money and adulation. She wouldn't have a clue what happened in the real world. She'd probably never seen a third-world country, a refugee camp, or how a natural disaster could devastate a community.

She had indeed landed in Oz. And here was the goddamn Wicked Witch of the West.

She nearly choked when Terry called out, "Hey, Austen. Could I have your autograph, please?"

Austen turned her head toward Terry with a wink. "Sure. Whatcha name?"

"Terry...with a y." She thrust over her backpack.

Austen gave a laugh and scrawled her signature on it. When Terry took it back, Austen smiled at Merritt and gestured to her pack. "Hand yours over and I'll sign it too, babe." Her eyes held not even a hint of recognition.

Merritt shook her head, unable to stop her glare. "No thanks."

Austen looked surprised, then her eyes narrowed ever so slightly. "Suit yourself." Abruptly, she swung her head away and called out to the crowd. "Gotta go, folks." She turned to a pretty Asian woman with long straight jet-black hair, who stood beside her with a briefcase. "Let's go, Rose. Ring Mick and tell him we'll be outside in a minute."

When she moved, two men in suits appeared immediately, flanking her on either side as an airport official led them down to a private exit. They watched her go before they made their way outside to board the bus to the domestic terminal for their flight to Canberra.

They were barely seated before Terry, clearly bursting with curiosity, asked, "What on earth have you got against Austen Farleigh, Merritt? You were kinda rude to her."

"I'm just in a shitty mood. That's all."

"Come off it. I know you too well to believe that. You acted like you knew her."

"Well, she didn't act as if she knew me," snapped Merritt.

Terry threw her hands in the air. "Whoa! Don't get your panties in a knot."

"Sorry," said Merritt ruefully. "Just let's forget about her."

"Okay. But you must admit she is fuckiiinnnggg hot!"

"I guess," said Merritt with a wan smile.

All her anger gone, she slumped into her seat despondently. *She didn't even recognize me.*

CHAPTER TWO

Eleven years earlier. The University of Virginia.

"Your father expects you home for his birthday, Merritt."

At the intractable tone of her mother's voice, she knew this time it was pointless to argue.

"I'll try," she said. "But I can't stay long. I've a hundred-page research paper due at the end of the week."

As a second-year med student, it was quite true her study load was heavy, but it was only an excuse. The truth was, she hated going home. It was always the same. Her mother invariably quizzed her about who she was dating, while her father went through her grades with a fine-tooth comb.

She'd learned early in life that being Senator John Harrington's daughter wasn't much fun. No matter what she did, she never managed to live up to his expectations. He demanded perfection.

The founder of Flybynite, a company that produced night-vision devices, he'd made a fortune from big defense contracts. Ideal for the military, their revolutionary night goggles weren't powered by batteries, instead by an internal piezoelectric charge generator.

Astute and abrasive, her father thrived in the political environment, and had won his US Virginia Senate seat at the age of forty-two. He was a handsome man, as fair as his wife was dark. A former Miss Delaware, Gloria Harrington had lush black hair, striking dark long-lashed eyes, smooth ivory skin and a tall shapely figure. With her light ivory skin and brown hair, Merritt was a combination of both gene pools.

"Make sure you do," her mother said. "Jason will be coming to the party."

Merritt thinned her lips. Jason had been one of the blind dates her mother had arranged. He was good-looking—she had to give him that—but that was where it ended. She wished she could just come out and say it. But God knows how her father was going to take her being a lesbian. Nausea lodged in the pit of her stomach when she visualized *that* reaction.

After they said their goodbyes, Merritt tapped off the phone. She still had an hour to collect her research books and be gone before Austen Farleigh's CD signing was due to start. She slipped on her comfortable Manolo flats before she hurried to the stairs. Anything higher and she would have done a face plant. At five feet ten, she steered away from high heels whenever possible.

When she reached the McGregor Room, she stopped in her tracks and stared at the door. When was it ever closed during the day? Then to her dismay, she heard music and voices inside. This particular library, dubbed the Harry Potter room, was her favorite place in the college to study and usually as quiet as a church.

She checked the time again. The signing must have been moved up. She hadn't a hope of getting her books now—staff as well as students would be lining up for a chance to meet the charismatic rock star. The whole college had been buzzing about her visit for weeks. For not only was Austen a sensational singer, she was an inspiration for young people. After a meteoric rise in the music world, she had reached star status by her early twenties.

She was also one of the most photographed people in showbiz, her perfectly symmetrical face, spectacular tats and lithe body a paparazzi dream. And if the tabloids could be believed, her exploits in the bedroom were as legendary as her performances on stage. No woman, young or old, seemed immune to her charms.

Not that Merritt had to worry about that. Austen would hardly give a dork like her a second glance.

Her hand on the doorknob, she heard a voice inside giving orders, "Closer, great. Looking good. Perfect...perfect!"

Curiosity niggled. Instead of retreating down the corridor, she opened the door and slipped inside.

A half ring of bright studio lights shone on a woman dressed completely in black. Perched casually on a stool in front of the long bookcase against the left wall, she was strumming a guitar and singing softly. A cameraman, his face damp with perspiration, was enthusiastically snapping photographs from every angle.

Even though the scene wasn't provocative, sexuality seemed to billow out of her like steam. And there was no mistaking who she was. The trademark tattoos glistened and writhed down her arms as if they were alive in the artificial lighting. Merritt sucked in a breath, feeling slightly off-center at the sight. The singer looked incredible: her body taut and terrific, her hair rich with purple spikes, her eyes dark and brooding.

She watched quietly in the shadows until, unable to suppress a sudden tickle in her throat, she coughed. Immediately, the photographer turned to stare at her.

With a glare, he lowered his camera. "What the fuck do *you* want?"

Merritt sucked in a breath, feeling like she was in one of her dreams when everyone was dressed, and she was in her underwear and wanted to run but couldn't. "I'm sorry," she stuttered out, acutely aware Austen Farleigh had turned to stare at her. "I'm so sorry." With her head down, she finally found her feet and stumbled out of the room.

Unable to wipe the vision of Austen out of her mind, an hour and a half later she crept back to the McGregor room. This time it was packed, all signs of the photo shoot gone. The library's couches and overstuffed chairs were pushed to the side, and in their place stood two tables. Laughing and chatting with her fans, Austen was busy signing autographs at the smaller one. Stacks of CDs were lined up on top of the other table, where an attractive dark-haired woman wearing bright coral lipstick sat taking orders.

Merritt shuffled to the end of the line, figuring she'd better buy a CD if she wanted to meet the singer. She craned her neck to catch a glimpse of her through the crowd around the table. Austen was clearly enjoying herself, flirting outrageously as she scrawled a personal message for each customer. Her laughter was infectious, and Merritt suddenly envied her. She had never been able to let herself go like that.

She dug in her wallet for her credit card, bought the CD and shifted over to the end of the other line until it was her turn.

"Well hello, gorgeous."

Tongue-tied, Merritt blinked at Austen. Up close, she was even more stunning than her photos. Merritt could see the dimples in her cheeks, the smooth lightly tanned skin and the little cleft in her chin. Self-consciously, she pushed her CD across the table and shyly gazed into the grayish-green eyes looking up at her. It was like looking into the ocean depths— Merritt knew from her biology classes that it was a very rare color. Lucky woman.

Austen flashed her a grin as she slowly swept her eyes from Merritt's face, then down her neck to linger on her chest. Merritt shifted self-consciously. It took an effort not to cover her breasts with her arms at the blatant perusal.

She forced back her discomfit and muttered, "Hi. Would you sign this CD, please?"

"And you would be?" asked Austen with a smile.

"Merritt."

She regarded her with a distinct gleam in her eye. "That's pretty. And what do you do for kicks, Merritt?"

"Pardon?"

Austen leaned forward and winked. "Fun...what do you do for fun?"

"Oh…fun. Um… I'm a med student with a heavy class load, so I don't go out much," she replied, and then flinched. She sounded like a geek.

Austen pulled a sympathetic face. "Poor you. Having to study all the time must suck. What's there to do around here anyhow?"

"There's plenty…shows, sports, parties, bars. If you walk around the campus, colonial history is all around you." She added bashfully, "If you're interested in that kind of thing."

"For someone who supposedly doesn't get out much, you seem passionate about this place. Hey…I tell you what. Why don't you show me around?"

"Gosh, I can't do that," Merritt stuttered, feeling heat flush into her cheeks.

"Hurry up!" came a strident call behind her.

Embarrassed, Merritt turned around and mouthed, "Sorry."

She reached for her CD, but Austen quickly covered her hand. "And why not?"

"Because…well…um—"

"What say after the concert you meet me backstage and you can show me your favorite spots? C'mon, you know you want to." Her voice had lowered to a silky tone.

"Next! Next! Next!" the people behind chanted.

"C'mon, babe. The natives are getting restless."

Her resolve flagging, Merritt bit her lip and slid her hand free. She was useless when put on the spot like this. "Well, I guess I could get my work out of the way before I—"

"Good, then it's settled. What's your last name for the backstage pass?"

Merritt paused for a moment, not sure why she had agreed to this, or even if she actually had. "Harrington," she answered reluctantly.

"See you later, Merritt Harrington," said Austen and handed her the autographed CD. "Next please," she continued smoothly, looking to the person behind Merritt.

Realizing that she had been adroitly dismissed, Merritt moved out of the way. She cast a last look at the singer chatting up another girl before she headed out the door.

"*I'm a med student with a heavy class load*," she chanted, cringing as she hurried down the passageway.

She must have sounded so pathetic.

* * *

Merritt very nearly didn't go to the concert. Part of her wanted to hide in her room, complete her assignment and veg out with a couple of movies. But the other half was dying to see Austen again. If she were completely honest, she was fascinated by the rock star. After much soul searching and indecision, she changed into her white dress, black ankle boots, and black leather jacket. She arranged her hair into her usual messy bun, thinking how much she hated her mousy hair as she jammed in the pins. Finally, when she studied her reflection in the mirror, she dithered again, then added her chunky blue necklace for color.

She flashed a look at the time and picked up the pace. Once through the Roman pergolas, she made her way into the back row of the John Paul Jones arena. The concert was already underway, the stage alive with bright flashing lights and pyrotechnics. Austen was belting out one of her Grammy winners, and as usual for a performance, was dressed in studded black. Her tank top was tight, her leather pants low over her hips and her boots mirror-polished. She looked edgy, magnetic, and kick-ass bad.

Two electric guitars, a bass, drums, and an electric keyboard formed the band.

Merritt's body immediately reacted to the music. Her feet tapped, her hips swayed, her hand slapped her thighs. The wail of the guitars and the beat of the drums were loud, frenetic, mind-blowing. Austen was the consummate performer, capturing the audience with her unique voice and onstage antics. She was everywhere, swinging, gyrating, striding across the floor as if she owned the world.

Merritt sat mesmerized as the concert flashed by in a blur of noise. She had never been to anything like it. When it was over, the entire audience rose to their feet in one block. They went wild, clapping, screaming, piercing the air with whistles. Caught up in the moment, she put two fingers in her mouth and let fly a few whistles too.

With a wide smile, Austen swaggered to the edge of the stage and opened her arms in a victory salute. She swung into an encore, which brought the house down.

When the crowd dispersed, Merritt wasn't sure if she had the nerve to go backstage. Forcing down her anxiety, she climbed the steps with her pass in her hand. When she showed it to the guard at the door, he waved to the woman from the CD table.

She immediately made her way over to Merritt. "Hi. I'm Katie Bell, Austen's business manager. She asked me to look out for you. Follow me…she's out the back."

A wave of pleasure swept over Merritt. *Okay, keep cool. Austen hadn't forgotten me.* "Oh, right. So she…um…still wants a tour?"

"Absolutely."

"Great," Merritt said, her stomach tight. Half of her was numb and the other half wanted to give a skip of delight.

Austen was outside on the phone at the side door exit. She looked up with a grin and motioned for them to take a bench seat while she leaned up against the wall blatantly staring at Merritt. Merritt shivered.

Katie patted Merritt's arm and winked. "I'll leave you two alone."

Merritt, torn between saying "Please stay" and "Ciao", simply whispered hoarsely, "Thank you."

Austen stuffed her cell phone back in her pocket. "Hi, babe." She pushed off the wall and moved closer.

Too close for comfort. Merritt shuffled backward awkwardly and hastily dug the paper out of her purse. "I…I put together a list of a few places most people like to see when they're here."

Austen raised an eyebrow. "Ah…you wanna play the tourist guide." She plucked the sheet out of Merritt's fingers with a flourish. "Let's make this more interesting, shall we? What do you think I'd like to see?"

Merritt gave an involuntary swallow when her list disappeared into Austen's rear pocket, then pulled herself together. Right, this probably was more fun. "Old Cabell Hall and the Amphitheatre."

"Why?"

"Your major would have had to be music," she stated emphatically.

"Fuck no," said Austen with a grin. "I didn't get the opportunity to go to college. I had to stay home and work."

"Well I'm glad you've succeeded with your music," said Merritt shyly. "Your concert was incredible. I loved your singing before, but now…wow, it'll always be special."

"Thanks, babe. That's a very sweet thing to say. It was fun out there tonight. The audience was one of the loudest we've heard. My favorite stop so far on this tour. But our band still has some ways to go before we get right to the top. We've done the States and now we need international exposure. We're off to Europe at the end of the year. We've got a gig in Rome before we tour the rest of the Continent." Austen leaned toward her, eyes hooded, "Now that's all about my career. What say we just start walking and see where it takes us, hmm? Follow the yellow brick road…make our dreams come true." She hummed a tune.

Merritt stared at her mesmerized and nodded.

As they strolled through the historic buildings, Austen took her hand. They talked quietly, sharing things like it was a first date. Caught up in the moment, Merritt lost all track of time. But she was acutely aware of the hand nesting in hers, the thumb rhythmically stroking her palm, the contrasting hot touch against her cool skin.

After nearly an hour, Austen gave her hand a squeeze. "Time we found somewhere to relax. The guys are having a party, but I'd prefer just the two of us. Do you know somewhere private we can go?"

Merritt went weak at the knees. Austen wanted to spend more time with her. She wracked her brains. "Um…there's a small lounge in my apartment building. It'll be empty this time of night. Everyone will be either in bed or out partying."

"Perfect," Austen purred in her ear.

The lounge was on the far side of the building, not as popular as the bigger rec room, but Merritt loved it. It was quiet and comfy and as she predicted, empty. Austen immediately turned on the lamp in the corner and switched off the main light. She sank into the lounge, her face soft at the edges in the glow. "Sit with me, babe."

"Um…would you like a drink?"

"Nah. I just want to chill out. I'm a bit stuffed after the performance." Austen patted the space beside her. "Come here, babe. I really like you a lot. You're not like other girls. There's something about you." She pinned her with a gaze that had an unspoken invitation of hidden delights.

Overawed, Merritt sat down self-consciously, though careful not to be too close. This cozy room wasn't such a good idea. She hadn't a clue how to handle this. Twenty-three years old and her sexual experience was woeful. To appease her mother, she'd gone out on a couple of blind dates with boys. They had never gotten past heavy petting, which she'd hated. Early this year, she'd dated a girl who was just as inexperienced. Remembering their fumbles in bed still made her cringe. After a month they'd called it quits, promising to keep in touch. Merritt had never heard from her again.

She wasn't so naïve not to know Austen was in another league entirely from college girls. The woman was supposed to be a goddess in bed. She knew she was completely out of her depth and hoped she didn't make a total hash of it.

She sunk into the chair. *Relax! Relax!*

Austen immediately leaned closer and whispered, "May I take your hair down?"

She nodded dumbly. When the pins were tugged out, her hair tumbled to her shoulders.

"Beautiful," Austen murmured, fanning out the strands with her fingers. She gathered the hair to one side and lightly touched her lips behind her ear. Goose bumps rippled across Merritt's neck and her toes curled.

When she felt the lips ghost up her neck and heard the husky voice in her ear, "Can I kiss you?" Her stomach knotted.

"Umm…okay," she agreed, bobbing her head nervously.

Austen inched forward, her breath warm on her cheeks, her lips a hair's breadth away from hers. Finally, slowly, she dipped that last distance to brush them over her mouth. Delicately, like the touch of a butterfly wing. But she didn't linger there, instead moved over her eyelids and cheeks. When she claimed her lips the next time, she was firmer, more possessive.

The aching pressure of the lips on hers made Merritt's skin tingle, her heart race. Austen's tongue pushed between her lips, and she immediately parted her mouth. The stroking tongue sent shivers down Merritt's spine. She squirmed, relishing how good it felt. Desperate for more, she looped her hands over Austen's shoulders to pull her in closer until their breasts were touching. She deepened the kiss. Still Austen didn't hurry her maddening strokes.

Completely turned on, Merritt took the initiative. She grasped a fistful of hair, pulled Austen's head even closer, and sucked her tongue deep in her mouth. Swirling her tongue around, flavor flooded her mouth. Austen tasted sweet, with a touch of peppermint and a hint of tobacco.

Addictive.

When they came up for air, Austen murmured, "Fuck you're hot. I could kiss you all day."

Needing no second invitation, Merritt sealed their lips together again. This time it was Austen who moaned.

When they pulled apart, Austen said breathlessly, "Do you want to see my tats?" Without waiting for an answer, with a quick twist she hoisted her tank top over her head. Merritt stared, captivated at the sight of the perfect small breasts encased in the black sports bra. Though she had never seen the point of marking her body, Austen's tattoos were the sexiest things she had ever seen. When she flexed her muscles, they rippled through her skin as if they were alive.

"You can touch them," Austen whispered in her ear.

Very gently, Merritt ran her fingertips lightly over the ink, tracing each intricate line.

When she looked up, their eyes locked. Her heart tripped as a slow smile spread over Austen's face. Then her shirt was deftly pulled open, her bra loosened, and Austen's hand was on her breast. Merritt arched into her, overwhelmed how good it felt. She groaned, skating her hand over the muscles of the lithe back. With a swift movement, Austen spread her body on top of her. She pinched a nipple, then rolled it in her fingers until it was hard as a gemstone. She bent down and licked it with her tongue.

Light-headed, Merritt took a deep breath when she realized she'd forgotten to breathe. The waves of sensations kept coming as Austen cradled her breasts in her hands, and squeezed as she worked the nipple. She played her like a guitar, gently strumming her until she was as taut as the strings.

When Austen sucked the nipple hard, Merritt braced her hand on the side of the seat as the exquisite tingles shot like arrows to her clitoris. She gasped. *Wow!* She'd never felt anything like it. Her skin was so sensitive, it felt like she was ready to burst into flames. The muscles in her pelvis automatically tightened when Austen's right hand reached her navel. Her body on fire, Merritt was beyond thinking rationally as the hand crept down and lightly massaged her lower abdomen. She begged for more.

Just as Austen's fingers slipped between Merritt's legs and hit the bundle of nerves, they both jerked as calypso ring tones from a phone broke the quiet. When Austen paused, Merritt huffed out. "Please...please don't stop."

"Sorry babe, I gotta answer this. Only a few people have this number." Austen pulled her hand out Merritt's pants and dug the phone out of her pocket. After a glance at the ID, she sat up straighter. "What's up, Ellie?"

Without a backward glance, she climbed off the couch and moved away to the kitchenette to take the call.

Her body nearly exploding with arousal, Merritt tried to relax back on the couch. She had never experienced anything like the ache burning between her legs.

When Austen answered, "No kidding. You're filming in Rome the same time I'm there? That's fucking fantastic." The words were muffled but loud enough for her to catch.

After a short pause, Austen spoke again, "Sure I can talk. I'm not doing anything important. Pretty boring, actually."

Merritt flinched. Hadn't she felt anything?

The next words were an even a lower blow. "I'm at UVA in Charlottesville. You know the scene. College students fawning all over you."

Merritt's entire body clenched in horror. *No, no, no. This can't be happening.* It was perfectly clear now that the singer had no idea she could hear her. Her eyes began to sting.

"Yeah, yeah. Of course, I'm behaving myself. I always do," Austen said with a laugh.

The next time she spoke, her voice had lowered to a purr. "Sure, babe, it'll be good to see you too. We'll do something special, just you and me. Take care now."

Totally mortified, Merritt got to her feet and adjusted her clothing.

Austen whipped round at the sound. "Hey…where are you going?"

"Anywhere but here." She could barely get the words out her throat was so clogged.

Austen stared at her as though she was putting two and two together. She made a wry face. "You heard?"

"I couldn't help it. You hardly tried to be quiet." Merritt's hurt was changing quickly to intense anger. Tonight, her entire world had turned upside down. What she had known, or imagined she'd known about sexual desire, was nothing like this encounter. These had been the most intense physical and emotional feelings she had ever experienced. And in the space of that phone call, the arrogant singer had dismissed them as nothing.

Austen moved forward quickly and grasped her arm. "Don't go. I'm sorry. Let me make it up to you. I promise I'll give you something special to remember me by."

Merritt yanked her arm free. "You already have. Now get away from me."

"You're really going?"

"Damn right I am," she gulped out and fled to the stairs leading to her apartment.

In the corridor, she scrambled in her pocket for a tissue as the tears began to fall. She felt so *stupid*.

And *used*.

A searing pain hit her hard. Naturally Austen wouldn't have been genuinely interested in a geek like her. What had she been thinking? She felt like screaming. How could she have been so naïve as to let a woman like that seduce her for kicks? She was probably in there laughing about it. Gloating. Well, there was one thing for sure. She was never, ever, going to be so gullible again.

Hell could freeze over first.

And that was exactly where that bitch Austen Farleigh could go.

CHAPTER THREE

Ignoring the loud banter in the back of the band's hire bus, Austen stared out at the rolling countryside en route to Canberra. It was great to be back, good to be able to perform in Australia again after so many years. She hadn't realized how much she missed her own country. Waves of nostalgia had been hitting her hard ever since they'd left Sydney behind. The sights were all too familiar. Her childhood home had been on a farm outside Cowra, a country town west of Sydney. She could nearly smell the pungent cow manure, the sweet hay, and the distinctive scent of warm fresh milk.

But when she recalled the early hours in the milking shed, day in day out, seven days a week, the sentimental feelings vanished. They had been hard times. There were no breaks when it came to dairy cows. They had to be milked twice a day, come rain or shine. The summer months weren't too bad, but the harsh winds and cold frosts in winter cracked her hands so badly it hurt too much to play her guitar.

She drifted back into her memories. How desperately she had wanted to get away from that life. But there hadn't been a choice. She had to leave school at sixteen to work full time on the farm. Times were tough, money too short for her to go on. They couldn't afford to employ a worker and there were two more kids to feed in the house. No matter how much she and her mother argued with him, her father refused to see that the small farm was no longer viable.

Two months before her seventeenth birthday, Austen couldn't stand it any longer. Desperate, she knew if she didn't get out soon her dreams of becoming a singer would never happen. If she wanted to make a life for herself, it was time to go. She'd packed her clothes and guitar, along with the pile of songs she'd written. Ignoring her mother's pleas and her father's angry shouting, she'd walked out the door to catch the bus to Sydney.

It had been a rainy dull day, her spirits as gray as the world around her. She had her entire savings, enough for two months' living expenses if she was frugal. After the driver let her off in the city center, she'd bought a burger and fries special from McDonald's, booked into a backpacker hostel and cried herself to sleep. Her mother's anguish was imprinted under her eyelids as she drifted off. She vowed that if she ever made the big time she'd make it up to her family. Give them a life without worry.

And even though over the following months she suffered waves of homesickness that was the end of the tears.

The day after arriving in Sydney, she found an ad on the hostel notice board for a bar attendant and took a bus out to the pub. It was a dump on the wrong side of the city, but it was work and the manager didn't ask questions about her age. As sleazy as his bar, he was a hefty guy with a beer belly and a droopy nicotine-stained mustache.

After blatantly examining her from head to toe, he didn't ask for her ID but merely said, "Ten bucks an hour. Cash. You can start tonight."

It sounded like a fortune. When she nodded, he flicked his head toward the bartender. "Harry will show you the ropes. Uniforms are in the back. Your shift starts at six."

Austen soon learned that "bar attendant" was a euphemism for "waitress with benefits." The skimpy uniform barely covered her ass and her boobs, making her feel like she was on the menu as well. She lasted two nights, fired for tipping a drink over a customer who shoved his hand up her skirt.

After that, she cut her hair short, bought two men's plain shirts to wear with her jeans, and learned how to swagger. Nobody was ever going to mistake she was interested in males again. She came out of the closet proudly. Then she applied for a position at the coffee shop near the hostel. The wage wasn't great, but enough to live on and pay for music lessons.

Finally she got a break. A big one that changed everything.

Her music teacher was a retired techno singer with good connections in the industry. She was a stout woman in her early sixties, the looks that had kept her on the stage long gone. But she'd been a remarkable teacher who could get the best out of her pupils. She clearly had seen something extraordinary in Austen, for after eight months of lessons, she'd introduced her to a friend who owned a popular nightclub.

Austen changed her name, figuring there was no way she could be called Meg McRoberts if she wanted to make it. And she had complete faith in herself that she would reach the big time.

Within six months, she was the star act.

Four months later she joined a rising rock band called Black Heat, who were looking for a lead singer. They were a good bunch of guys who had a unique sound and were going places. She spent most of her precious savings at a tattoo parlor, tinted her hair blue and bought some fancy black clothes. If she was going to become well-known, she had to stand out.

After their first album and a country-wide tour, they never looked back. When bookings flooded in after the album reached number three on the charts, they moved to the States to chase the big money. Basing themselves in New York, they rented a condo in Brooklyn and hired a business manager who doubled as their agent. Katie Bell was young, smart, and progressive, already making a name for herself in the music industry with several up-and-coming clients on her books. That had been their wisest move. She took over their bookings, organized their record label and made them superstars.

Austen's popularity eventually eclipsed the band's. Four years later they became officially known as Austen and the Black Heat. The boys hadn't argued, aware it was her charisma that had taken them into fame.

A voice broke into her thoughts. "You look rather pensive," Katie remarked as she lowered into the seat beside her and handed her a Coke.

Austen pulled herself out of her reverie and clipped the tab off the can. "Thanks, just remembering. I was brought up on a dairy farm not all that far west of here. It's taking me back."

"No kidding? I had no idea. All these years you've never talked about your childhood. I thought your parents had always lived in Port Macquarie."

"No. I bought them the house for their retirement. Dad always liked fishing and he finally realized that the only way to survive in the dairy industry was to get bigger and computerized. He was too old to adapt. Mum, bless her heart, couldn't wait to leave." She smiled to herself. Her mother had blossomed when they went to the coast, no longer washed out and overworked. It took a while, but her father became happy too, embracing retirement. Catching the surprised expression on her manager's face, she added defensively, "I also gave my sister and brother the education I never got."

"Well, well. A dutiful daughter. You're surprising me today."

Stung, Austen took a sip. She was sorry now she'd shared the information. She liked to keep her professional and private life separate. Even though she and Katie had worked together for years, she wanted to keep a piece of herself to herself. "There's a lot about me you don't know."

"Geez, Austen. What's not to know? You're always in the news."

Austen's temper rose. "For fuck sake, Katie, you of all people shouldn't believe all the shitty media."

"But you have to admit there are plenty of photos out there to prove my point." Katie gave her a sidelong glance. "Tell me.

Why haven't you found a special someone amongst all the women?"

"For your information, I was in love once." As soon as the words left her mouth, she wanted them back.

"Really?" exclaimed Katie with a gleam in her eye. "Who was she? What happened?"

Austen shrugged, feigning nonchalance. Her love for Eleanor Godwin was a thing of the past, but entirely her business. "Just someone. No one you've met. You know the saying… win a few, lose a few. Do you have any *business* you'd like to discuss?"

Katie put a hand over her heart. "Sorry, I didn't mean to pry. I actually do want to run a few things by you. When do you want me to book your return flight to New York?"

"Our plans have changed. The guys have chartered a boat in Cairns for a fishing trip and want to take five weeks off instead of three to catch up with their friends and family. I want to too. The extra weeks will give us more time."

"For God's sake, Austen. Now you dump this on me. I've lined up interviews with Ellen and Jimmy Fallon in those last two weeks."

Austen sizzled out a heated breath. "Give me a fucking break. We've been working nonstop for months. You'll just have to reschedule the talk shows. It's not negotiable."

"Fine," Katie agreed testily.

"When are you flying home, Katie?"

"I'm staying in Canberra for a while. It seems to be a nice place to take a vacation, and I have an uncle who's an Aussie now and lives in Queanbeyan. It'll be great to catch up with my cousins. I've arranged rooms at the Hyatt for you, Rose, and myself for a week. I've reserved the Presidential suite for you… it has a piano if you need to work. It's also the only suite that has a kitchenette," she gave a little snicker, "but knowing your efforts in the cooking department, that will be a waste. If you want to stay on for a few more days let me know. The guys won't be staying at the Hyatt…I've booked them into an apartment to give them room for all their gear." Katie got up from the chair. "I'd better let Rose talk to you now. I know she has a few things for you to sign."

Austen turned her head to watch her weave her way back to her seat. She was surprised she'd even come—she hadn't accompanied them for years. Sometimes her business manager was a puzzle. She was attractive, elegant, and stylish, yet at forty-one she hadn't settled down with anyone. Austen knew she was bisexual, and often wondered if she had a thing for her. Once, a few years ago, they had both been drinking and Katie had kissed her. Austen had gently pushed her away. One rule she never broke—no sex with the staff. Katie had laughed it off, claiming she just wanted to see what the fuss was all about. Since then, Austen never knew where she exactly stood with her.

Rose, briefcase in hand, sat down beside her. The Chinese American, with her good humor and unflagging politeness, was a solid friend. The band's lawyer for five years, Austen was also employing her for her personal business. She had made Austen a great deal of money, over and above the CD sales, tours, singing gigs, and endorsements.

Rose snapped open the briefcase. "I've got papers for you to sign. The sale of the refurbished Manhattan apartment. The buyer is paying the full asking price and has accepted the property on an as-is basis. And the acquisition of that industrial warehouse in the Bronx. I've read through the contracts. No problems, they just need your signature. I'll have a few more items to review with you in the next day or so. After that, it'll be nice to have the opportunity to see Canberra for a week before I fly to China."

With a grin, Austen signed her name on the dotted line. "There. You've now made me richer than Croesus."

"Ha…don't give me all the credit. You're smart, Austen, that's why I admire you so much. I've seen celebrities flush their fortunes down the toilet."

"Yeah…well. I've been dirt-poor. I don't want to be that way again."

Rose carefully put the documents back into the case. "I wish you'd tell people about your philanthropy. I'm sick and tired of reading trash about you."

"Hey. That's what gets people to my concerts. They love knowing what scandals I get up to, and who's on my arm and at what function. If only they knew I prefer a quiet night at home with a good homemade meal occasionally. Being a pleasure monger can be so exhausting." She gave an impish grin and wink. "Well, most of the time."

Rose regarded her curiously. "Don't you ever get sick of the attention? The constant barrage of snapping cameras?"

"More so now that I'm getting older. But that's what people want. Show biz is all about your image." Austen contemplated her thoughtfully. She wasn't normally a sharer, but Rose was a good friend and discreet. "You know, Rose, when I was younger, in my early twenties and a rising star, I *was* the woman they made me out to be. I lived in the fast lane, shagging every woman I could. And make no mistake…there were plenty who were dying to be bedded by me. I couldn't get enough of the sex, the adulation of the fans, and what money could buy."

Austen paused for a moment, taking a deep breath. It wasn't so easy facing a few home truths. "You've got to understand how it was. When you haven't had anything, then getting everything at once makes you crazy. I was like a dog let off a leash."

Rose regarded her compassionately. "Everyone likes a good time when they're young, Austen."

"True. But you know me. I like to do things in a big way," said Austen ruefully. "But eventually it all hit the fan. My image had become my brand and my lifestyle rebounded on me. I didn't make it to first base with the woman I really wanted. My reputation had pretty much tainted hope of any sensible woman looking at me as relationship material. I'm still seen as the bad girl who plays hard, but I'm not the shagging machine they make me out to be."

"I've never thought you were, Austen. I imagine under that hugely extroverted personality of yours, you're probably very choosy. You're a charming people person and the woman who gets you will be very lucky. You have enough money to do what you like, so find yourself a wife to share a home with and cook your dinner when you're home."

"I might just do that." Austen peeped at her slyly. "You've never been interested?"

"Good heavens, no. Nanna Lan would have a fit if I brought you home."

"Just kidding. Is your grandmother still trying to get you hooked up to a nice Chinese gentleman?"

Rose heaved a long sigh. "Yes. Now that I'm visiting China, she's ecstatic. She has three for me to meet. I don't have the heart to tell her I'd prefer a woman."

"You should. Maybe she'll send over a nice Chinese *lady.*"

"Ha. No hope of that. Her mahjong cronies would be scandalized."

Austen patted her arm gently. "Seriously though. You're thirty-one, too old to be still in the closet."

"I'm out with my friends and at work," Rose said defensively. "But you're right, it's going to be hard to tell my family."

"We'll think of a strategy."

"I won't be holding my breath. My parents still have ties to the old country with my grandmama living over there, and China doesn't recognize LGBTQ rights." She rose from the seat. "I need to get some rest. I hardly slept on the plane."

When Rose had gone back to her seat, Austen closed her eyes, put on her headphones and zoned out into her own thoughts again. All her life she'd wanted security, which meant money. But now she had plenty, she wanted something more. Something to make her heart sing again. She'd been thinking a lot about that lately. Thirty-five years old, top of her game, but was she even capable of truly loving anyone again?

Then she remembered the woman at Sydney airport. She had made her sit up and take notice. It had been a long time since anyone had.

After arriving dead tired from the long flight from New York, she had been going through the motions with the crowd of enthusiastic fans when the two women appeared. They'd taken her by surprise—certainly not the usual autograph junkies. They looked professional, mature, and judging by their drawn features, had just disembarked from a long trip as well. The cheery one with the short blond hair was nice-looking, but she wasn't the one who caught her eye.

It was the tall slender woman beside her, the one frowning at Austen.

She wasn't a conventional beauty, but stunning. Her eyes were a deep blue, her wavy brown hair shone with unusual bronze highlights, her lips were kissable and full and her chin stubborn. As Austen studied her face, she had a feeling she'd seen her before but dismissed it. She'd never forget this one. When the blonde had asked her to sign her backpack, she'd been more than happy to oblige. It'd given her a reason to offer to autograph the other woman's bag. Then she'd intended to quietly ask her where she was staying in Australia.

When she'd answered with a bald *no* and a look of intense dislike, Austen was flabbergasted. When it sank in that she'd been brushed aside as if she wasn't worth the time of day, her initial annoyance turned to mortification.

It had been the crappiest feeling she'd experienced for years.

CHAPTER FOUR

Merritt gazed out the window, admiring the splendid oaks and elms that lined the suburban Canberra avenue. Halfway along, the taxi turned into the driveway of a palatial three-storied brick manor house. She stepped out, the southern sun warm against her face, the scent of spring blossoms on the breeze. She breathed deeply, the air pristine after the thick pollution in Lima.

The front door opened, and her mother walked onto the porch. Merritt gazed at her fondly. Gloria Harrington had lost neither the grace nor the looks that had won her the beauty pageant all those years ago. Now in her late fifties, she was a well-preserved elegant woman, with a figure as trim as it had been in her twenties. Merritt knew she worked hard to stay that way—Senator John Harrington would demand his wife remain an asset to his political career.

She had often wondered, especially in later years, if her mother was happy. There always seemed something a little sad about her, something not quite right in her efforts to appear the perfect wife. Not that Merritt blamed her. She never could understand how she could live with her father.

Then she was in her mother's arms, hugging her tightly. "Hi, Mom." She sniffed back a tear. She'd missed her. With one trip after another, she hadn't been able to see her for seven months. Too long. Her father hadn't been home that time. She hadn't seen him for over a year.

"Hello, dear. It's wonderful you were able to come." Gloria pulled away to examine her and her forehead wrinkled into a frown. "I hope you've been looking after yourself. You've lost weight since I last saw you. And you look very tired. I'm really pleased you're having this break with us. I can make sure you're getting your rest and eating properly."

"No need to worry. It's been a difficult few weeks and a long trip, that's all."

Gloria turned to Terry. "Welcome, Terry. It's lovely to see you again."

Terry thrust out her hand with a cheery smile. "Great to see you again, Mrs. Harrington. And thanks for having me. I'm so looking forward to seeing Canberra. I've never been here before."

"We're pleased to have you, Terry. I hope you have a very enjoyable stay. I've put you girls in the loft...you'll have the whole floor to yourselves. Your suitcases arrived two days ago... they're upstairs in your rooms. I'm sure you'll want to freshen up before dinner. We normally eat around seven thirty, so come down at seven and we'll catch up over a drink beforehand."

To their pleasant surprise, the loft was a sumptuous three-bedroom suite, with a huge lounge entertainment area, a kitchen, and a well-stocked bar. So delightful that Merritt would have been happy to spend her vacation there reading and trying out recipes. Cooking had been always a passion. She wished she had someone to come home to. There were nights when she would stretch out her arm, willing not to find an empty space. But then reality would hit—she was alone.

But now she was leaving DWB and would be settled in one place, it was time to seriously look. A few of her friends, straight and gay, had successfully found partners with online matchmaking sites. It was worth consideration.

With a whoosh Terry threw herself into a plush leather lounge chair. "Wow. Talk about living in the lap of luxury. This is going to be soooo hard to take."

"Isn't it just?" Merritt said with a grin, savoring the moment. She wasn't looking forward to seeing her father. It had been so long, she knew she was going to get the third degree. She gestured toward the bar. "Help yourself to a drink. I'm going to take a shower and change for dinner."

"Okay. I'll have a drink before dressing. Not casual, I presume?"

"Something nice…just no jeans. My father expects us to be a little dressy at dinner," Merritt said, adding apologetically, "in this day and age, that must seem a little pretentious."

"Not in the slightest. I actually think it's rather nice." Terry laughed. "I didn't imagine we'd be eating in front of the TV."

"God, no," Merritt called out as she walked through her bedroom door.

It was a charming room with a cream and pastel blue color scheme, and a large window. The queen-sized bed was covered with a plump duvet and a pile of throw pillows, while an elegant Italian lamp sat on the quaint bedside table. A thick ornate Persian rug stretched across the polished wooden floor.

She tested the bed, thankful it was soft. Like heaven after living so rough. Without a good sleep to unwind, she knew she'd overload. Knowing her father, she wouldn't be relaxing much here. No doubt there would be a constant stream of guests to entertain at dinner most nights.

She slid off the bed to shower.

When she emerged from her bedroom, Terry was already waiting, dressed in her favorite blue number that flattered her curves. Merritt had on the double-breasted pantsuit she'd bought at Saks Fifth Avenue in New York on her last visit. When she'd slipped it on, she was immediately hooked. The color and stylish cut gave her a wonderful feeling of confidence.

Terry raised an eyebrow. "Wow. Don't you look great."

Merritt gave a twirl. "I loved it as soon as I tried it on." She hooked her arm through Terry's. "Come on, let's go eat."

When they entered the sitting room, her mother gestured toward a mahogany drinks cabinet in the corner. "You get what you want, Merritt. There's a sauvignon blanc opened, or a selection of beers and spirits. I'll have the wine."

"A scotch and dry, thanks," said Terry.

"Right-o. I'll join Mom with the wine." Merritt skimmed her palm over the smooth wood. "Great bar," she remarked with an approving hum.

Once they had settled down in the chairs with their drinks, Gloria immediately asked, "How are *things*?"

"Everything's fine," Merritt answered, knowing full well the *things* she referred to was DWB. And that her mother didn't wish her to elaborate. She had objected profusely when Merritt joined the organization and had shied away from any discussion about her work ever since.

"Peru was really shit…um…awful," piped up Terry. "There were times when—" She cut off her sentence as the door swung open and John Harrington strode in.

Merritt had to admit he made a distinguished figure. Though fifty-nine last birthday, he looked still in his prime: tall and fit, with classical handsome features and hair tinged with silver at the temples. He seemed to command the room with his presence alone.

She rose to greet him, giving him an awkward peck on the cheek. Her father didn't like showing affection. "It's good to see you, Merritt," he said. "I trust you had a good flight."

"Not too bad. I managed to get some sleep on the long leg across the Pacific," she replied, though she didn't know why she bothered. He wasn't listening. He was studying Terry, a hint of hostility in his expression. Which wasn't surprising. He'd always disliked Terry, partly blaming her for Merritt's sexual preference.

And that made Merritt's blood boil. As far as she was concerned, he was a hypocrite of the highest order. She would never forget, or forgive him, for the scene when she came out to him.

* * *

October 6, 2014 had been a day to remember. The state of Virginia had finally passed the bill legalizing same-sex marriage, and her father had been a leading advocate for changing the law.

She had been so proud of him for his stance on human rights, especially LGBTQ issues. On reflection, she should have known that a leopard didn't change its spots. Her father was a homophobe—his public face was entirely different from his private one. "Home devil and street angel" certainly applied to Senator John Harrington. If she hadn't been so swept away with all the hype surrounding the landmark decision, she would have realized that being up for re-election, he needed to court the liberal vote. America was changing, the old moderates making way for the younger progressive voters. And her father was an astute politician.

But she hadn't been thinking and had taken his speeches on face value. So, she had rocked up to Sunday dinner with her prepared revelation.

After the main course was cleared away, she began tentatively, "I have something to tell you both."

Her mother looked at her with a hopeful smile. "You've met someone?"

She cleared her throat. "Um…not exactly."

Her father glanced at her with a frown. "What does that mean? What does he do?" He narrowed his eyes. "He's not married, is he?"

Merritt cursed herself for being so nervous. This was even harder than she had anticipated. "I'm not having an affair with a married man. In fact, there is no *he*."

"Has something happened at work? Is that what this is all about?" her mother asked, her face dissolving into disappointment.

"No."

"Well, out with it," her father interjected impatiently. "Dessert will be here in a minute."

"Okay. I'll just say it. There is no *he* because I'm a lesbian."

Merritt didn't know what she had expected, but it certainly wasn't the violent diatribe that spewed from his mouth. The tongue-lashing went on and on, and at one stage she thought he was going to hit her. She cringed back in the chair, but thankfully, he managed to get control of his temper before it went that far. Finally, he slammed his fist down on the table and ground out, "Never ever mention this again in my house." Then he stormed out of the room.

Shell-shocked, Merritt sat folding her napkin in squares, staring at the table. When she raised her eyes to look at her mother, she was devastated to find she was crying.

"Don't, Mom," she begged.

"Why didn't you tell me before this, Merritt?"

Merritt looked at her miserably. "Because I was afraid how *he* was going to take it. He campaigned for gay marriage for Christ sake, and I thought he wouldn't mind. Or at least would understand," she sniffled. "Why would he support us, then act like this? He's a fucking fraud."

"He just overreacted. He'll come around."

She stared at her mother, horrified. Did she really think he would? Didn't she see she had been too busy placating her husband over the years instead of protecting her daughter? "Why don't you ever stand up for me? You let him bully me."

Her mother's face crumpled. "It's not that simple."

"Rubbish!" Without another word, Merritt ran from the house.

* * *

As the night progressed, her father must have decided Terry was going to be an asset at the ball as a DWB doctor, for he slipped into his expansive affable persona. He knew how to dazzle, flashing Terry a grin occasionally, white teeth and all charm. It wasn't long before she became starry-eyed with the attention. He seemed genuinely interested as she related their various humanitarian missions. It felt oddly like betrayal to see her friend so wrapped up in him, but she didn't blame her. Nobody was immune to his charisma.

Merritt flicked a look at her mother occasionally. She seemed to be interested as well, though paled when Terry described the distressing bits. It struck her that maybe her mother wasn't as strong as she'd always thought. Just because she was a respected, composed society matron, didn't mean she was in control of her private feelings. Merritt had long since forgiven her for not defending her, especially when Merritt had come out of the closet. It seemed too mean to hold a grudge when she knew her mother loved her dearly. And she was her only child.

By the time dinner was announced, Merritt had adopted a philosophical approach. If her father wanted to play happy families for Terry, so be it. At least the absence of any conflict would make the vacation very pleasant.

"Right," said her father, offering his arm to Terry. "Shall we adjourn to the dining room? I know you girls would have brought gowns for the big gala dinner and ball on Friday night, but what about getting something new? Gloria intends taking you shopping tomorrow, so I'd like to give you a treat. Charge the dresses to me."

"That's very kind of you, Senator," said Terry with a blush.

"Nonsense. It'll be my pleasure. And I'll expect you to charm the guests. There'll be delegates from across the Asia-Pacific region. You can be US ambassadors. Who better to represent our fine country than two humanitarian doctors?" He flashed a winning smile. "It'll be fun too. There'll be dancing, plus a very special highlight for the night. I've engaged Austen Farleigh and the Black Heat to play." He squeezed Terry's hand. "And call me John."

Merritt froze, not hearing anything more, her mind in freefall.

Oh…my…God! Austen will be there.

CHAPTER FIVE

"Wow," exclaimed Terry as their black Audi glided to a stop outside Parliament House. "This is something."

Merritt nodded as she eyed the impressive Great Verandah with its rich red granite paving. The huge Aboriginal mosaic on the forecourt was equally as eye-catching. With difficulty she climbed out of the car, the clinging gown and killer heels hard to handle after her comfy field fatigues and boots. Terry stepped out with far more elegance, she noted enviously. They waited on the sideline while the senator, with the ease of a seasoned politician, fielded questions from the crowd of reporters. She had no idea why there were so many press present, but surmised someone important must be coming. Then it clicked. Of course. They'd come to see Austen.

"It's like watching a masterclass on diplomacy," whispered Terry.

"He's had a lot of practice," said Merritt dryly, smoothing her gown while she waited. She still wasn't over the fact that the dress and accessories cost over three thousand dollars. And

Terry's had as well. When they had hesitated over the price, her mother had murmured with a satisfied gleam in her eye, "Buy up…your father's paying. It's Australian dollars, after all."

And they had. Terry loved shopping, which had made her mother's day. Merritt was impatient, never seeing the point of continuing to look once she found what she wanted. Today though, she was resigned to go without complaint. After they browsed Canberra boutiques all morning, Gloria took them to lunch and afterward to an exclusive showroom in a side street off the City Mall. Merritt suspected this was the intended destination all along, and her mother had simply drawn out the experience.

Hidden in the Aladdin's cave were a selection of hot-off-the-catwalk pieces with hefty price tags. They emerged with gowns fit for princesses. Terry had chosen a vibrant V-neck asymmetrical royal-blue satin dress with cascading ruffles. Merritt's was far less flamboyant—a very elegant form-fitting silver ankle-length gown with a low-cut lace bodice. With her mother's ruby necklace to set it off, it looked spectacular.

On the way home, Terry's eyes had misted over. "I've never felt so in love with a dress before."

Merritt chuckled. "You must really be desperate."

"I am. I hope we're still going out on the town tomorrow night," Terry asked with a hopeful look.

"You bet we will."

Merritt snapped back to the present when her parents moved again. Once through the stringent security check, they made their way into the huge foyer for predinner drinks. She gazed around, impressed. Everything in the space was marble: the floor, the numerous columns, and the two impressive staircases on either side that led to the Great Hall. Being the hosts, they were one of the first parties to arrive, but soon the room was bursting with high-profile guests, the air filled with the rich scent of a hundred perfumes.

She was commandeered immediately by her father, while Terry accompanied her mother. With a fixed social smile, Merritt tried to keep up with the introductions. She noted Terry remained mainly in the one place with her mother. Just her luck. Merritt was being whisked from one guest to the other. Most greeted her with bows or handshakes, but the delegate from Thailand offered the traditional wai. Pleased she'd taken the time to practice, she smoothly returned the gesture. She joined her hands against her chest, keeping them high to acknowledge the woman's superior rank and bowed her head. She was rewarded with a smile of approval from her father.

As they moved through the crowd, it was clear that her father wanted to greet as many people as he could, but Merritt found it tiring. She politely held a short conversation with each guest, though some had accents so thick she had to lean in to understand them. Finally, in need of a break, Merritt slipped off to the restroom.

When she emerged from a toilet stall, she lingered at the washbasins with the pretense of touching up her makeup. She was applying another layer of lipstick, when a slim Asian woman came up beside her and caught her eye in the mirror. Merritt recognized her immediately—she had been with Austen at the airport. She nodded and slid her eyes back to the lipstick tube.

A soft American accent echoed in her ear, "Hi."

Merritt swung her gaze back to the woman. "Hello," she answered as she studied her quietly. She liked what she saw. The woman had a timeless quality about her: a pixie face that glowed with a serene warmth, and shiny black hair caught in an up-do style with a few escaping strands that floated like gossamer over her ears. Very fetching and pretty. Her gaydar pinged—there was no mistaking the flicker of interest in the woman's eyes as she dropped a quick glance to Merritt's cleavage.

"I couldn't help noticing you at the airport the other day. You looked really tired," the woman remarked as she squirted soap over her hands.

"I was," Merritt replied, unable to keep the anxiety out of her voice at the memory. "We'd just flown in from Peru."

At her tone, the woman looked up to watch her reflection in the mirror. "I take it that the visit was stressful?" she said and then blushed. "I'm sorry. That was rude of me to ask."

"No…it's fine. I work with Doctors Without Borders. An assignment in the Andes. An avalanche buried a village…It was devastating."

"Ah. I read about it. Dreadful thing to happen to those poor people. You're a doctor?"

"I am. I'm Merritt Harrington. It's very nice to meet you," she replied with a smile.

"Senator Harrington's daughter?"

"Yes."

"I'm pleased to meet you, Merritt. My name is Rose Wang. I have a law practice in New York. Where's home for you?"

"I live in the Washington DC area, though I do visit New York quite a lot." Merritt tried to be casual as she added, "You were with Austen Farleigh at the airport?"

"Austen's a friend and one of my clients."

"She certainly has a dynamic personality."

"She does. Nothing much upsets her." She looked at Merritt curiously. "Why didn't you want her autograph?"

Merritt cleared her throat, feeling her face heat. "Um…I find all that fan stuff a bit over-the-top. It's just not for me. So… how long do you plan to stay in Canberra?"

"I fly to China next Thursday."

"What part of the country?"

"Guangdong. It's south on the Pearl river."

Merritt smiled at her. "Believe it or not, I've been there on a five-day tour from Hong Kong. It looked like an extremely fertile area, with every available piece of land under cultivation, even the slopes of the hills. The paddy fields were so pretty."

Rose smiled happily back. "It's one of the most important agricultural regions in China. My parents emigrated to America when I was only two, but I've been over to see my grandmama and other relatives quite a few times. I find them fascinating, so different from the people at home."

"I know what you mean. Tonight is the first time I've had the chance to meet so many Asians. They're so very…well… formal." Merritt paused and changed the subject. Rose had ties to China, and she didn't want to appear critical. "Have you been here before?"

"To Sydney but not Canberra. I'm going to sightsee mostly. You?"

"No big plans. I'm here to just chill."

A little frown furrowed into Rose's brow. "I'm not holding you up, am I? I'm sure you have more people to meet."

Merritt met her eyes with an amused gaze. "To tell you the truth, I came in here for a break. I'm not a people person like my father."

"I was escaping too," said Rose with a giggle. "One of the guys from the Chinese delegation was being overly friendly," she pouted prettily, "and he wasn't taking the hint I wasn't interested."

"Don't worry. We'll be going upstairs for dinner in a minute and you won't be sitting at his table. The delegates are in the VIP section."

"That's a relief. I guess we'd better be going. I'm sure someone will be looking for us."

"I suppose we should. Look, Rose. Um…my friend Terry and I plan to go out tomorrow night to one of the bars in town. If you've got no other plans, you're welcome to join us." The words just popped out of Merritt's mouth before she even thought about what she was saying. She blinked rapidly, having no idea why she'd done something so odd and inexplicable as to ask Rose, a stranger, to come out with them. Perhaps it was the way they had talked so comfortably, or simply just the result of the two glasses of champagne. But whatever the reason, she realized she didn't want to rescind the invitation.

Rose's eyes widened in surprise, and her face broke into a shy smile. "I would like that very much. We're staying at the Hyatt."

"Great." Merritt searched in her pocketbook for her phone. "Shall we exchange numbers?" Once done, she slipped the phone away. "I'll call you tomorrow at noon. Guess I'd better make an appearance again."

When she emerged into the foyer, her father was nowhere in sight. She noticed Rose was joined by a curvy woman who looked effortlessly elegant, all New-York sophistication. Her hair was long and sleek with the glossy look of an expensive cut and a world-class colorist. Her dress was form-fitting with a low bodice encasing full breasts. Merritt studied her, wondering why she looked a little familiar. She couldn't quite place her, but then lost sight of them as they disappeared up the far staircase.

She craned her head over the crowd until she saw Terry making her way up the opposite flight of marble stairs with her mother. Merritt hurried to catch up. Gloria flashed an affectionate smile and slid her arm through hers. "John has already escorted Madame Yin into the hall. We three can go in together."

At the top of the sweeping staircase, they stood for a moment at the door to admire the Great Hall. It looked brilliant, with the dazzling decorations and banks of sumptuous flowers. The lighting was muted, lit by glowing lamps on the tables and a light over the huge Arthur Boyd tapestry on the far wall.

"The tapestry is entirely handmade," Gloria said, slipping into the role of tourist guide. "It represents an Australian eucalypt forest, and apparently it took two years to make."

"It's fabulous," murmured Terry.

"It is," agreed Merritt. She swept her gaze around the room, across the gowned women and tuxedoed men, to lodge on the musical instruments on the stage fronting the dance floor. She wondered at the small fortune it must have cost to bring Austen and the Black Heat over here. Having seen so much real poverty, it always irritated her how governments wasted money on such excesses.

Merritt found herself seated between the Indonesian Minister of Trade and the US Ambassador to the Philippines. The men were good company, and she kept up her side of the conversation as they worked their way through the banquet. To her surprise, after the first course Austen appeared on stage with a guitar in her hand. The rest of the band was nowhere in sight. Merritt felt a thrill of excitement. She was going to sing solo.

Austen perched on the stool in front of the microphone under a single cone of light. She waited for the applause to die down before she said, "I'd like to entertain you with some light background music while you eat, folks. This first song is one I wrote a few years ago. I hope you like it."

She strummed a few chords and began to sing. It was a love song, delivered quietly. This was a new side of Austen she'd never heard. Gone was the swaggering arrogance. She looked softer, more vulnerable. It was one of the most incredible songs Merritt had ever heard—full of warmth and glowing light. Notes shimmered in the air. With her low husky voice, Austen was mesmerizing as she crooned out the lyrics.

Merritt tipped back her head and closed her eyes to imagine an expanse of stars, a raindrop on a petal, a snowflake falling. They swirled around as they merged into the tune. Seductive, breathtaking. She snapped open her eyes to find Austen staring straight at her.

Suddenly, Merritt was that naïve girl again all those years ago, slightly overweight and very earnest. When Austen smiled, she was overcome with a physical yearning, an aching to be touched. She dropped her gaze to the table and breathed in deeply.

Damnit! Things hadn't changed.

Though she was no longer that innocent girl, her emotions were the same. The torch she carried for this larger-than-life singer hadn't dimmed one iota.

CHAPTER SIX

Austen stared at the woman sitting at the front table. Her eyes were closed, and she had a dreamy expression as she listened to her song. She couldn't believe it—her mystery woman was here.

Excitement flickered through her. Though she tried to ignore it to concentrate on her singing, her eyes kept wandering back to the table. The woman had an eye-catching quality about her. The candle lamps cast soft shadows on her face, golden highlights danced on her shining hair. Her silver dress sparkled like fairy dust, the plunging neckline promising hidden delights. But Austen doubted they would easily be shared. She looked unattainable, like a painting only to be admired.

When she opened her eyes and their gazes locked, the others in the room ceased to exist. Transfixed, Austen was lost in the depths. When the woman gave her an enigmatic look, then dropped her head, the loss was so acute she nearly missed a note. She couldn't remember the last time she had that reaction to anyone. Ellie maybe, but certainly not someone she hadn't even met. As she sang through her repertoire of dinner music, Austen was more circumspect. She concentrated on her performance—time enough later to find a way to meet her, to figure out what it was about her that was different from other women.

But try as she might, she couldn't ignore her. Questions kept rolling through her mind. Who was she? Why was she at this stuffy diplomatic do? She must be someone important to be sitting at the VIP table. Austen couldn't see her as the wife of either of the men she sat between. They looked old enough to be her father, especially the Indonesian guy who had a face lined like a map. But she was holding her own, not fawning over them as she quietly talked, which meant she must be used to interacting with powerful people.

Their band usually avoided formal affairs. Diplomatic functions weren't their scene, but Katie had set up the engagement with an offer too good to refuse. A hefty fee for one night, plus their accommodation and first-class flights. They had taken the gig, figuring it was a chance to see their families and friends as well as have a vacation. Since they had been working nonstop for months, the break was timely. It also gave Austen the opportunity to sing some of her own compositions that she'd written for the solo guitar. Over the years, she'd had few occasions to bring them out.

As she sang, Austen glanced around the room, watching the multinational guests, noting how the staff weaved through the tables with practiced ease. Her gaze rested for a long moment on the huge tapestry. But as if on a string, her eyes were pulled back to that woman. She hadn't looked at Austen again as she chatted with her dining companions. Oddly, it seemed as if she was deliberately ignoring her and it was becoming irritating.

After the dessert was cleared away, Austen finished the last song in her solo segment. When she rose to take a bow, she was greeted with enthusiastic applause and couldn't help feeling a flush of pleasure. Even with a high-powered audience like this, she hadn't lost the flair for captivating a room. It had been a long time since she had been enthused about a receptive audience. And finally to be able to showcase her own work was a real high. For years, the concerts had been all the same, nothing to stimulate her anymore: same costumes, same type of songs, same screaming fans, same type of venues, only different cities.

She gave herself a mental shake. When had she become so jaded? She barely ever thought about the early times, when the shouts, whistles, and stamping feet were aphrodisiacs she couldn't get enough of. When she would study the Billboard charts like others studied the stock market. Now that she'd made it, she didn't bother. The freshness and thrill were gone, the ass-kissing barely registered now.

After a last bow, the cone of light was extinguished. As she tucked the guitar behind the drums at the back of the stage, she glanced at her watch. In half an hour the boys would be coming on to start the dance music. If she wanted to meet the mystery woman, now was the opportunity. Just how presented a problem—this was hardly the type of place to just rock up and introduce herself.

On the way down from the stage, she spied the blonde who had been at the airport. Austen had to search for the name before it came. Terry. She sat on the other end of the table between a gray-haired Asian man with glasses and a striking older woman with a classy wedge hairdo and a diamond necklace with matching drop-earrings that must have cost a fortune. When their gazes met, there was no mistaking the definite gleam of interest in Terry's eyes. She clearly batted for her team.

Austen veered toward her. Not only to have the opportunity to meet the mystery woman's friend, but to see a friendly face as well. While she was adept at mixing with all sorts, diplomats were on another level. And though she was comfortable in her own skin, she doubted she'd have anything in common with this lot.

When Terry rose with an open grin, Austen spread on the charm she reserved for special people, "Hey there. Terry isn't it? From the airport?"

"Yes. Terry Westbrook. I'm flattered you remembered," she replied coyly.

"Ah…you're not someone I'd forget in a hurry." Flirting had always been second nature to Austen.

"That's nice of you to say," murmured Terry, her eyes crinkled with pleasure. She turned to her dinner companions. "I'd like you to meet Mrs. Gloria Harrington, the senator's wife, and Mr. Ji Zhang, the Chinese Ambassador for Trade."

Zhang rose and bowed. "I'm very pleased to meet such an accomplished singer, Ms. Farleigh."

Gloria clasped her hand warmly and said softly, "It's lovely to meet you, Austen. Would you have a drink with us?"

"Thank you, I'd like that," Austen answered.

Gloria raised a finger, and a waiter appeared with a chair and an extra glass. After he poured her a glass of wine from the bottle in the ice bucket, Austen nodded her thanks and settled somewhat nervously into the seat. These two were way out of her class. Gloria reeked of old money, northeastern US by her accent. Austen's ear for dialects came with her pitch-perfect voice. All dignity and formality, the Chinese guy didn't look like he could crack a smile.

She needn't have worried. They didn't treat her like an idiot who thought economic solutions came from an ATM machine. Gloria Harrington was the perfect hostess, putting her at ease immediately. Austen's glued-on smile became genuine as she found she was actually enjoying herself listening to Terry's amusing Doctor-Without-Borders anecdotes and Zhang's dry witty remarks. In the spirit of things, she threw in her own stories of their on-tour calamities.

Gloria looked at her curiously when she talked about the band. "I understood you were a rock singer, but your dinner tunes were more like folk songs. Poignant and full of passion."

Austen felt herself flushing. "Thank you. They're my own compositions...not exactly rock music. But we're so tied up with concerts and recordings, I don't get to sing them much. One day I intend doing a solo album," she shrugged, "but with the band's commitments, it's hard."

Gloria patted her hand. "You should. They're wonderful. I have a daughter here whom I know would love to meet you." She gave a little chuckle. "I'm sure she'll jump at the chance to have a break. She must be maxed out with small talk by now."

She gestured to someone at the other end of the table. Austen swung round as her mystery woman rose from her seat.

Immediately, with a bow Zhang got up from the chair. "I'll stretch my legs while you talk," he said politely and wandered off.

Austen caught a sharp breath, strangely tongue-tied. As tall and regal as her mother, the daughter looked in complete control. The dress was eye-popping, molded to every curve of her delectable body. The neckline dipped low, with a large ruby nestled in her cleavage like a ripe plum waiting to be plucked. A tingle of desire lodged low and deep, and she had to drag her eyes up to look at her face. For a world-tilting moment, Austen was back to when she was seventeen, shy and awkward.

When she heard Gloria say, "Austen, this is my daughter Merritt," instead of her usual flirty answer, she only managed an indecipherable, "Pretty name," and offered her hand.

Merritt grasped it for the briefest possible second.

Austen cleared her throat. "And what do you do, Merritt?"

The blue eyes regarded her coolly, her face fixing into uncommunicative lines. "I'm a doctor."

"She works with me," offered Terry.

Austen searched for something to say. She knew zilch about medicine, so she stuck to what she knew. "Have you ever been to one of my shows?" she asked, then wished she hadn't. It sounded like she was self-absorbed.

A noncommittal look settled on Merritt's face. "I saw you once many years ago."

At that snippet, the hairs on the back of Austen's neck twitched. There was something about the way she tilted her head and studied her that was familiar. It nearly came, but in the next second it was gone. Surely, Merritt couldn't have been one of her casual one-nighters? She doubted it. Just because Terry was a lesbian, didn't mean this woman was as well. She wasn't giving out any signals. "Oh…right. Well, listening to us again can be a trip down memory lane."

Merritt didn't reply, merely pursed her lips. Austen swore she actually looked angry, though she hadn't a clue why. There was a little awkward pause before Gloria asked, "How long will you be staying in Canberra, Austen?"

"I'm on a five-week vacation after tonight, though I haven't made any set plans where I'll spend the time yet."

"Canberra is a lovely place. There's plenty to see here."

"I grew up not too far away from here, but I'll be happy just to chill for a while. We've been on tour for months," Austen said. Then out of the corner of her eye, she caught movement on the stage. *Damn!* The boys were taking their places. Her respite was over, and she hadn't established any sort of connection, hadn't even reached first base with Merritt. She drained the rest of her drink. "That's my cue."

"Maybe we can get together after you finish?" Terry suggested.

Relief left Austen almost light-headed. Ignoring Merritt's less-than-enthusiastic look, she grinned. "That sounds great. I've two friends here who'll be glad of the company too." Before Merritt could refuse, she said her goodbyes and hurried to the stage.

They took their places, waiting for the formal part of the evening before they played. After the Prime Minister's welcome, the guest speaker, Senator John Harrington, strode onto the stage. Austen stared at him in surprise. She had presumed the slightly harassed-looking man sitting next to Merritt was her father, not this guy with movie star good looks and buff body. He waited for the polite applause to die down before he began. But his rhetoric wasn't any different from speeches she'd heard many times before. The need for cooperation, the value of global trade…blah, blah, blah. She groaned and switched off. She'd momentarily forgotten this was a political event, but it was being driven home now.

Considering how attracted she was to his daughter, Austen took a good second look at Harrington. He was the quintessential politician, polished and articulate. But underneath, there seemed something about him that was off: too smooth, too—she searched for the word—too *practiced*. When he finally wrapped up his speech, he turned with a fixed smile to introduce the band.

To her surprise, it smacked of disapproval. Taken aback, Austen felt a stab of satisfaction as a resounding roar went up through the room. He hadn't commanded anything like the enthusiastic welcome *they* received.

She waved and bowed before she met his gaze. And there it was again, written all over his face. Real dislike. She didn't have to be a rocket scientist to know why—she'd met enough homophobes to recognize one. No matter what bullshit he had spouted to the crowd in the introduction, a self-made very successful lesbian didn't fit into his tidy upper-class world of the well-educated heterosexual.

She wondered why on earth he had engaged them. But then maybe he was just out to impress, or prove a point, to the other countries. They were, after all, superstars.

Once they began to play, the rest of the night passed quickly enough. They swung into dance mode, with a little more restraint than if they were performing at a rock concert. As a certain brilliance was expected nevertheless, Austen was determined not to disappoint. Tonight, she was out to impress, so she put her heart and soul into her performance. The audience was very receptive, not as staid as she first envisaged. Though they started out with a measure of decorum, they rapidly got into the swing of things.

She noticed Merritt didn't lack partners, which wasn't surprising. She was a breath of spring amongst the older women. She hadn't hooked up with any particular man, though Austen had to clamp down her jealousy when one clasped her too tightly. But later in the night, Austen noticed she was beginning to look at her more often. Hope blossomed. Perhaps she wasn't so immune to her as she tried to make out. Maybe she was interested after all.

At two in the morning, they wrapped it up with one of their award-winning songs. Many older guests had gone home, but there were still enough people to keep the bar open.

"Fook, that was a long night. I'm stuffed," grunted Mick, the lead guitarist, as they stacked the instruments to the side of the stage.

Austen gave a tired sigh. "I'll say. I'd forgotten what a drag a ball could be. My throat is so dry I can barely swallow. A beer will go down well."

"You bet. No partying for me tonight though," he said with a grimace.

She dug him in the ribs. "Getting old?"

"Yeah…well…we aren't twenty anymore."

"No, that we're not. I'm going to go over and have a drink with the girls. I'll catch up with you guys on Sunday at the barbeque."

"Okay. See you there."

She gave them a wave before turning to the crowd to search for Terry. She was already heading her way, dragging Merritt by the arm as she walked.

"Hey, babes," Austen said. "I'll just grab a beer and we'll join Katie and Rose if that's fine with you."

"Sure," Terry answered brightly, but Merritt seemed to be more interested in something on her shoes. "Where are your friends?"

Austen pointed toward the back of the hall. "That way."

"Right. You two head over and I'll get the drinks if you like. You must need to sit down," Terry offered. "Another vodka, Merritt?"

"Make it a half. I've had more than enough."

Terry made a clicking sound with her tongue. "'Bout time you let your hair down." She disappeared to the bar.

Austen stood awkwardly, watching Merritt who studiously avoided her eyes. Then the words just popped out of her mouth. "Would you have dinner with me one night next week?"

Merritt raised her eyes and regarded her solemnly. "I appreciate the invitation, Austen, but no thanks. Terry will be waiting with the drinks. Coming?"

Subdued, she trailed after Merritt who seemed to know where she was going. When they arrived at the table, Rose leaped up with a smile. "Merritt. I was hoping you'd join us. This is Katie."

Austen stared at them. How did they know each other? What was she missing? She sat down and scowled as a smile was quick to blossom on Merritt's face for the other two women.

"Hi, Rose. Lovely to meet you, Katie."

"Every time I looked you were dancing with a different partner," said Rose, giggling.

Merritt leaned in and elbowed her. "Yeah…well. I was keeping the American flag flying. You were very popular too, I noticed."

Rose gave a chuckle that turned into a strangled groan. "Must be my looks. I got dinner invitations from half the Chinese contingent."

They all joined in the laughter as Terry arrived with the drinks. Austen quickly downed her beer, her mood plummeting as Merritt kept up a bright chatter with the others, but barely acknowledged her.

After another round, Merritt rose to her feet. "I'm off. Jetlag still has a hold on me. Are you coming Terry? Stay if you want. I'll give you my backdoor key."

Terry cast a look at Austen. The invitation was plain in her eyes. In another time, Austen may have taken her up on the unspoken offer. Terry was attractive, sexy, and looked like she knew how to have a good time with no strings attached. Not tonight though. Terry wasn't the one she wanted. Instead, she stood up. "I'm completely wiped, so I think I'll head back to my room too and hit the sack." She glanced at Merritt to find her studying her keenly. Relief was plain on her face.

Austen winced. For fuck sake, did Merritt think her friend needed to be protected from her?

"It's time we all went to bed," said Katie with a yawn. "I'll call the cab. Do you want one as well, Merritt?"

"I see my mom's on the move." She looked at Terry who nodded. "We'll catch a ride with her. Dad will no doubt stay on. He always says the best business is done at night over a glass of brandy. Thanks anyway."

As Katie dialed her phone, Austen watched Merritt and Terry join Gloria, who threaded her arms through theirs in a motherly way, like a hen gathering her chicks.

"I'll see you later tonight, Merritt," Rose called from the door.

Austen jerked to a stop.

Merritt had asked her out? When the hell did that happen? Was it an actual date?

CHAPTER SEVEN

"You girls have a wonderful time," Gloria called out from the front door.

"Will do, Mom," Merritt said, giving her a wave before following Terry into the back of the cab.

After texting Rose that they were on their way to pick her up at the Hyatt, she sank into the upholstery, trying to tamp down her excitement. It had been a long time since she'd been to a bar or had a bed companion for that matter. Terry, she knew, was desperate to get laid. The scene at the end of the dinner flashed into her mind. It had been quite plain that Terry had wanted to go home with Austen. She had practically thrown herself at the woman. The relief Merritt had felt when Austen hadn't taken her up on the unspoken invitation, surprised her. She hated that she cared, but there it was.

Merritt stared out the window, trying not to rehash the gala. But it was impossible—she hadn't been able to get Austen out of her mind all day. Though her singing had been fantastic, it was the woman herself that was the fascination. There was something about her that just sent Merritt's heart racing and her body thrumming. Why she didn't know. She'd never had that reaction to anyone else. But seeing her up on the stage and talking to her, listening to her, the infatuation she'd harbored all those years had dug in even deeper. And the new feelings terrified her. But there was no way Austen would ever look at her other than for casual sex.

This had *heartbreak* written all over it. Blazoned in neon lights.

It was time she seriously looked for a stable loving partner. Someone like Rose.

She smiled over at Terry, catching her enthusiasm as her friend gazed out the window. Not for the first time, Merritt thought what a great pity they weren't romantically interested in each other. They were the best of friends, liked the same things and worked in the same profession. All the components of a perfect relationship, except for the most important ingredient: sexual attraction. It would be like making a cake with plain flour instead of self-rising.

As usual, she was happy to leave the night's planning in Terry's hands who was the self-appointed guru of all their entertainment activities. Merritt often thought that if Terry hadn't been such a good doctor, she would have made a perfect activities coordinator on a cruise ship. She had the knack of always knowing exactly the best places to go, no matter what city. Tonight, they were off to have dinner at The Tipsy Bull, then on to Mooseheads nightclub. Or as Terry quipped, they were going to "Get loose at the Moose."

They had crawled out of bed at nine a.m., spent the morning talking with her mother, and in the afternoon, Gloria had treated them both to a two-hour session at a luxury spa. After a massage, mineral soak, facial, manicure, and pedicure, they had floated home on cloud nine. It was amazing the power of pampering to reduce stress. Merritt had felt better immediately, the tension from the last month had eased, along with the last of the jetlag.

Tonight, she was ready for a good time. Thankfully, she didn't have to make excuses to her father for not being at dinner. He was away for two days on business.

When their taxi pulled up Rose was waiting at the pickup zone outside the Hyatt. Dressed in a red silk dress with matching red heels, and her glossy black hair piled messily on top of her head, she looked very cute.

"Mmmm…nice," murmured Terry.

Merritt chuckled. Terry's gaze wasn't on Rose's face, it was fixed on her smooth thighs under the short skirt. Merritt dug her in the ribs and whispered, "Down doggie," and scooted over to give Rose room. As she sank into the seat next to her, Merritt caught a whiff of her perfume, a mixture of jasmine and orange blossoms, delicate like Rose. "Nice dress. It looks like it was made just for you," she said.

"Thanks, Merritt." Rose smiled, showing her perfect white teeth. "Hi, Terry. Love the leather."

"Hey, Rose." Terry slid her hands lovingly over the top of her legs. "They're my favorite dance pants." She leaned over the front of the seat to the driver. "The Tipsy Bull, please."

As the taxi moved off, Rose turned to Merritt with a smile. "Thanks for asking me out, otherwise I'd be stuck in my room tonight. Katie's gone off for a couple of days with a cousin and Austen's in a huff about something."

Terry glanced at her in surprise. "What's she cranky about?"

"I've no idea what's upset her. Nothing normally fazes her."

"I imagine if she was going to lose her cool, she would have done it years ago with the paparazzi. There are pictures of her everywhere," Terry said.

"How true. Those cockroaches never leave her alone. Quite frankly, she has the patience of a saint… I wish sometimes that she'd just tell them where to go," Rose said with a snort, and smothered a chuckle. "She has enough colorful language to send them running for the hills."

Merritt eyed her curiously. "Why doesn't she, do you think?"

"She's a pragmatist, especially about her career. She just accepts that's the price she has to pay for stardom."

"You seem to know her very well," said Terry. "Merritt said that you're her attorney."

"Austen's my client. I represent the band as well. She's also a good friend." Rose hesitated a moment before she went on. "Don't believe all the trash you read about her. She's a great person and very generous. Her foundation offers scholarships in the performing arts for underprivileged girls, and as well, she helps lots of people out, including LGBTQ groups."

"So the bad-ass rocker is an old softie," Terry remarked.

"I didn't say that exactly. She has a strong personality…no pushover that's for sure."

"Not the womanizer they make her out to be?" Merritt asked, unable to keep the skepticism out of her voice.

Rose pursed her lips. "Come on, Merritt. It's gossip."

"You've never been interested?" Even though Merritt knew the question was too personal, she couldn't help asking it. It was bugging her—for some reason, she really needed to know.

When Rose raised an eyebrow, and Terry exclaimed, "Hey, that's a bit nosy," Merritt felt her cheeks go hot. "Sorry. That was out of line. It's none of my business."

"No, it's fine," said Rose softly. "She's not my type." She cocked her head and peeped up at Merritt. "Do you have a lady, or perhaps a gentleman at home?"

"No, but if I did it would be a lady."

"Ah…that's nice to know. So…what do you like doing? I get the vibes you're not a wild party girl."

"No, she's not," shot in Terry. "It's like pulling teeth to get her to go clubbing." She leaned over to Rose and said conspiratorially, "Do you want to know her big secret?"

Rose's eyes widened fractionally as she nodded.

"The lady likes to cook," announced Terry.

Merritt put her hand over her heart. "It's true. I cannot tell a lie. I'd rather stay in and cook for friends than go out."

Rose's face blossomed into a wide smile. "As it happens, I love to cook too. What's your specialty?"

"I'll answer that," Terry interrupted with a snicker. "She picks up recipes in every place we've worked and tries them out on me. I've eaten snails, grasshoppers, and a lot of unrecognizable things. The soup in Mexico was so hot, I had to guzzle a glass of water after each spoonful."

"For heaven's sake, will you never stop whining about that," exclaimed Merritt. "Just because my Spanish needs work and I added a few more chilies…"

"A *few* more! C'mon Merritt, you said later you put in an extra *half a cup*. I was letting off fire for days."

Merritt made a face when Rose dissolved into laughter. "Every cook has a disaster occasionally, Rose, as you well know. When you're in the DC area and I'm home, come for dinner and you can judge for yourself."

Rose's answer was cut short when the taxi pulled over to the curb. Merritt handed over her card. "I'll get this. You can have the first round, Terry."

"Deal."

The Tipsy Bull was a popular place. The waitress led them out to a patio to a table in front of a wall of shrubs and lights.

"This is perfect…brilliant. How did you find the place?" asked Rose.

"One of the nurses in Peru recommended it. She said not to expect anything too posh, but the food was to die for," said Terry. "What do you want to drink? Gin is their specialty."

Merritt perused the drinks list and exclaimed, "Will you look at this. It's a gin encyclopedia. There're tons and tons of gin mixtures, and I'm going to have one of these Tipsy-Tempting cocktails. The Mint Julep will go down well." She passed over the menu to Rose.

"The Fizzy Ting sounds delicious."

"I'll start off with the Passion and Vice," said Terry and waggled her eyebrows at Rose. "Hopefully, it'll be a prelude for things to come."

Rose smiled. "You wish. But I can't let you pay for mine,"

Merritt placed a hand firmly on her arm. "No way. Terry agreed to get the first round. It's not often I have a win."

"Okay. But I'll make it up to you later, Terry." Rose must have realized what she'd said, for when Terry tittered, her cheeks flushed pink.

That set the tone for the night. They started with an incredible sourdough with whipped ricotta and worked their way through a selection of tapas. They kept up a steady banter through their meal, and by the time they joined the line into Mooseheads, they were in full party mode.

Merritt thrust her wrist to be stamped by the bouncer at the door, then moved aside to wait for the others.

"Hurry up. There's a dance screaming my name," Terry urged Rose, who had been asked for her ID and was fumbling in her purse.

Merritt squeezed her arm when he finally waved her through. "Lucky you for looking so young."

Rose chuckled. "You should have seen his face when he found out I was thirty-one."

They didn't linger at the bar but headed upstairs to the nightclub. Loud music and wall-to-wall people greeted them as they stepped inside. The high-ceilinged room with flashing blue lights was rocking with revelers. The crush in front of the door didn't stop Terry. She pushed through the throngs of people like a woman on a mission. But when Merritt followed her through the jostling crowd, the image of the Peruvian avalanche suddenly shimmered before her eyes. She broke out into a sweat as momentary panic gripped her. But then Rose tugged her elbow, the flashback vanished as quickly as it had come. She shrugged it off, though reminded herself she needed to have a psych evaluation before she went back to work.

By the time they caught up to Terry, she'd reached the other side of the bar where a group of women were congregated.

"Bingo," Terry muttered. "Lesbian corner." She gave the women a wave.

"I'll get the drinks," said Rose. "What'll you have?"

After they rattled off their orders, she disappeared to the bar. "She's lots of fun. I'm glad you invited her," said Terry.

"Me too. It was a spur-of-the-moment thing and she's great company," replied Merritt, turning her head when one of the women called out, "Would you like to join us?"

"Yeah, we'd love to," Terry called back. And before Merritt could say a word, she'd dragged her over with her. Merritt just shook her head. Terry was phenomenal. Here for two seconds and they'd already joined a party.

Most of the women looked to be in their twenties or early thirties, and two in their late thirties. Rose arrived with the drinks and they swapped names. The group turned out to be military personnel from the Australian army medical corps, and when they discovered she and Terry were doctors with Médecins Sans Frontières, they were embraced unreservedly into the fold.

It didn't take long to be whisked off to the dance floor. Merritt's partner, June, was a major and a physician. One of the older women, she was tall, with fair skin, strong features and a straight military bearing. She reminded Merritt of a Swedish doctor she'd worked with in the Philippine earthquake: a commanding presence and solid as a rock. June also knew how to move, with some extraordinarily complicated steps.

Lights, lasers, and strobes flashed across the room, punctuated with confetti bursts. Merritt became lost in the dancing. At one stage, she spotted Terry dirty dancing between two women, their arms wrapped around each other in an erotic sandwich. Bodies twirled, and every so often, Rose came into view, moving in perfect synchronization with the music. She had a natural grace.

Every twenty minutes, the DJ would give them a break to top up their drinks. At the beginning of the next set of songs, seeing how popular Rose was, Merritt grasped her hand before anyone else could jump in.

"I was wondering when we'd get a chance to dance together," Rose leaned close and shouted in her ear over the noise.

"You're in demand. I had to wait my turn."

Rose gave her a wide smile. "You too."

They swung together, their steps in harmony, and Merritt was sorry when the dance ended. She took a drink break, watching the petite lawyer as she was whisked off by a stocky woman who seemed very taken with her. Rose was hard to read, treating each partner with scrupulous civility and charm. Merritt wondered what she thought of her, and if she was interested. It was hard to tell. But it would certainly be excellent to have Rose as a friend. They seemed very like-minded.

She was pulled out of her musings when Terry dragged her out of the chair. "C'mon, let's dance."

Midnight came and went. She stopped to grab a bottle of water, drank most of it, then poured the rest down her front. One of the nurses took her hand and they were back in the thick of things, swinging hips and waving arms in time to the blaring music. Tipsy now, Merritt closed her eyes, dancing off by herself into the crowd as she let the throbbing beat wash over her.

Suddenly, she felt a body press against her back and heard a throaty voice in her ear. "God, you're sexy."

A thrill rushed through Merritt. There was no mistaking the voice or the alluring cologne that wafted over her shoulder. Everyone else was forgotten. When the hands clasped her hips possessively, pulling her in closer until their pelvises were pressed tightly together, she clenched her jaw and shuddered.

"Austen," she gasped out. "What are you doing?"

When Austen took the tip of her earlobe in her mouth and lightly sucked, a spurt of need hit Merritt quick, sharp and low. Her heart flipped. She jerked away, and immediately her body protested the loss of contact. But when the hands on her hips lost their grip, Merritt stumbled. Suddenly aware a few dancers had stopped to stare, she forced herself to calm down and turned to face her. What she saw in Austen's eyes, she knew was reflected in her own.

Desire.

She turned abruptly and fled.

As she pushed through the dancers, Merritt felt completely rattled. The truth was unnerving. One touch from Austen had the power to send her libido into orbit. There was no way she had been prepared for the full-bodied hormonal rush, or the unexpected intensity of her physical response. Heat scorched her skin and her groin had clenched at the contact. Now her mouth felt parched and the ache in her belly was a wide stretch of longing.

Cool off, she ordered herself, as her heart still bumped against her rib cage. After an internal struggle, she managed to get some sort of control over her feelings. She wished she hadn't drunk so much. The old saying, "When the wine's in, the wits are out," was so true. She could hardly think straight normally when it came to Austen, let alone when she'd had a few too many.

Suddenly, somewhere to her right a loud crash reverberated above the music. With a startled gasp, Merritt twisted her head to look. For an awful moment she was back on the mountain, hearing a landslide in the distance, wondering if the vibrations would ricochet along a ridge and send the ice and mud above them sliding down. When the images vanished, she let out the long, painful breath she had been holding. She had no idea what the noise had been, but as no one had taken much notice, she guessed it was part of the sound effects.

She continued on, now feeling more subdued than flustered.

As she reached the edge of the dance floor, she felt a firm pat on her butt. It was as if she'd been doused with a bucket of cold water. Her head cleared. She stopped dead in her tracks and turned to give the young guy standing behind her a long hard stare. He stepped back quickly, lifting his hands in apology before he melted into the crowd.

Without a backward glance, she hurried away from the dancers and circled the bar. June was sitting alone against the wall, nursing a beer. Merritt pulled a seat up beside her with a heavy sigh. "Not dancing?" she asked.

"I'm taking a break. Not as young as I used to be," June answered as she eyed Merritt closely. "You look upset. Something wrong?"

"I'm fine."

"Nonsense. I can see something's bothering you. Want to talk about it?"

Her emotions still raw, Merritt's first inclination was to refuse. But she hesitated. June was not only a doctor, but also a high-ranking officer. She would no doubt be well versed in counseling her troops. She angled her head to study her. Deep-set eyes, strong square jaw, hair cut stylishly short and makeup subtle. A calm, strong face radiating empathy. And Merritt needed to get some troubles off her chest. June mightn't be able to help with her personal turmoil, but she could with her professional stress. She would have been in many dangerous situations, and familiar with facing death. "I wouldn't mind discussing something," she began tentatively.

"I'd be happy to listen. Let's go out on the patio and you can tell me all about it. It's too loud in here to hear each other and I could do with some fresh air."

Merritt nodded and followed her outside to a corner nook away from the noise. They leaned over the railing, standing close together for an intimate chat. After a deep breath, Merritt began. "It's work-related and I'd value your professional opinion. My last assignment was horrendous and I'm having some flashbacks."

June tilted her head to scan Merritt's face. "What happened?"

"We were called to an avalanche in Peru. It had buried an entire mountain village."

"I saw the news footage. It was appalling. Tell me about it."

"Two thousand people lived in there. Only four hundred and two were dug out alive. But that wasn't the worse of it. It started to rain…and I mean *really* rain with zero visibility. It went fucking on and on. No helicopters could get in, so we had to keep the survivors alive on the mountain in the cold and wet until more rescue crews arrived to help. Moving the injured down the mountain was the worst." She related the events of the horrendous trek, every agonizing detail, not glossing over how difficult and distressing it had been.

Abruptly, she began to shake as the images overwhelmed her.

June took her arm firmly. "Take a deep breath. That's it… in…out… in…out."

Merritt gulped in the air, blinking away the threatening tears. After a moment the panic subsided and she relaxed.

"Good girl," murmured June. "Do you want to continue?"

Merritt nodded. "Yes. I need to get this out. I've been bottling it up."

"Go on. But stop if it gets too much."

Merritt looked at her with a grimace. "The worst of it was, all the time we were on that awful mountain I was thinking there could be another landslide anytime. Every noise had my teeth on edge. I was terrified." She slumped against the railing, her heart racing. "On the way down, despite our efforts, another twenty-one died before we reached Huaraz. We tried, but we couldn't keep them all alive. It was really shitty to be so helpless."

June clasped her hands, the warmth soothing Merritt's now ice-cold skin. "Hey, don't be so hard on yourself, Merritt. Of course, you were scared—who wouldn't be. No one expects miracles in situations like that. Just think about those you saved." She gave her hands a squeeze. "Tell me…what's triggering the flashbacks?"

"Loud noises. Bustling crowds."

"That's usually what sets off this kind of response. How long have you been working for the DWB?"

"Two and a half years."

"Full time?"

"Yes."

June looked out over the city as she turned over the information, and then gazed back to Merritt. "That's a long stretch. Field missions can burn you out. I'll give you the name of a friend of mine here in Canberra who'll help you. She's the best counselor I know for your type of stress. I refer my staff who have trouble adjusting after their overseas tours to her."

"Thanks. I'd appreciate that."

"If you give me your phone, I'll put in her name and number. Make sure you tell her I sent you and she'll fit you in." She gave Merritt's arm a reassuring pat. "Even though this is the first time you've had anything like this, you shouldn't ignore it."

"I won't. And thanks, I appreciate your help," Merritt said as she handed over her phone. She took a quick glance at June's left hand. Her ring finger was bare.

June gave her a lopsided grin. "Glad to hear you're sensible. Doctors are the worst for ignoring their health. Me included. Now come on inside and I'll get you a drink. We could both do with one. What will you have?"

"A half scotch and dry, please," Merritt said, forcing her mind firmly back into the present. As she idly watched June walk to the bar, she thought what a nice, all-round package she was. She wondered if she was seeing anyone. And what a pity Terry was leaving for New Zealand in a week. June would be ideal for her. A steadying influence. Not that her best friend ever took up with women like her. Which was a shame. Someone like June would be a far more suitable partner than all the good-time girls Terry insisted on dating.

There was no more time to dwell on things when she heard a babble of voices nearing from the dance floor.

"Where did you disappear to?" asked Rose, her face flushed pink from the exertion.

"I got a little claustrophobic out there and took a break. It's been years since I was out on a dance floor that crowded."

Rose swept her hair back into order and grinned. "It's been a long time for me too. I forgot what it was like. I'll sleep well tonight."

Merritt glanced over at Terry who had her arms around the waists of two nurses. She doubted her friend was going to get much sleep tonight.

At the sound of excited chatter from the cluster of women, she craned her neck to see what was causing the commotion. When her eyes lit on the object of their attention, she stared in alarm.

Ohmygod!

Austen was approaching, her face creased in an easy smile, her body gliding gracefully like a black panther. She was easily the most alluring woman in the room. Merritt swallowed, trying to ignore the tingles that rippled across her skin. She plastered on a nonchalant expression as she stood back in the corner while the others swarmed around the rock star. After Rose introduced her around, she was monopolized by the army women and, not surprisingly, nobody was interested in dancing again.

"We're throwing a barbeque at three tomorrow afternoon," Austen announced after she had settled in. "Everyone's welcome and bring your mates. The boys in the band would love some feminine company too. There's a pool if you want a swim." With a winning smile she rattled off the address.

"Do you want us to bring drinks?" asked someone in the crowd.

"No. We've ordered plenty."

"The ultimate lesbian poster girl," June murmured in Merritt's ear.

Merritt looked around to find June behind her, her mouth quirked in a sardonic grin. "She is at that," she replied, eyeing June closely. "You don't seem impressed."

"I love her music but she's far too full of herself for me. Besides," June raised a hand and slowly tucked a strand of hair behind Merritt's ear, "alphas aren't my type."

Merritt blinked, not knowing how to answer. The last thing she wanted to do was lead June on, and it was now clear the soldier fancied her. She opened her mouth to change the subject, then broke off when she heard the all-too-familiar husky voice in her ear. "Hey, Merritt. Who's your friend?"

"Um…this is June, Austen. She's the commanding officer of the medical corps."

"June Bergin," June said, thrusting out her hand.

Austen shook it, and deliberately moved closer to Merritt until she was a hair's breadth away from touching her. "Great to meet you, June."

Merritt smiled, watching them size each other up as they exchanged small talk. When Austen closed the gap until she was touching Merritt, June's forehead creased into a frown and her lips tightened. Merritt's skin tingled. She wanted to move away, but she didn't want to make a fuss about it. So she stayed put, trying to ignore her body that seemed to have a mind of its own. It was straining to press closer into Austen. Finally, she couldn't stand it any longer and excused herself to go to the restroom.

Brooding over the liberties Austen was taking with her, she joined the line to the toilets. By the time it was her turn to enter a stall, she was seething. How dare Austen act so possessively. She hardly knew her, and on top of that, had completely forgotten their encounter at UVA. And *that* memory lapse was beginning to piss her off.

As well, she had made it clear she wasn't interested when Austen asked her on a dinner date at the ball. But obviously, Austen wasn't going to take no for an answer. She clearly wasn't used to rejection. Well, she was going to have to get used to this one.

After fussing with her hair and applying fresh lip gloss at the long mirror above the hand basins, Merritt stepped out into the corridor. Austen was leaning casually against the wall outside, her eyes pinning her the moment she left the room.

Merritt ignored the intense look and said gruffly, "There's no line now."

"I was waiting for you."

Merritt crossed her arms, hugging her elbows tightly. "Oh? Why?"

"Come on, babe, you must feel the chemistry between us. It's off the charts."

Immediately, the hunger was back. Merritt ruthlessly quashed it down. "Is that one of your pickup lines?"

Austen's eyes changed, the green faintly deepening. She moved forward until there was less than a foot between them. Nearly the same height, Merritt couldn't help herself. She dropped her gaze a fraction to the full lips. Immediately, a spark flared. Her reaction was not lost on Austen. Her mouth spread into a sultry smile. "How about this then. I'd like to give you a long, slow kiss, the kind that slides over with melting sighs and heats up your blood. And I want to taste you."

Merritt shuddered. She already knew how Austen tasted. She carried the flavor inside her. Eleven years and she still couldn't rid herself of it.

Without another word, Austen took Merritt's face in her hands, and pressed her lips lightly against hers.

It took an enormous effort for Merritt to step away. Austen's lips were so soft, so perfect, so right. "Please…don't…touch me. Nothing's going to happen between us, Austen. Tempting, but I don't do casual."

"Who said this was casual?"

"It's hardly anything else. Just think of yourself as forbidden fruit."

"Ohhhh," murmured Austen. "Forbidden fruit am I? Just remember we crave what we can't have."

Don't I know it, Merritt inwardly groaned. "Maybe, but we're not going there. I'm leaving to go back to the others now."

Austen looked solemnly at her. "I won't give up that easily."

"It won't do you any good. I'm sorry," Merritt said and hurried off down the corridor.

The others were making moves to leave when she returned. With a smile, June edged her to the side. "May I take you home, Merritt?"

Merritt froze, then caught the beseeching look Rose was throwing at her. She gave a sigh of relief at finding a way out of refusing without being hurtful. "Thanks for asking, June, but I did promise I'd see Rose home. Will you be at the barbeque tomorrow?" She glanced at her watch. "It's after midnight so I'll rephrase that to tonight."

"I definitely intend to now."

"Good, then I'll see you there." She waved to Rose. "Are you ready to leave?"

"I'm ready. What about Terry?"

Merritt glanced over at her friend. She caught her eye and tossed her head in the direction of the door. Terry shook her head with a grin. "She won't be coming home with us, Rose."

Without comment, Rose raised a delicate eyebrow. Austen was nowhere in sight when they said their goodbyes. After Merritt booked an Uber, she hooked her arm through Rose's and they made their way downstairs. To her surprise, Austen appeared at the bottom of the steps. She glanced at their joined arms and said quietly, "I can give you a lift to the hotel, Rose."

"Merritt has offered to take me home, thanks all the same, Austen."

"Yeah, well, great. Just so long as you're being looked after."

"Our Uber will be here in a minute," said Merritt. She waited for Austen to move aside so they could continue to the exit. She did, seemingly with some reluctance.

The night air was cool, and they were pleased to see their ride arrive almost immediately. They climbed into the backseat, quiet for a while as they watched the lights of the city through the window.

Rose was the first to break their companionable silence. "I had a wonderful time. Thank you so much for inviting me. I definitely need to get out more often. Laughing, dancing…not working."

"It was fun, wasn't it?" Merritt glanced at Rose. She looked unruffled and elegant. "You were very popular with the girls… one in particular."

Rose groaned. "She was nice but persistent. I'm pleased you're giving me a ride home."

"Me too."

"Terry's not so…how shall I put it…not so circumspect."

"No, she isn't," said Merritt with a chuckle. "She's a free spirit. And has enough stamina to satisfy both those ladies."

Rose made a little clicking sound with her tongue. "Something like that is foreign to me. I was brought up very strictly in the old Chinese ways. My parents are traditional about such things. Honor and shame are very important in our society."

"Do they know you prefer women?"

"No," Rose whispered. "But they love me. When I find someone I want to spend my life with, I will tell them."

Merritt reached over and squeezed her hand. "Whoever wins your heart will be a lucky lady indeed."

On impulse, she kissed Rose softly on the lips. It was intended as a friendly goodnight gesture between friends. But Rose immediately took her face in her hands and deepened the kiss. She was forced to move away from Merritt a moment later when the car glided to a stop outside the Hyatt. "That was nice," Rose whispered. "I'll see you at the barbeque."

"Would you like to go with Terry and me?"

"Great. I hate walking into a party alone."

"We'll pick you up at three here if you like. I'll text you when we're on our way." She watched Rose walk inside the doors before she gave her address to the driver. Settled back into the seat, she thought about how her body had reacted to tonight's two kisses.

Rose's mouth had been soft, her perfume tantalizing. But there had be no sparks. Not a one. Austen's kiss had been just as brief, yet her body had felt the sizzle right down to her toes. Merritt tugged at her seat belt in frustration.

She was never going to get Austen out of her system at this rate. Maybe, she should just go out with her and be done with it. Their infatuation would be certain to burn itself out. They were hardly suited.

CHAPTER EIGHT

Austen cracked her eyelids open at the knocking on the door. Blearily, she glanced at the clock on the side table. Eight thirty. With a groan, she ran her hand through her hair. It felt like she'd only lain down five minutes ago instead of four hours. At another series of raps, this time louder, she swung her bare legs over the bed and padded to the wardrobe for a gown. When she opened the door, Rose was outside with two takeaway cups. "Safe to come in?"

"I'm alone," said Austen testily.

"I've brought you coffee, double strength," Rose said with a chirpy smile.

Austen ushered her inside and accepted the steaming cup. "Thanks. But if it's one thing I hate, it's cheeriness this time of the morning. Especially when I'm feeling like a zombie."

"Have you forgotten we're having breakfast at nine with the director of the Australian National Academy of Music?"

Austen winced. She'd completely forgotten. *Blow!* Why did she have those last vodkas? Totally stupid. And what possessed her to agree to a breakfast meeting? "I didn't give it another thought," she said grumpily. "Let's try to make it quick, shall we? I haven't the energy to waste on bullshit."

"Aren't you in a happy mood this morning?" Rose said with a smile. "What time did you get to bed?"

"I only stayed for another hour after you left."

Rose arched an eyebrow.

"Okay. Make that two."

"Sorry. I should have reminded you. It's been a while since we arranged the meeting."

"Not your fault. I should look at my appointment book more often." Austen gave her a toothy grin. "Believe it or not, it was the last thing on my mind last night. I'll have a quick shower and see you downstairs in half an hour. Where do I go?"

"The management has kindly set up a table for us in the Griffin Room on the ground floor. It's open only in the evenings, so we'll have complete privacy."

After Rose disappeared out the door, Austen took another swig of coffee, feeling the caffeine work its way into her veins. There was nothing like that first hit in the morning. A hot shower and the rest of the cup, and she felt half human again. She dressed quickly, brushed her hair into some semblance of order and walked to the lift.

The guests milling around the reception desk stopped to watch her as she entered the lobby. She wished sometimes she could go out in public and be invisible. But she refused to hide, or let others dictate how she was going to lead her life. One of the hotel staff immediately appeared at her elbow and led her to a room off to the side. Austen glanced around appreciatively as she made her way to their table. With its heritage design, classic comfortable furniture, and glowing fireplace, the Griffin Room looked cozy.

Dr. Gena Stanislaw, the Music Academy's Director, was at a table chatting with Rose and climbed to her feet to greet her. She was a fortyish, uptown woman, sleekly dressed in a well-cut gray business suit, and wearing a pair of edgy glasses. She also had credentials as long as her arm. As she shook Austen's hand, her eyes fixed on her tattoos. When she caught the hint of disapproval in the woman's expression, Austen flexed her muscles to make them twitch.

The waitress appeared, her eyes wide in awe as she gazed at Austen. "Are you ready to order, ladies?"

Austen flashed her a wink. "A black coffee, eggs Benedict and bacon, please."

"Avocado on toast, thanks, and a pot of tea," said Rose.

"I'll have a half-strength flat white with Zymil milk, extra hot, and the flourless organic pumpkin pancakes," Gena said. Austen smiled to herself. Smart *and precious*.

The waitress threw Austen a timid smile before she bustled off.

"I understand you wish to give a donation to our trust fund for the Academy bursaries, Austen," Gena said.

"I do. I would like it set up as an endowment fund solely for disadvantaged kids from the country areas."

The director gave a small smile. "Our finance department manages a great many bequests and donations. Yours will be in good hands and we'll respect your wishes."

Austen caught her eye and held it. "I have no doubt you will. I chose your organization out of many. Music is obviously important to me, and I'd like to make sure the road is made a little easier for gifted country kids who would otherwise not get that chance. This a large donation and I'd like to be sure it is used for its specific purpose."

Gena cleared her throat. "How much exactly?"

Austen reached for the pen on Rose's folder and scrawled the figure on a paper napkin. She tossed it across the table.

When she ran her eyes over the figure, Gena swallowed. "Oh…right. Of course, Austen. Do you want the trust in your name?"

"No. Call it Country Kids Music. I'm to remain anonymous. But there is one important stipulation. My mother will be an executive of the trust. Your board will have complete autonomy in the choice of recipients, as long as they fit the criteria. Just so you run it by her before finalizing your choice. Rose has a portfolio of suggested investments that she'll discuss with you. There'll be plenty of money for lots of underprivileged kids to have a chance in music, and for the trust to be self-perpetuating."

"We have experts—" Gena began, then clamped her mouth shut when she caught the look on Austen's face. She turned to Rose who had the folder open. "I'd like to hear what you've put together, Rose."

As they discussed the financial details, Austen tuned out. A picture of Merritt slipped into her head and she embellished it. Merritt sprawled naked on her bed, a stethoscope around her neck. Her hair fanned out on the pillow, her finger beckoned to Austen. "Come here, my love, and I'll listen to your heart."

Caught up in her fantasy, it struck her that there was something not quite right about the location. When she moved the scene to a lounge, it seemed a better fit. Fragments of memory floated in. Where had she heard Merritt's name before? The doctor part seemed familiar as well. She felt a shiver of apprehension. Was Merritt one of her past one-night hookups? She didn't look the type you'd pick up in a bar. Austen never denied the fact that she'd played fast and loose with sex and alcohol in those early days, and the names and faces were a blur now.

Breakfast arrived, giving her no more time to daydream. She went through the motions of being pleasant, waiting for an excuse to access her phone. When Rose produced her notes again after the plates were cleared away, she excused herself. "I have a call to make. I won't be long."

Once out of sight, she brought up the Internet. When she typed in *Merritt Harrington* on Facebook, there wasn't a profile. She closed the app and retyped *Doctor Merritt Harrington* in the search bar. Most of the information was centered around her father, with a few mentions of her work with DWB. Austen hit the image button. The pictures were of Merritt at disaster areas with medic teams, or with her father. She was pleased to see there were none with an obvious love interest.

She scrolled down.

If she hadn't been examining each picture closely, she would have missed it.

Nearly at the bottom of the page, there was a shot of her standing next to her father at her graduation from medical school. Merritt was dressed in an academic gown and mortarboard, and though much younger and fuller in the face, she still had a special something that was appealing. Austen squinted to read the certificate she was holding, just able to make out *The University of Virginia.* She glanced up at the stately building behind the crowd. She'd seen it before somewhere on tour.

A lightbulb flashed and the memory flooded in.

Oh crap!

The girl at the CD signing who had caught her eye. Nerdy, sweet Merritt. How she had enjoyed the time they had spent together walking around the historic campus with Merritt as her enthusiastic tour guide. Then the scene in the lounge. Eleanor's phone call. How she had treated the girl badly, led her on, and then dismissed her as though she was nothing. All because Austen was trying to convince Eleanor that she wasn't sleeping around. And who had she been trying to kid anyhow? Eleanor would have been blind not to have seen the paparazzi's work in the tabloids. The joke had been on Austen. Ellie had never wanted her as a lover. It was just wishful thinking on her part.

She flicked her thoughts back to that concert and signing session. Out of all the fans, something had drawn her to the shy girl. And when Austen had started her full-on seduction, she was surprised how passionately Merritt had responded to her kisses, to her touch. It had been a huge turn-on. But in her arrogance, she had ruined it all. Had broken the girl's trust for someone she never, or would ever, have.

No wonder Merritt avoided her now. She wouldn't have forgotten what happened—or forgiven her. Not that she blamed her. One didn't make allowances for that sort of behavior.

Despondent, Austen clicked out of the 'net and made her way back to the table. Apparently well satisfied with the discussion, Gena was talking animatedly. Austen wasn't surprised. Rose was a financial whiz.

The business concluded and after a few more pleasantries, Gena stood up from the table. "I'll be off. It was lovely to meet you both, and once again many thanks for your very generous donation, Austen. You will make a lot of young people very happy." And with a, "I'll keep in touch," left the room.

"Want another coffee?" asked Rose.

Austen nodded. Less time to sit in her room and feel guilty. "Yes please. Were you happy with the meeting?"

"She was a bit of a pain to start with but had a grasp of figures."

"Do you think it's in good hands?"

"Yes. She has the students' welfare at heart."

"Then the money will be well spent." Austen paused and eyed her friend guardedly. "How did you enjoy last night?"

"They were a great bunch of women. I had a ball."

"It *was* great fun. I'm glad I went there. Um…you and Merritt seem to be good friends."

"We have a lot in common."

Austen felt a bite of jealousy. She closed her eyes. *Don't go there.* But she couldn't help herself. "You like her?"

Rose blushed. "Good heavens, Austen, I've just met her. She's very nice and easy to talk to."

"Just asking."

Rose tilted her head to look at her with a knowing smile. "The ladies liked *you.*"

"Oh, yeah. That just goes with being in showbiz. People go ape over celebs."

"When have you been so modest," Rose teased.

Austen shot her a grin. "Sometimes I can be."

"So…when do you plan to visit your folks?"

"Five days before I fly back." Austen waved her fingers. "That's plenty long enough. Any longer and they start picking at me about my lifestyle."

"I can—" Rose's next comment was cut short by the waitress reappearing.

The young woman shifted from one foot to the other then produced a pen and CD from her pocket. "Um…I wonder if I could have your autograph, please, Austen?"

Austen held out her hand. "Sure, babe. What's your name?"

"Connie."

Austen scrawled a few words and handed it back with a wink. "There you go, Con."

After the girl disappeared, Rose reached over and squeezed Austen's arm affectionately. "As much as I admire your fame, I don't envy you. You don't have any privacy."

"Aw…she was nice. She probably took ten minutes to gather the courage to ask me. The only people I despise are the losers who troll me on social media."

"Are they hard to ignore?"

Austen shrugged. "Nah. I've learned not to bother reading their psycho shit."

"Good for you."

"What are you planning to do for the rest of the day?"

"I've got some paperwork to finish. You?"

"I'm going to pick up a hire car at one. I'll need wheels to get around. You wanna come over with me and have a few drinks with the band before everyone arrives?"

Rose shook her head. "Thanks all the same, but Merritt's picking me up."

"Oh…right," Austen grunted out, taken by surprise. *Crap!* Rose wasn't wasting any time. The way she handled herself at the diplomatic dinner, Merritt would fit right into her traditional Chinese family. And she bet Rose was thinking just that.

But then again, maybe it was Merritt who was doing the chasing. She didn't know why that last thought was much more upsetting.

She'd just have to think of a way of getting Merritt's trust back.

And that was going to take some doing now.

CHAPTER NINE

For the fourth—and as far as she was concerned the last—time, Merritt shook Terry's shoulder. "Get up. It's after three. If you don't get your butt out of the bed this minute I'm going without you."

A groan echoed from the pillow and a bloodshot eye opened. "Oh…hell. I feel like I've been put through a wringer." Catching the darkening frown on Merritt's face, Terry threw back the sheet and crawled over the side of the mattress. "Okay, okay. I'm getting up."

Merritt sent another message to Rose. *She's finally surfaced. See you in half an hour.*

A smiley face came as a reply. The lawyer was certainly pleasant-natured. Merritt suspected she wasn't much of a party girl and didn't care if she was late. She could relate to that.

She turned to Terry who was moving at a snail's pace. "I'll get your clothes while you're in the shower. What do you want to wear?"

"The skinny blue jeans with the rips in the knees and the cream T-top."

"I'll run the iron over them. Apparently, there's a pool, so put on your bikini underneath if you want a swim. I won't bother, but I know how you like the water."

"Okay. Thanks," Terry muttered, her voice thick and husky.

Merritt just shook her head. It had been obvious when Terry arrived in a taxi at nine this morning that she'd had an all-nighter. Her hair was sticking up at odd angles and her eyes popping out of her head. Gloria hadn't batted an eyelid. Her face crinkled in amusement, she merely insisted Terry eat something before going to bed.

Thirty minutes later, showered and dressed, Terry was ready. Merritt always marveled how she had the ability to recover so quickly after a heavy night. It was the same after a particularly grueling day at work. Super resilient. This afternoon though, she was walking a little gingerly.

When she saw Merritt studying her gait, she merely laughed, unembarrassed. "I used muscles I didn't know I had last night. Those army girls sure have stamina. Must be all their field training." She looked at Merritt wistfully. "Um…any chance of a coffee before we go?"

"Nope. We'll get you one on the way, lover girl. The Uber will be here in a sec."

* * *

Merritt looked around appreciatively as they made their way along the pathway. Nothing beat Mother Nature for providing the perfect setting. The apartment complex had bungalow-style guest units scattered amongst lawns, trees, and flowers. Now it was spring, the gardens exploded with colorful blooms and delightful floral perfumes.

When they reached the outdoor entertainment area, Rose murmured, "The boys in the band are staying here, and booked the outdoor area for the night."

"It's great," Merritt remarked as they stopped to take it in. The spacious yard was filled with wooden tables and chairs, two large gas burners on one side, and a fenced pool set into lush greenery on the other. A tantalizing smell of grilling chicken wafted in the air.

The party was rocking, not the sedate barbecue she had envisaged. There were about fifty or so guests, as many men as women. And they were a mixed bag: jocks, musicians, and even a few bikers in leather gear and big boots. The army contingent stood out from the other women who were nowhere near as athletic looking.

Merritt searched the crowd for Austen. She was lounging against the pool fence, holding court with a group of scantily clad young women. Merritt felt a twinge of annoyance tinged with jealousy. That'd be right. Once a flirt, always a flirt.

Behind them, swimmers were splashing noisily in the pool. On the other side of the lawn, a group of adrenaline junkies were playing some ridiculous racing game that involved crawling on their hands and knees and swerving around pegs while balancing a four pack of open beer cans on their backs. Every time the pack fell off, there was a spray of beer accompanied by a chorus of shouts and cheers from the spectators. Merritt hadn't seen anything so brainless since college.

"Hype party," Terry said. "I'm going for a swim. What about you two?"

"Not for a while," answered Rose. "I'll have a drink first."

"Me too," said Merritt, spotting June waving from a table.

"Fashionably late," said June with a smile as she moved two extra chairs into the circle.

Merritt sank down beside her. "Hey, there. We had a holdup. It looks like everyone's in party mode."

"They're really starting to warm up. Austen hasn't been stingy with the alcohol."

"She's very generous," said Rose.

"She sure is," June said, then groaned. "Christ, I feel old watching those young things galivanting around in their skimpy shorts and tops."

Merritt chuckled. "At that age you flaunt it."

"I'm just envious. We have a couple of bottles of champagne in the ice bucket. Would you and Rose like a glass, or maybe you'd prefer something else?"

"Champagne sounds super," said Rose.

Merritt looked at her dubiously. It was a bit early for her, and anything bubbly always went straight to her head. June waved a glass, so not wanting to appear a spoilsport, she said with a smile, "Oh, what the heck. Why not? Fill 'er up."

Four glasses later and very giggly, Merritt was having more fun than she'd had for ages. With an endless supply of jokes, their table was soon as raucous as the rest of the crowd. Since Austen had only said a brief "Hello" when she delivered a plate of chicken kebabs, it was clear she'd given up pursuing her. Merritt ignored the sharp pang of regret. It was a good thing, she told herself. They weren't on the same page—not even on the same planet.

She was laughing at a joke, when a sporty guy at the next table called out, "You soldier girls want to take us on in a crab race? That is, if you've got the balls for it." This was followed by hoots of laughter from his buddies.

Merritt hoped they would ignore him, but he'd hit a nerve with June. With a gleam in her eyes, she cast a look around the table. "What about it, ladies?"

"Yes, ma'am," they chorused.

"Okay, you're on," June called back.

"Right. Six to a side. You can't crawl in a straight line... you have to circle the three pegs. If your pack drops off you're disqualified. There's a three-minute time limit."

Merritt looked around nervously. There were only five army women, which meant the sixth would have to be either her or Rose. She glanced over at the pool, wishing Terry was here. This sort of mindless thing was right up her alley. Then when June announced, "One of you will have to be our sixth," she looked beseechingly at Rose, who immediately shook her head. "Don't even go there. I'd be hopeless at it. You're fitter than me."

"Then it's settled," June said, grabbing Merritt's hand before she could protest. "You'll be fine. Don't bolt out at the start or you'll lose the beer. You can go last so there's no pressure."

"Yeah, right. Easier said than done," muttered Merritt, wondering how the hell she was even considering doing something so ridiculous.

Soon it got even worse. The races were one-on-one, so instead of being with the field, she'd be in the spotlight. Until she lost her cans that is, which wouldn't be long. After the champagne, it'd be too difficult to keep her balance. Sober—maybe. Four champagnes later—hardly likely.

When the first two lined up and began racing the length of the grassed area, everyone crowded around to watch. To Merritt it seemed like running a gauntlet. She studied the crawlers carefully, noting how they moved while keeping the pack upright. It was actually like a graceful dance. As the competition heated up, the onlookers became louder. And then it was her turn. The scores were tied. So much for no pressure.

June sidled up beside her. "Just go easy. You can do it."

Resisting the urge to swear, Merritt smiled weakly. "Will do," she said and sank onto the grass.

She eyed her opponent, an athletic type who barely looked more than twenty. He had a smug smile as he dropped down on all fours beside her. After giving her an appraising look, he muttered, "I'm going to beat your ass."

Catching a glimpse of his well-developed abs when he stretched his body into position, she chewed the inside of her lip. No doubt he would. "Yeah…you can try," she snapped back.

Someone balanced the pack of beer on her back, the weight of the full cans enough to make it stable. Though not enough that a sudden movement wouldn't send the lot flying.

An expectant hush fell over the crowd, followed by cheers when the starter yelled, "*Go!*"

Remembering her instructions, she started off cautiously, ignoring her rival who moved quickly out of the blocks. Perspiration trickled down her neck as she strained to move smoothly. The grass was slippery with spilled beer, which didn't help. It was a long three minutes. Halfway there, she was way behind. Talk about the hare and the tortoise. It seemed all over as she watched her opponent take the turn around the last peg. He had it in the bag.

Then it happened. He made the turn too fast and his load wobbled. He stopped quickly to get his balance, but it was too late. The cans toppled off. This was accompanied by groans from his teammates and derisive hoots from the onlookers.

She gave a chortle. *Slow and steady wins the race.* At tortoise speed, she continued on. But then she heard June shout, "Hurry up. You've only got three seconds to get there."

Damnit! She'd been too slow. The finishing line was still about a yard and a half away.

Desperately, she lunged forward. Her hand went from under her, and with a cry she sprawled facedown into the grass. Dirt shot up her nose. The pack toppled off as she collapsed with a whoosh. Clearly startled at this sudden turn of events, the onlookers went quiet for a second before they exploded into gales of laughter.

For a long moment she lay winded. She squinted an eye open, letting out a muffled groan. Not only was the finish line still a foot away, the tins were on their sides at her left shoulder, the beer trickling in a little stream under her chest. She could feel it soaking through to her nipples.

Sonofabitch! Not only had she let the side down, she was going to stink of beer and look like a contestant in a wet T-shirt contest. Feeling humiliated, she pushed up into a sitting position. As she struggled to rise, she accepted the helping hand that someone thrust in front of her nose.

"Thanks," she said gratefully as she was hauled to her feet. "I'm—" She bit back the next words when she saw she was clasping Austen's hand.

"Are you all right?" Austen asked.

"No bones broken. Just my pride."

Austen gave a little chuckle. "It did look funny."

"Huh! It's not as easy as it looks."

"You're a good sport, babe," Austen said, brushing her cheek with her knuckles before taking a step back.

Merritt took a hitching breath, momentarily befuddled by the warm feeling the simple gesture evoked. But the mood was abruptly broken when June pushed between them and took Merritt's arm. After glancing at the hand on her arm, Austen turned away and retreated into the crowd.

Terry's voice came over the babble of voices. "Geez, girlfriend. What's with the Rambo act? What's in the stuff you're drinking? I've never seen you do anything like that."

"And you won't see it again. I made a complete mess of it."

"Nonsense," said June. "You acquitted yourself very well. Besides, we didn't lose…it was all declared a draw."

When a wolf whistle pierced the air, Terry appeared at her side with a towel. "Better cover your chest. Your assets are showing."

"Damn," she mumbled, looking down at the soaked shirt that was clinging to her curves. Her nipples were standing up through the wet material like soldiers on parade. Hastily, she draped the towel around her neck, fanning it over her boobs.

"I'm going back in the pool," said Terry. "I won't be needing the towel for a while."

"Okay, thanks. I'll bring it back after I wash my top." She smiled at June. "I won't be long. We passed a guest laundry on our way in."

She wandered off back down the pathway until she reached the amenities block. Relieved to see a dryer, she quickly stripped off her top to wash it. Intent on removing the stains, she didn't notice that she had company in the room until a throaty voice whispered in her ear, "I've been wanting to get you alone all afternoon."

"*Austen!*" Merritt yelped. "You nearly gave me a heart attack."

"Then I'd better give you mouth-to-mouth," she said with a chuckle, leaning over to brush her lips down her cheek.

Merritt pushed her away playfully. "Behave."

"But you smell so good."

"I smell like a brewery."

"Hmm. I can only smell *you*. It's intoxicating."

"You're incorrigible. Look…we've already had this conversation. I'm not interested in anything casual."

"Yes, I know. But what say we just go out and get to know each other. Have dinner, catch a movie, whatever you like."

Merritt slowly relaxed her defensive stance. "Sorry, Austen. I've promised Rose I'd sightsee with her until she leaves Thursday."

Austen stiffened. "You and Rose are going on dates?"

"Well… not exactly dating per se. She's darn good company so we're going to do the touristy things together. There're plenty of interesting places to see in Canberra…the War Memorial, the National Mint, the Science Museum."

Austen's eyes had lost their coolness and were now pools of emotion. "I get that you and Rose have become friends, but why are you pretending there's nothing between *us*?"

Merritt was silent for a moment, then made up her mind. It was time for the reckoning. "Because you have the capacity to hurt me. I met you years ago at The University of Virginia. I was just an inexperienced college girl and after you seduced me, you treated me like I was nothing. And you've never given any indication that you've even remembered me."

"When I saw you at the airport your face was familiar, but I had no idea where I'd seen you. Then this morning it came to me." She looked guiltily at Merritt, and said in a voice low and rough, "I was a complete asshole that night. I'm sorry Merritt. I know nothing will excuse my behavior, but you've got to believe I'm not that person anymore."

"How can I believe *that*?"

"Come out with me and I'll prove it." Austen tilted her head, gazing at her with undisguised longing. "Will you?"

Merritt swallowed, every hormone clambering for her to agree. But her brain won the battle. "Ask me again on Thursday. I…I can't commit now. I'll think it over."

"Okay…I'll wait. We'll exchange numbers at the table." Austen moved closer. "In the meantime, may I kiss you? Just a goodbye-until-next-time one?"

Merritt had barely finished nodding when Austen's mouth sought hers, at first gentle but quickly became intense. Merritt stilled in her arms, then couldn't help herself. She answered with an urgency of her own. When their tongues tangled, it forced a groan, though she didn't know if it came from her or Austen. Finally, she found the strength to tear her mouth away. "Oh, God," she gasped out. "I can't…I want… Oh, I don't know what I want anymore. Darn you, Austen. You ambushed me."

"I know. I couldn't help myself," Austen said, though she looked more smug than sorry. "I'd better get back to the party and leave you to clean your shirt, although," she waggled her eyebrows, "I do like you in that sexy lace bra."

She flashed Merritt a sultry grin and was gone.

CHAPTER TEN

The air had cooled since night had fallen, the setting intimate under the glow of lights. Austen swirled the beer in her glass as she looked around, thinking how much she had missed this. Back on home soil with laid-back people. No pressure. Feeling more relaxed and energized in a way she hadn't been in a very long time, she turned to Mick who was scarfing down a burger. "Ready for the jam session later on?" she asked.

He swallowed the last of the bun, then scrubbed his fingers with a paper towel. "Yep. We've two acoustic guitars, the small keyboard, Keith has that tin whistle of his and we managed to borrow a bongo drum for Max. Everything else has been packed to be shipped back to the States."

"Great." She glanced at her watch. "It's eight fifteen. We'll start about ten."

She made herself a steak burger, piling on the fried onions before settling down on a stool with her plate. While she ate, she watched Merritt chatting with the women at the far table. Her mind drifted back to their kiss. She had meant it to be quick and soft, just a taste, but it had developed into so much more. So very quickly. And how ardently Merritt had kissed her back had taken her by surprise. She had been so responsive it had taken Austen's breath away, turning her emotions into knots.

Austen regarded Merritt steadily, trying to figure out why she was so drawn to her. Her physical appeal was easy enough to explain. Merritt was smart, charming, attractive, with a dash of vulnerability that made her very approachable. Everything Austen liked in a woman. It had been years since she'd been this attracted to anyone. She'd had enough of the posturing young things who wanted nothing more than their moment of fame on her arm. They were a dime a dozen.

But Merritt had managed to stir up feelings she'd kept buried for years. And while Austen knew she would be the perfect date to spend time with on her vacation, she also intuitively sensed she'd better be wary too. The good doctor may be persuaded to have a few fun dates with her, even perhaps share her bed, but she would hardly want a lasting relationship with a rock singer with a reputation. She had more class than that. Especially with a father in politics, one who would hardly condone his daughter being involved with her.

At the sound of a female voice calling, "Hey, Austen. You wanna go for a swim?" she glanced over at the three groupies at the pool entrance. The honey-blonde in the skimpy bikini was looking at her with a sexy pout that promised more than just a swim.

A brief smile crossed Austen's face before she shook her head. "Nah. Maybe later, babe," she called out, and turned to glance again in Merritt's direction.

It was obvious she had heard, for she was staring across at Austen. When she caught her eye, Merritt glanced away quickly. Austen felt a flush of warmth. No matter how much Merritt protested, she wasn't so immune to her. The next second she wondered what she was doing here when she all she wanted to be was with Merritt. With no more hesitation, she gathered up her plate and glass, working the crowd as she sauntered over to the table.

The women greeted her enthusiastically. After giving everyone around the table a cheery wave, she fitted in a chair next to Rose, directly opposite Merritt.

"Hey there," she said softly, looking over the table at her.

Merritt licked her lips before offering a smile of her own. "Hi."

June casually draped her arm around the back of Merritt's chair and said, "It's nice you've joined us."

Appearing uncomfortable, Merritt moved forward and placed her elbows on the table. Austen automatically leaned over the table too, catching a trace of Merritt's enticing scent. She felt heat sparking between them, causing a tiny shiver to run along her spine. Merritt made a whispered humming sound that made her suck in a breath. They could have been completely alone, as everything faded into insignificance for Austen except for the deep blue eyes staring into hers.

Fuck, the woman can turn me on with just a look.

Rose's voice broke the spell, "Fabulous party."

Suddenly aware she was way too close to Merritt, Austen hastily retreated. With a warm smile, she shifted her attention to Rose. "The boys wanted a blowout before heading off tomorrow afternoon. Katie organized everything."

"Well, it was a lovely gesture," said Rose, then gave a low laugh. "Where did they pick up this crowd? They're an odd assortment, especially the bikers."

Austen glanced across at a big bearded man in black leather who was chewing Mick's ear. She chuckled. "They're HOGS, not members of any infamous bikie gang."

"They know them?"

"The guys in the band are Harley enthusiasts. It's quite a fraternity. They plan to go on a road trip on bikes."

"Really? I presumed they were going to rent a car." She looked at Austen curiously. "Do you ride bikes as well? I know you love extreme sports."

Austen nodded. "I've a Triumph in the garage. I take it out occasionally, but I much prefer fast cars."

"I heard you drive that red Porsche of yours at a blistering pace."

"Guilty as charged," Austen said with a grin. "I love speed."

"What did you rent here. A sports car?"

Austen pulled a face. "As much as I would have liked to, I went for something more practical. A Range Rover, in case I want to go off-road." She turned to address the others at the table. "What's everyone drinking?"

For the next two hours, the women joked and drank, their teasing banter amusing, quick-witted and sometimes razor-edged. Though often the medical jargon went over her head, Austen couldn't remember when she had enjoyed herself so much over the course of an evening. Merritt looked completely relaxed. Her lurking tension had seemingly faded away. As she laughed at something one of the nurses was saying, Austen sat back to simply enjoy watching her. It was the first time she'd seen her so unguarded and she liked what she saw. She'd obviously washed her face in the laundry, for it was devoid of any makeup. It glowed with a healthy freshness, the smattering of freckles across her nose looked totally cute.

As though conscious of her regard, Merritt turn to look at her with hooded eyes. Unbidden, a song popped into Austen's head, a slow ballad that spoke of unrequited love. She tapped out the tune on the tabletop, both hands were flying over the wooden surface. Her mother always said her hands were her best features. Long, slender, and strengthened by years of hard work, they were perfectly made for guitar playing.

As she sang quietly, the women fell quiet. When she finished, she turned to the sound of strumming behind her. With a bow, Mick offered her the acoustic guitar. Austen lovingly ran her hands over the polished frame. "Shall we give the folks a few tunes?" she said with a wide smile.

"Let's go," he agreed.

She perched on a stool in the center of the four band members. "Better try to keep it low," she murmured. "We don't want the neighbors complaining."

As she plucked out a tune, everyone crowded around, including the swimmers who had quickly emerged from the pool when the word spread Austen was going to sing. As she focused on the chords, she reveled in the familiar feeling of anticipation at the beginning of a performance. She lived for her music.

The band pounded out a lively accompanying beat as she began. One number followed another, and it wasn't long before people were dancing. She couldn't help her own response to the music, unconsciously swaying and tapping her feet as she sang. Soon everyone was up, flinging themselves about on any available space on the lawn. She suspected there were a few ring-ins from the other apartments as well. The crowd had definitely swelled.

Like a moth to a flame, she followed Merritt with her eyes. She watched as June took her hand and pulled her into the throng. She was fascinated by the way Merritt moved when she danced: how her hips rocked seductively to the beat, the subtle shift of muscles as she spun, the enticing sway of her breasts. Every so often, Austen caught a tantalizing glimpse of white skin above her waistband, causing a jolt of arousal. And Merritt was totally unaware of the effect she was having on her. It went beyond a physical pull. In fact, Austen was beginning to feel she had never felt like this with anyone.

When they began a slow number, she was sorry she had included it. Though one of their biggest hits, it gave June an opportunity to pull Merritt into her arms. She wanted to stomp across and yank them apart, but instead cut the song short. When she abruptly moved into a faster one, the band stumbled before picking up the tune. Out of the corner of her eye, Austen could see Mick throw her a questioning glance but ignored him. Finally, to her relief one of the guys from the ridiculous crab race moved in on Merritt, cutting June out.

Merritt didn't seem to hesitate, moving to face him with a sway of her hips. Austen snickered to herself. *Suck that up, Major!*

By the time they wrapped up the music with their favorite finale, it was very late in the night. The dull stress ache beginning behind Austen's eyes only served as a reminder how frustrated she had become watching Merritt. Now she had to wait and see with whom Merritt was going home. Merritt said something to Terry, who shook her head. The next minute, Terry went off with her two army friends.

As she passed over the guitar to Mick, three young women from the pool approached. She swore under her breath. There was no escape, no hope of avoiding what she knew was coming. The blonde was more forward than most. She immediately stepped close, curled her fingers around Austen's arm, squeezed lightly and whispered in her ear, "Let's go to my place to have our own party."

Austen took a moment to study her. In her early twenties, the girl was the very definition of sex-on-a-stick: blond shoulder-length curls, a curvy nubile body and full breasts that nearly burst out of her top. Not feeling one iota of attraction, Austen just wished she'd go. "Sorry. Some other time, babe," she said, gently pulling the hand off her arm.

The girl looked like she was going to argue, but gave a sniff and said, "Your loss," before she sauntered off.

Austen turned back in annoyance and looked straight into Mick's twinkling eyes. "Well, well. You've got it bad to knock that one back," he said in his best Irish brogue.

Austen narrowed her eyes. "I don't know what you're talking about." But she knew all right—he could read her like a book. Mick was her best friend. Sporting red hair, a fair complexion and a temper to match, he had arrived in Australia as a backpacker from Mullingar in Ireland. He had become like a brother over the years with the band.

"Shit, girl, you didn't even look once at that hot babe. Yet, you looked like someone had stolen your favorite toy when the doctor went off to dance with that army bird with the stick up her ass."

Austen made a wry face, knowing there was no point denying it. "Merritt's not interested."

"Don't you believe it. She glanced over at you often enough."

"Huh! That's only because I was singing," she said morosely.

"Fuck me, Austen. You can be a stubborn woman sometimes. I'm not one to give advice, but it's about time you stopped shutting yourself off from people."

"What the hell's that supposed to mean?"

"Come on...you damn well know what I'm talking about. When in the last ten years have you had a single relationship? Jesus, can you name anyone that wasn't a one-night stand?"

"Neither can you," she snapped.

"I'm not judging you. This life, with all its perks, is hard on relationships. But I can see you're different with Merritt. All I'm saying is, if you're experiencing real feelings then don't ignore them. Do something about it."

All at once, Austen felt like she was sixteen again, wanting something but unsure how to get it. "She's out of my league," she muttered.

Mick broke into a spurt of laughter. "Since when has that ever stopped *you?* You've never hesitated when you've wanted something." He peered over her shoulder. "Everyone's starting to go. I'd better say goodbye."

Austen looked around the yard for Merritt. After a couple of sweeps, she caught sight of her in a secluded corner talking with June. A few minutes later, June gave her a peck on the cheek, though from her body language she wasn't too pleased. Austen gave a silent whoop. The major wasn't taking her home. Her joy, however, was short-lived. Merritt joined Rose and spoke in her ear. Rose nodded with a smile and entwined her arm in hers. When they headed her way, arm and arm, Austen winced.

Merritt was going home with Rose.

Of course she was, *damnit.*

She painted on a smile, though it became harder to keep in place as they neared.

"We're going home," said Rose brightly. Merritt avoided her eyes.

"I hope you had a great time. I'll see you tomorrow for breakfast, Rose?"

"Sorry. Merritt and I are planning to see the city. We're starting early, so we'll have breakfast on the way."

Austen swallowed her disappointment. "Oh, right. Have fun."

CHAPTER ELEVEN

Merritt sat outside on the deck, nursing a cup of coffee. She leaned back, lost in her thoughts. The past three days being tourists with Rose had been fun. The first morning they had taken a double-decker bus to view the city sights, and in the afternoon had gone on an off-road tour to see the local wildlife. Since she had never seen a kangaroo, she thought the experience was amazing. The next day was great fun—a hot air balloon flight for an hour, followed by a culinary tour. They had dined that night at a seafood restaurant where she'd had the best coral trout she'd ever tasted.

Today, after meeting her mother in town for morning tea, they'd visited two of the city's biggest draw cards, the War Memorial and National Art Gallery. Tonight though, her father had requested Merritt and Terry dine with them. She wrinkled her nose in annoyance as she recalled his curt text. As always, he managed to make it a decree rather than an invitation. Thankfully, Terry was quite happy to have a night at home. Merritt dropped Rose off at her hotel in the late afternoon, promising to see her off at the airport in the morning.

She took a sip of coffee as she thought about Rose. She was just the nicest person. Attractive, charming, successful, and they got along extremely well. Though she knew Rose wanted to pursue her interest in her further, Merritt had softly suggested they would be much better as friends. Rose hadn't pushed the issue, but all the same, Merritt still felt guilty that she had hurt the gentle woman. But her heart wanted what her heart wanted. And it wasn't Rose. Not for the first time did she curse Austen. She had ruined her for anyone else.

She closed her eyes, and images of the party chased around in her head. It'd been the best time. Once she'd gotten over her embarrassment, she could even laugh about the race. It was the most mindless thing she'd ever participated in and perhaps the most fun. The crowd of women had been entertaining, though June had been a little hard to shake. Merritt gave a chuckle at that. The major was used to being obeyed and didn't like being told *no*.

But the highlight of the night came the instant Austen began to sing. Merritt had been captivated. She had been phenomenal, with her stormy, drop-dead gorgeous looks and her husky powerful voice. Not to mention her lithe tattooed body was the stuff of fantasies. When Austen looked at her with that slow, sexy smile, Merritt had had an inexplicable urge to throw herself at her feet.

And then there was the *kiss*. Merritt tried not to think about *that*, or her reaction to it. But her thoughts drifted to it on their own accord and she trembled. As soon as Austen's mouth had touched hers, she had been acutely aware of the current that ran between them. So tangible that she could feel the electricity shoot from her lips to her groin. Her former lovers hadn't been able to do anything remotely like that to her. She had tingled in the most embarrassing way for minutes after it was over.

Merritt exhaled, shifting uncomfortably in the chair as she tried to make sense of her emotions. She wished for something— but what exactly? That Austen was more like Rose? That she didn't have a reputation as a bad girl? No, she didn't want those things. She liked that she was edgy and her own woman. She liked that she was unique, that she lived by her own rules.

Whether Merritt agreed with Austen's lifestyle choices wasn't the issue, or even her business for that matter.

Suddenly, the veil of confusion dissolved, and it became crystal clear what she wanted. She wished Austen would look at her and for once see the person underneath, not just a woman to take to bed for a night.

Merritt gave a self-deprecating sigh. *If wishes were horses, beggars would ride.*

She didn't know how long she remained tangled up in her thoughts, but when she opened her eyes her mother was standing in the doorway. "Oh, you're out here, dear. Where's Terry?"

"Upstairs getting ready for dinner. She'll be down shortly." She began to rise from the chair, but her mother waved her back. "Stay there and I'll join you. It's a lovely night. Would you like a drink?"

Merritt lifted her cup. "I'm happy with a coffee. I'll have a glass of wine with dinner."

Gloria settled down into a deck chair with a smile. "I'll wait for dinner as well. It'll be served in half an hour. Your father has just arrived home." She gave a sigh. "It's so nice to get off my feet. The garden party for the diplomatic wives this afternoon was rather tiring. There was no quiet time…they all wanted a piece of me."

They sat for several minutes in companionable silence, Merritt staring sightlessly into the distance. So caught up in images of Austen, it was awhile before she realized her mother was watching her. She was studying her as if trying to read something in her face. Merritt smiled hesitantly at her. "What?"

"I'd love to know what's put that look on your face." Gloria raised an eyebrow. "Or whom."

Merritt ducked her head to hide the blush. *No, you wouldn't, Mom.* "Trust me. It's nothing interesting," she said off-handedly.

Maybe too casually, because her mother glanced at her sharply. "Hmm. Perhaps you should have asked Rose to dinner tonight?"

Merritt rolled her eyes. "God, Mom. Can you imagine how Dad would give her the third degree? She's too nice a person to have to put up with his crap."

"So, Rose and you are—?"

Merritt let the unspoken question hang in the air for a moment before she replied firmly, "Rose is just a friend. She's been great company and I'll miss her when she goes to China tomorrow. Hopefully, we can catch up when I go back home."

Gloria tilted her head on the side. "But something has happened. You can protest all you like, but I can tell when things are different with you." She leaned across and took her hand gently. "I'm here for you, dear, if you want to discuss anything."

"I know, Mom. And I love you. But I really don't have anything to tell you."

"Okay. I won't press you further. Do you have anything specifically planned for the rest of your vacation? I thought we might do a few things together when I'm not tied up with this trade summit. Your father and I have more engagements, but I'll certainly make time for you."

"I'm just glad to be able to relax. On Friday, I have an appointment with a counselor to help me de-stress after the last assignment."

When her mother didn't reply, Merritt patted her arm. "It's nothing to worry about. It's just something we have to do sometimes." Pleased to see her mother brighten at the words, she added reassuringly, "I'm going to have a lovely time reading and using the kitchen to experiment with some new recipes. I'd like to try a few Peruvian dishes."

Gloria made a face. "You're not going to serve us llama, are you?"

"Llama isn't a common dish in Peru," Merritt replied with amusement. "They eat a lot of fish and chicken. Their recipes are very tasty, full of limes, chilies, and spices. I'll cook dinner for us one night."

"That would be nice, but make sure it's not too hot for your father. You know how spicy food upsets his stomach."

Merritt gritted her teeth. Sometimes her mother needed a good shake. When was she going to stop pandering to a man who treated her like chattel? But she held her tongue for now, knowing it would only upset her to argue. But she made a mental note to have a serious talk with her before she left.

Terry appeared at the door and she turned her attention to her.

"Hey there," said Terry in a bubbly voice. "You look ravishing, Mrs. H."

Merritt smothered a grin. Whatever Terry had been up to the last few days, had improved her good mood even more. Gloria preened and gave Terry a warm smile. "I think it's about time you called me Gloria. It's nice to have you home again, Terry."

"Umm…I've been staying with a friend for a couple of days."

"I imagine you and Merritt would like to have a day together before you fly to New Zealand on Friday."

"Yes, of course, Gloria," murmured Terry, a look of unease flashing across her face.

Merritt let her squirm. Terry clearly had a date tomorrow, which probably would go into the night. "We could go sightseeing," she said sweetly. "I know how you love museums." She ignored Terry's glare and continued, "Or perhaps we could visit Parliament House and watch a debate."

Terry was saved from replying when the housekeeper appeared at the door. "Dinner is ready to be served, Mrs. Harrington."

"Thank you, Janice," Gloria replied and rose to her feet. "I'll get your father, Merritt. You girls go to the dining room when you're ready."

"Watch a fucking parliamentary debate?" hissed Terry as soon as she was out of sight. "That'd be worse than watching paint dry."

Merritt snickered. "Got a hot date again?"

"As a matter of fact, I do."

"The same two girls?"

"Only one. Jordan," replied Terry.

Merritt raised her eyebrows in surprise as a blush crept over her friend's cheeks. "Good for you."

"She's super nice. She's going to try to get a week off and come to New Zealand with me."

"That's great."

"She's actually pretty awesome."

Merritt smiled, pleased she'd found someone, though she couldn't imagine a lasting relationship coming from a ménage à trois. But then again…she chided herself. How would she know? Terry always claimed she was too prudish. And maybe she was presuming that Terry had had a threesome and it wasn't true. But did it matter anyhow? "And you're pretty amazing yourself, girlfriend." She gave her a nudge with her elbow and entwined their arms. "Let's go and eat."

Dinner with her father was as enjoyable as it ever got. He was at his charming best. Something must have put him in a good humor, she mused. Maybe he'd had a wild night out with some of the trade delegates while he was away. She wouldn't put it past him to go to a strip club occasionally. But whatever it was, it made it easier on her mother, which was all that concerned her.

After they'd had a nightcap on the terrace, she was ready for bed. Tucked up under the covers nearly asleep, her eyes popped open. *Hell!* Tomorrow was Thursday. How could she have forgotten *that.* D day—time to give Austen her answer about going out with her. She pulled the pillow over her head. It was a given that she'd never be able to refuse. She hoped Austen, though, had some doubt. It wouldn't do to appear too easy. But if she imagined Merritt was going to leap straight into bed with her, she had another thing coming. It wasn't going to happen.

But now she was wide awake, her entire body throbbed at the thought of Austen pressed against her. She groaned, swung her legs over the side of the bed and padded to the bathroom. She searched in her toiletry bag until she found what she was looking for. Once she was between the sheets again, she turned it on. It hummed pleasantly.

* * *

At nine in the morning, the taxi driver dropped Terry and Merritt off at Canberra International Airport to bid farewell to Rose.

She had already checked in with Air China and was waiting with Austen in the crowded departure lounge. Austen wasn't wearing her customary black, instead was dressed in faded blue jeans, a loose white long-sleeved shirt buttoned up high and a Yankees' baseball cap. With a pair of wraparound sunglasses covering half her face, she was just one of the crowd.

Rose rushed forward to give Merritt a hug. "I'm going to miss you."

"Me too," Merritt said warmly. "Do you have time for coffee?"

"My plane's boarding in twenty minutes so I'd better get going. Make sure you call me when you get back home."

"Will do. And don't forget that you're coming over to my place to try out my cooking."

"I won't forget," she promised. After giving Austen a long hug, she disappeared up the escalator.

Austen waved her hand at the coffee shop. "Can I entice you ladies to coffee and some decadent sweets?"

"You bet," said Terry with a laugh. "I've had enough exercise in the last few days not to have to worry."

Merritt nudged her with her shoulder. "Stop bragging."

Austen chuckled. "Good for you."

After they decided on their orders, Terry rose from her seat. "I'll get it."

Merritt watched her go to the counter, conscious that Austen had her eyes pinned on her.

"Have you decided, Merritt?" she asked softly.

She swiveled back to look at Austen and nodded. "All right. Let's have one date and see where it goes."

"Today? Now?"

Merritt gave her a shy smile. "I guess so. Terry is going over to her friend's place, so I'm free to do whatever you like."

Austen's face brightened, replacing her slightly anxious look. Had Austen actually been worried she wouldn't say yes? She felt a little giddy at the thought. "That would be great," said Austen softly, taking Merritt's hand and rubbing her thumb gently over her knuckles.

At that moment, Terry appeared. She took one look at their joined hands and frowned.

Merritt hastily pulled hers back off the table. Terry's smile reappeared as soon as they began to chat again. Two cups of coffee later, Austen excused herself to go to the restroom. An almost imperceptible change came over Terry as soon as Austen wandered off.

"Austen Farleigh? What the hell are you thinking?"

Merritt shifted self-consciously in her chair. "What do you mean?"

Terry shook her head incredulously. "I'm not blind. You were holding hands with her. And you've both been acting kinda weird ever since we sat down. Trying to half ignore each other but not succeeding, if you know what I mean. You be very careful, Merritt. She's earned her reputation. She'll eat you up and spit you out."

"I can handle myself," Merritt protested weakly.

"Do you think you'll be able to? You're not in her league when it comes to experience." Terry ran her fingers through her hair, a habit showing her frustration. "I thought you and Rose hit it off."

"Rose is nice but just as a friend," Merritt replied defensively. "Austen and I were just talking about getting to know each other better, not to go on a dirty weekend. I don't know why you're carrying on."

Terry looked at her pleadingly. "You're my best friend and I don't want you to get hurt. Just be careful."

Merritt nodded, the defensiveness gone, a wry note in its place. "I will. I know the pitfalls."

"If I wasn't so worried, I'd laugh. My friend is a goddess among women. She's got Austen Farleigh to date her."

"Oh, give me a break," Merritt retorted with a grin. She couldn't stay annoyed with Terry. She was protecting her back. She'd go out with Austen today, then after that...*who knows?*

CHAPTER TWELVE

Austen grasped Merritt's outstretched hand to help her climb down from the jetty into the fiberglass boat. Powered by an electric motor, it was small and compact, with a fixed table amidships, ideal for a picnic.

"This is so cute!" Merritt exclaimed.

"I hoped you'd like it," said Austen, waiting for her to be seated before she settled beside her, the tiller between them.

Austen pressed the starter button and the motor came to life with a purr. Once the boat had glided from its mooring bay into the open water, she rummaged in her carry bag and passed Merritt a bottle of water and another baseball cap. "Here… you'll need these."

"Thanks." Merritt turned the cap to look at the logo. "Ah, ha…another Yankees cap. You're a fan?"

"Yep. Love baseball. Love the Yanks. What about you?"

"You're kidding me. I'm from Washington. Go Nats."

Austen chuckled. "We'll have to go to a game one day."

It was only when pink tinged Merritt's cheeks that Austen realized what she had said. And it had just come out. But strangely, the thought of Merritt in her future felt as natural as taking a breath. But she'd better be careful. Merritt might be the first woman for years she was interested in getting to know properly—*but long term?* She changed the subject hurriedly, "Are you happy to motor on for a while before we eat? It's not exactly a speedboat though."

"Suits me. It's so peaceful."

Austen nodded in agreement, feeling completely chilled out. Any more relaxed and she'd be asleep. Damn, but it felt good to have a break from the fans and photographers. There was always something about water that drew her in, soothed her nerves. Lake Burley Griffin was no exception. It was pretty as a picture, the water glass under the cloudless sky. Grassy verges came into view, sloping gently like a green mat to the water's edge. A pathway ran along the foreshore, wending its way through parks and gardens. A few cyclists and walkers were braving the noonday sun, but mostly people were in the picnic areas under the shady trees.

"How far around the lake?" asked Merritt, who looked equally as relaxed.

"Forty kilometers."

Merritt gave a lazy smile. "What's that in miles?"

Austen did a quick conversion in her head. "Nearly twenty-five."

"That's a long way for an artificial lake."

"Bloody oath it is."

"I love the Aussie slang," Merritt said with a chuckle. "Was it hard getting used to our way of speaking when you moved to the US? Australians use a lot of words we don't, particularly slang."

Austen shrugged. "It was and it wasn't. You adapt quickly enough. You know the old saying—when in Rome. But every time I come home, it seems natural to Aussie-speak again. I guess it's all in the mind. My mother has a friend from Scotland. She's been in Australia for forty years, but as soon as she talks about Scotland, her voice changes into a thick brogue. Weird!"

Merritt looked at her searchingly. "Do you intend coming home to Australia for good eventually?"

"Ah, the million-dollar question," she said offhandedly, but her hand tightened on the tiller. She'd avoided even thinking about it. She loved her apartment in New York, loved the bustle of the city, the nightlife. But would she want it for the rest of her life? Damnit—how had the conversation got so personal so quickly? "To be honest, I don't know. It'll depend I guess."

Merritt looked at her as if she wanted to ask more, but merely said, "Sorry, I probably shouldn't have asked."

"No…you're fine. What about you?"

"I'd like to be closer to Mom for a while. Once my contract's up, which will be four months after this vacation, I'll probably apply for a position at a hospital on the East Coast somewhere. Washington, Boston, New York. I'll have to look into licensing requirements and openings. I don't know yet."

"So, what do you do for kicks?"

Merritt burst into laughter. "You asked me that very same question when you signed my CD at UVA."

"And what did you say?"

"That I had to study." She gave a wry shrug. "You must have thought I was such a dork."

"Hardly. You were the one I wanted out of all those college students," she waggled her eyebrows, "and some staff members as well."

Merritt gave her a light punch on the arm. "You're so full of yourself. What happened to the Ellie you were talking to on the phone? Did you see her in Rome?"

Austen deflected the question. "You've a good memory. We went our own ways. You haven't answered me. What do you like doing?"

"I like to read, cook, watch movies, and I'm a sports fan." She eyed Austen watchfully. "Pretty boring?"

"Why would I think that?"

"It's only natural that it would sound mundane to you. You live an exciting life."

Unable to help herself, Austen curled her fingers around Merritt's wrist. "Don't be silly. That doesn't make you boring. You're one of the most put-together women I've ever met. Let me give you a few facts about myself. I'm thirty-five years old with no tertiary education. I left home when I was sixteen, because if I hadn't, I would have been stuck in the back blocks forever. I made my way in the music world with equal amounts of talent, hard work, and luck. I'm highly competitive, push things to the limits far too much and have done a few things in my life I'm not proud of."

Merritt gave her an appraising glance. "Is there anything else you think I should know?"

Austen's eyes glinted. "I find you very interesting and I'd like to get to know you better."

"Can I ask you a personal question?" Merritt said, gazing solemnly into her eyes.

"Fire away."

"When are you going to feed me? Because I don't know about you, but I'm starving."

Austen broke into a laugh. "I can see a good spot to anchor over there. I've got lunch in the basket."

Changing direction, she glided the boat under a weeping willow that hung like a silvery green curtain over the water's edge. She cut the motor and tied up to a branch.

"A perfect little shady nook," exclaimed Merritt.

"Yep, it is. Completely private as well. Something I've learned to value very much," Austen said, reaching for the insulated cooler under the table. She flipped open the lid and laid out the food, pleased to see the catering agency had lived up to its reputation for superb gourmet food. The spread looked amazing: smoked salmon and cream cheese, baguettes, green salad, raspberry-glazed chicken breast and a brie and fruit plate with Grand Marnier cream. The feast came complete with silverware cutlery, tablecloth, and two crystal glasses.

She opened the light Riesling, poured two glasses and handed one to Merritt. "Here's to a wonderful vacation."

"Cheers," said Merritt, clicking their glasses together. She took a sip as she surveyed the meal. "Wow. This looks really good."

"It certainly does." Austen rubbed her stomach. "A bit more upmarket than my usual burger and fries."

"You should eat better than that," chided Merritt.

"Ah," exclaimed Austen, genuinely wistful. "I can't cook to save myself, so takeaways are easier. But nothing beats home cooking. I miss my mother's meals."

Merritt didn't comment, merely giving a small smile as she neatly arranged the food onto her plate.

As Austen ate her baguette, she watched Merritt eat gracefully and efficiently, as she did everything else. How could anyone make eating an artform? A far cry from Austen's on-road meals with the guys in the band, who wolfed down their food.

"If you don't stop staring at me like that, I'm going to have a complex," said Merritt with a mixture of amusement and embarrassment.

"Was I staring?" said Austen teasingly.

"You know you were."

She winked. "Sorry, but I always stare when there's something worth looking at."

"You're a consummate flirt, Austen Farleigh," said Merritt with an eye roll, and added in a more serious tone. "I wish you'd drop the act and just be yourself. I'd like to get to know the real you, the woman underneath."

Feeling a little vulnerable, Austen acknowledged her request with a nod. "I'm sorry…force of habit. Let start again, shall we. Tell me how you and Terry met. You're obviously the best of friends."

For the next hour, they shared stories about their lives, getting to know each other like any couple on a first date. Austen didn't know whether it was simply a result of the excellent wine and food, but they talked comfortably without awkwardness. It was as if they had known each other for months. A first for her, as most of her interactions with women she was attracted to were a prelude to the night in bed to come. Flirting was the natural foreplay. She couldn't remember when she enjoyed the company of someone quite so much. They seemed to be perfectly in tune with each other. She tried to analyze why exactly Merritt was different but gave up after a while and leaned back to enjoy the day.

Finally, and somewhat reluctantly, she glanced at her watch. "We'd better get going if we want to see the sights."

Merritt quietly packed up, waiting for Austen to put everything in the cooler before she moved to the back seat again. This time she sat close enough that their thighs lightly touched. Austen felt a glow of contentment that Merritt had initiated the contact. She allowed herself to enjoy this unexpected pleasure, careful not to push it further. She knew instinctively, if she was going to have any chance with this elusive woman, she had to allow her to set the pace.

The rest of the cruise passed pleasantly as they took in Canberra's sights. At times they talked, at others they sat contently in a comfortable silence. Finally, Austen nosed the boat into the wharf where an attendant helped them disembark. After arranging for the management to return the picnic hamper, Austen reached for Merritt. "Let's get out of here."

"That was a great afternoon," murmured Merritt, accepting the outstretched hand.

As they sauntered out to the carpark, Austen tried to imagine what it would be like to be just like everyone else. No fans, no paparazzi, just living an ordinary life with a woman whom she idolized beside her. When her car came into view, she slowed her pace, reluctant to let Merritt go. "Have you anything planned for tonight?"

"I promised I'd have dinner at home. My parents are having a small dinner party and my father wants me there," replied Merritt. Austen thought she caught a note of reluctance in her voice.

"What time are you expected?"

"Seven o'clock."

"We still have time for a cup of coffee. They have a nice lounge at my hotel and the coffee's good. Would you like to come? I promise to get you home by six."

Merritt gave her hand a squeeze. "I'd love to."

"Wonderful." As she held the car door open for Merritt, Austen's phone rang. "Excuse me for a minute," she said.

Katie came on the line. "Hi, Austen. Where are you?"

"Just heading back to the hotel. What's up?"

"I was wondering if you wanted to go somewhere for dinner tonight?"

"Good idea." She looked over at Merritt who was strapping on her seat belt. After a minute's hesitation, she made up her mind. It would be nice for Katie to get to know Merritt. "I've got a friend with me if you'd like to join us for coffee in the outdoor courtyard of the tearoom. We'll be there in ten minutes."

"Okay. I'll see you there."

Austen pocketed the phone, and feeling content, got into the driver's seat and turned to Merritt with a smile. "Katie's going to join us for coffee."

* * *

Katie was already sitting at a table in the courtyard, and as always, her makeup was perfect and her dress elegant. She gave Austen a wave as she came through the door, but her smile faded when she caught sight of Merritt behind her. If Austen hadn't been watching her closely, she would have missed the reaction. But when it disappeared in an instant and Katie's expression reverted to amiable, she wondered if she had actually seen it.

"Hi, Katie," Merritt said with a friendly nod.

"Hello there, Merritt, it's nice to see you again." She looked curiously from one to the other. "Have you and Austen been somewhere?"

"We took a cruise on the lake in a cute little boat and had a picnic lunch."

Katie looked surprised. "You and Austen went on a date?"

"Well, yes."

Austen cleared her throat. "I'll place our order. Would you like anything to eat?"

"I couldn't eat anything more after that wonderful lunch. The Brazilian-blend flat white, please," Merritt said, flashing her a wide smile.

Austen couldn't help responding with a smile of her own. Realizing she'd gazed at Merritt a little too long, she turned to Katie hastily. "Katie?"

Her face now devoid of expression, Katie paused long enough for Austen to feel awkward before she said, "The same thanks, but with skim milk."

By the time the coffee arrived, Austen was pleased to see Katie was her old self again and she was going out of her way to charm Merritt.

An hour later, Merritt rose from the chair. "I guess I'd better be going."

"I'll drive you home," said Austen.

"No, no. It's easier if I take a cab. You stay here with Katie."

"I'll walk you to the door," Austen said firmly.

When they reached the lobby, she lowered her voice to a murmur. "Have dinner with me tomorrow night."

At first there was no response, but then she felt the warmth of Merritt's hand as it covered hers. "I'd love to," she whispered, and then she was gone.

Back in the courtyard, Katie was sitting stiffly in the chair, the muscles of her jaw clenched. "Senator Harrington's daughter, Austen? What the fuck are you doing? He's a very powerful man."

Taken aback, Austen stared at her. "So? What's it got to do with him? She's an independent woman in her thirties. I'm only taking her out, not marrying her."

"You're actually going to date her? I thought you were leaving on Saturday?"

"Change of plans. I've already told the hotel I'm staying on," Austen replied with a shrug.

Katie became instantly still, and after a stretch of silence, said in a flat voice, "It's none of my business but be careful."

"No, it's not your business. You're my business manager not my keeper, and Merritt has nothing to do with you."

Katie's eyes widened slightly, and she gave Austen a startled glance. "I'm sorry. I didn't realize—" Her voice trailed off.

Austen leaned forward, her eyes narrowed. "Let that be the end of it. Where are we going for dinner?"

"I've booked a table at Courgette for seven thirty. It's rated five stars."

"Should be good food," remarked Austen, but she knew dinner at the upscale restaurant would be nowhere as thrilling as the picnic in the little fiberglass boat.

CHAPTER THIRTEEN

Merritt couldn't remember how often during dinner she became lost in thought. It was proving impossible to get her mind off the day on the lake. Off Austen. So preoccupied, that her father began glaring at her and her mother kept sending her anxious glances. Their guests were the Singapore Minister for Trade and their Ambassador to Australia. Two interesting diplomats, but she still had to force herself to go through the motions of participating in the conversation. When they finally retired to her father's study for trade talks, she sighed in relief.

Gloria threw her a questioning glance. "You've been very distracted tonight, Merritt. I know you said yesterday you have nothing to tell me, but there's obviously something bothering you. Are you worried about your session with the counselor tomorrow? I know I've never discussed your work, but—"

"Mom," Merritt interrupted quickly. "I understand completely that you find it difficult when I'm in dangerous places. And it's probably time I did something less demanding and stressful." She reached across the table to give her mother a reassuring pat on the hand. "But I'm not worried about seeing the counselor. In fact, it'll be liberating to talk to a professional."

Gloria cast her an apologetic look. "It's just that…well…I worry. You know, you have your father's drive and resilience."

Merritt gave a little snort. "Really?"

"Of course. You've made me so proud over the years." She took a deep breath before she went on, "You know he'd like you to follow in his footsteps."

Merritt stared at her. "You're kidding me?"

"He's been grooming you for the political stage. Haven't you realized that?"

Merritt grew still, conscious her mother watched her carefully as she processed the information. "Is that what this is all about? Virtually ordering me to spend my vacation here? Carting me around with him at the gala dinner? Entertaining his guests?" She stared at her mother. *Why haven't I seen it before?* "But now that I think about it, he's being doing it all my life."

Gloria gave a delicate shrug. "I'm afraid so."

"It must have been a blow to his plans when I decided to go into medicine."

"Not really. Many doctors go into politics."

"So," Merritt said. "That's why he pushed me so hard." Understanding dawned and she ground out the next sentence. "And that's why he was so upset when I announced I was gay."

There was a long pause before her mother responded, "Your father is intolerant of many things."

"A bigot, you mean," Merritt said, unable to keep the bitterness out of her voice.

"He's old-school, Merritt. But I believe if you find a suitable partner who fits in with our lifestyle and friends, he'll come around," Gloria replied, reaching out with a hand to reassure her.

Merritt forced herself to stay calm and composed as she inwardly cringed. He'd never approve of Austen, a lesbian poster bad girl *and* a rock star. But another thought fetched a faint smile to her lips. She should ask her to dinner here one night, making it quite clear she was her date. He'd probably be incredibly angry and appallingly rude and that would be the end to any aspirations he had of getting her into politics.

"Maybe so," she said emphatically, "but I've no intention of ever following in his footsteps, Mom."

Gloria smiled. "I never thought you did."

* * *

Light rain began to fall as Merritt's taxi pulled up outside the inner-city office block. She made a dash for the lobby and cast her eyes around until she found the name she wanted on the brass directory on the wall. Exiting the elevator at the third floor, she walked down the hallway to the psychologist's office. With a deep breath, she pushed open the door. The waiting room was bright and breezy, decorated with five sleek modern chairs, a large abstract painting on the wall and a vase of fresh flowers on the counter. The receptionist, a young woman sporting dyed red hair and a pair of funky glasses, flashed her a welcoming smile.

As soon as Merritt filled out the new patient form, she was ushered into the therapist's office. She eyed her surroundings in surprise. While the reception area was colorful, the consulting room was stark: white walls decorated with only a clock, a desk, two plain armchairs and a brown leather couch. The polished top of the solid oak desk was devoid of any personal touches, simply a notepad, a computer, two pens, and a box of tissues. She was momentarily thrown. But on reflection, she figured there was a purpose that the room was so sterile. Nothing to distract the patient.

Dr. Angelica Turner wasn't what she expected either. She looked like a gypsy, with a tanned complexion, unruly curly hair and large loopy earrings that dangled nearly to her shoulders. A pair of reading glasses sat on the desk next to her computer. At a rough guess, Merritt put her somewhere in her mid-forties, though it was hard to tell. She had one of those timeless faces. She could have been on the wrong side of fifty for all she knew.

"Welcome, Dr. Harrington," she said, smiling. "May I call you Merritt?"

"Yes, of course."

"I'm Angelica. I'm very pleased to meet you." She gave her a friendly nod and flicked open the notepad. "I presume from your accent that you're American."

"Yes. I'm from the Washington DC area."

"Ah…I was there in the fall. The Virginia oaks and maples were simply glorious, masses of color. Tell me about yourself. Have you always lived there?"

Merritt settled back and chatted about her childhood and college days. Then went on to her work at the hospital and finally DWB.

"Tell me…why did you join?" Angelica asked, her dark eyes focused more on her now.

"Terry was the first to suggest it."

"Terry?"

"Sorry, I should have mentioned her before. We worked together at the Fairfax Hospital trauma unit and became friends. She came up with this idea and I went along with it. We're assigned as part of a team."

"Have you been with them for long?"

"Two and a half years."

"Quite a long spell for that type of work. I imagine when you're called to a disaster, the work's full on."

"It is. We're a trauma unit, so we're sent to places in crisis."

"I can imagine it would be draining, mentally as well as physically." Angelica jotted something in her notepad, then lifted her head to look at her again. "You said on the phone that June Bergin recommended me. What prompted her to suggest that you see me?"

Merritt shifted uncomfortably in her seat. Though the therapist spoke with a low pleasant voice, her eyes were watchful. "Um…I had a couple of episodes. Panic attacks. They didn't last long. It was at the nightclub where I met her."

"What set them off? Do you know, or were they just random?"

"I became squashed on the dance floor and then there was a loud noise."

"Ah...common triggers. Tell me, Merritt, have you had counseling before?"

Merritt nodded. "We're offered psychosocial care before and after every assignment."

"And have you availed yourself of the service?"

"We all attend the sessions. Terry and I usually go to a resort afterward to veg out. That does the most good."

"But not this time?"

Merritt expelled a shaky breath. "I came straight here from Peru and didn't have the opportunity for counseling. Which was unfortunate, because I actually need some help this time. My last assignment was frightening...really ghastly."

With a wave of her hand at the couch, Angelica said sympathetically, "Would you feel more comfortable if you were more relaxed?"

Merritt glanced over at it. Lying down was the last thing she wanted to do. She hated to be put in such a vulnerable position. She shook her head. "No, I'd prefer to sit here if that's all right with you."

"Whatever you feel happy with. Tell me all about that assignment."

Merritt didn't hold back, including every gruesome detail. At one stage when describing her fear of another avalanche, she fell silent. Angelica said nothing, simply waited for her to continue. To get through her story, Merritt fixed her eyes on a dangling earring, finding after a while it became hypnotic and dulled the pain. Finally, she ran out of words and trailed off into silence with a last, "So many dead." Tears welled up in her eyes and she blinked them back.

After a pause, Angelica sat back in her chair and began to speak. It was a relief for Merritt that her part was over. Reliving the ordeal had been upsetting and exhausting. "How did this experience make you feel?"

Merritt tried to gather her thoughts into a response. "Emergency work is total focus. When you're in the thick of a crisis, your mind is solely on your patients. That's where your training kicks in. Everything becomes automatic, you're tunnel-visioned. But truthfully, it was different up in the Andes. I was more conscious of my surroundings than usual. I'd been in dangerous places before, but this seemed different, more threatening. For the first time since I joined the service, I wanted to run away as far and as fast as I could, even before I started to work." She gave a shrug. "Perhaps I'd just had enough of it all… tired of death in strange places. And on some level I felt out of control and hopeless. I wasn't as good as the others at coping."

"The others?"

"Karl. Terry. And the nurses. They were all so calm. So competent." When Angelica didn't reply, Merritt felt compelled to elaborate. "After a while, I'd reached the end of my tether. The death, the stench, the mud…the fucking rain. All I wanted to do was get out of the place before the whole mountain came crashing down on us. I was scared, terrified really…"

When Angelica gazed at her kindly but remained quiet, Merritt's hands trembled. She twisted them anxiously into her lap. "I know that sounds weak," she breathed out in a small voice.

"No one's judging you," Angelica said encouragingly. "And it certainly wasn't a sign of weakness. Your mind had had enough."

"I'm a doctor, for God sake."

"I know, but that doesn't make you superwoman." Angelica jotted something in her notes then raised her head to look at her intently. "Tell me, Merritt, why did you agree to join DWB with Terry?"

"I guess because it was such a good cause. I'd be doing something worthwhile," Merritt said. She gave a wry smile. "To be completely honest, it sounded rather exciting. Being in exotic places, seeing firsthand things you only ever got to see on the news. Being right *there*. And it was something my father didn't have any control—" Merritt stopped talking abruptly, horrified at herself. Why had she mentioned him?

A gleam appeared in Angelica's eyes. She gazed at Merritt with an enigmatic smile. "Your father didn't want you to go?"

Merritt's heart sank as the therapist homed in on her slip. She plastered on her best bland mask and shrugged. "I haven't lived at home for years. I make my own decisions."

"And your mother?"

Merritt glanced quickly up at the clock on the wall. *Darn it—
still five minutes to go.* When she caught the therapist following
her gaze, she tried to concentrate back on the earring. But try
as she might, it was waving out of focus now as her eyes filled.
She swallowed and replied a little too harshly. "She found it
hard to cope with me being in a danger zone. She…um…never
discusses my overseas work with me."

"Never?"

Merritt cleared her throat. "No."

"Okay," Angelica said with a smile. "I think that's enough
for the day." She opened her computer and after a few clicks,
studied the screen. "How long will you be in Canberra?"

"Four more weeks."

"I'll fit you in for an appointment early next week. Would
Tuesday morning at ten suit you?"

Merritt nodded mutely.

"Great, I'll see you then," Angelica said, extending her hand.

Merritt shook it, forcing a smile. Dr. Turner wasn't going to
let her relationship with her parents go. That was clear.

Fuck! The meeting had been going well, she was getting
things off her chest. Why the hell did she have to mention her
father?

Mentally exhausted, Merritt decided to walk for a while to
clear her head. As the morning rain clouds had been swept away
by the easterly breeze, it was fine enough for a leisurely stroll.
And home was the last place she wanted to be after rehashing
her experience. Somehow, just being one of the many people
in the street put everything into perspective. She was, after all,
only a small piece of humanity, a small cog in the great scheme
of things. For an hour she wandered around window-shopping,
then on a corner as she waited for the traffic lights to change,
her phone buzzed a text.

Her heart gave a flutter when Austen's name popped up.

*Booked table at the Sage 7:30 tonight. Predinner drinks at the
Hyatt?*

A little frisson of excitement tingled through Merritt as she reread the message. A few drinks with Austen would be just the therapy she needed after dragging up all those ghastly memories.

Sounds good. What time?

6:30. Speaker's Corner Bar.

Merritt pressed the thumbs-up emoji, and with a renewed spring in her step, went to find a café to eat something before she went out to the airport.

* * *

When she walked through the glass departure doors, Terry was already inside with a cute sandy-haired woman beside her. Merritt recognized her from the nightclub as one of the women with whom Terry had gone home. She was glad Jordan was able to get time off to travel with her—she hadn't seen her friend this happy with someone for years.

Jordan turned out to be as shy as Terry was bubbly, and she found herself liking the young woman.

All too soon it was time for them to go. Merritt pulled Terry into a long hug and whispered in her ear, "I like Jordan. Look after yourself and I'll see you when we get home."

After giving Jordan a hug as well, she watched sadly as they went through security.

She was going to miss her friend.

CHAPTER FOURTEEN

As soon as Merritt's cab pulled up outside the entrance to the Hyatt a doorman, dressed in a 1920s uniform, opened her door. Before she walked up the short flight of stairs, she smoothed her knee-length cocktail dress, a recent acquisition from a shopping expedition with a college friend in DC. She knew it must look good, for her mother, a very fussy fashionista, had given her a nod of approval.

"You look very nice, dear. The blue sets off your eyes delightfully."

Thankfully, her father was fidgeting impatiently at the door, and Gloria had only time to ask quickly, "Where are you off to tonight? I thought you were staying in."

"I'm having dinner with a friend," replied Merritt, ignoring the niggle of guilt. She'd retired straight to her room when she'd arrived home, needing quiet time to regroup for her date. The therapy session, plus seeing her best friend disappear into the bowels of the airport, had left her feeling fuzzy-headed and out of sorts. She had deliberately not mentioned to her mother at breakfast that she was going out to dinner, to save the inevitable questions she didn't want to answer.

Gloria gave her one last curious look before she walked out with her husband to the car. Merritt watched the black Audi drive off, realizing she'd have to come up with some plausible explanation if she was going to continue seeing Austen. For all her mother's protestations that her sexuality didn't matter, Merritt doubted she would consider Austen the *suitable* partner. Though the rock star would be wealthy, maybe even richer than her family, Austen was hardly upper class. And the Harringtons were old Virginian stock, dating back to colonial times. Damn snobs in Merritt's book. One thing she had learned from working in the third world, snobbery was a first-world blight.

At the hotel desk, the receptionist directed her down the hallway to a small intimate lounge. Merritt gazed around appreciatively. The Speaker's Corner oozed charm, all wood, brass, and leather. Cushy chairs around low polished tables lined the walls and circled the fireplace. Since the nights had turned warm, there was a door open to a veranda.

Austen was leaning against the bar, her head tilted as she listened to the bartender. Merritt took a moment to study her before she made herself known. By the way the black suit fit snugly over her willowy frame, there was no doubt it had been tailor-made. When Merritt approached, Austen turned to reveal a crisp white shirt underneath the jacket. The top three buttons were undone, the colorful tattoo peeping out looking like an exotic necklace. Her only jewelry was a small silver guitar brooch pinned to her lapel.

She looked so dashing that Merritt's stomach fluttered like a swarm of butterflies. She quickly closed her sagging mouth. The suit might have a masculine cut, but there was no mistaking Austen was a woman. And a stunning one. A sudden sense of coming home engulfed Merritt. Without a thought, she stepped close and pulled her into a tight hug. Austen rubbed her fingers lightly up her back as Merritt sank into her. "I missed you too, babe," she whispered in her ear.

"That obvious, huh?" muttered Merritt, slightly embarrassed. She'd never been one for spontaneous displays. Especially in public.

Austen stepped back and gently brushed a strand of hair from Merritt's forehead. "Bad day?"

"A little," she said, wrinkling her nose.

"Let's get you a drink," Austen said. "Stephen here makes the best cocktails."

The bartender, a slim man in a fancy brocade waistcoat and red bowtie, flashed her a practiced smile. "What will you have, ma'am?"

"A margarita, please."

"And I'll have another single malt on the rocks," Austen said, then glanced at Merritt. "Would you prefer to sit inside or on the veranda?"

Merritt roamed her eyes around the room. Despite being a foreigner, everything about it seemed so familiar, she could feel the history in her bones. She imagined there would have been hundreds of political deals cut around the tables over the years. "Inside, please. It has a wonderful atmosphere and very cozy."

"Suits me. It's more private in here as well," replied Austen.

Merritt nodded. It must be dreadfully draining to be constantly besieged by the public. At least here in the upscale Hyatt, they catered for VIP guests and wouldn't allow her to be pestered by autograph hunters.

Austen led her to a secluded table for two in the corner. Once they were comfortably seated, she placed her hand over Merritt's fingers and squeezed lightly. Her voice dropped an octave. "Do you want to talk about what's bothering you?"

Merritt shook her head. "Not really. I saw a counselor this morning about my last assignment, which brought up a few unpleasant memories. I'd like to forget about it tonight. Tell me about your day."

Austen didn't remove her hand, nor did Merritt pull her fingers loose. It seemed so natural to remain connected, to be touching. "I didn't do much. After a few business calls, I went to the gym, had a swim and watched a couple of inhouse movies."

She feathered her thumb over Merritt's knuckles. "I was wishing you were with me."

Merritt held her eyes with a smile. "It's always better if you have someone to share things with." She added sadly, "Terry left for New Zealand this afternoon."

"You'll miss her."

"I will." She took a sip of her drink and asked, "What about you? Who's your best friend?"

Austen grinned. "Mick. He's a mad Irishman but as loyal as they come. We get on well. I don't have many close friends, lots of acquaintances though. It's hard to keep up friendships when you're always on the road. Mostly, I mix with other singers and industry people."

"Like Rose and Katie."

"Yeah. Rose is a real sweetie. Katie's not too bad, but she can be pretty moody at times. Now that her business is super-successful, I don't see much of her anymore."

"But she came out here with you."

"For a vacation and to visit her uncle. He moved to Australia with his family twenty years ago," Austen replied. Her eyes turned darker, greener. "You look beautiful tonight. Your dress is lovely…you're lovely."

Merritt felt the heat rush to her cheeks. There was no mistaking the approval in Austen's voice. *God help me, but I'm blushing like a schoolgirl.* She took another sip, remembering her mother's words. "A compliment must always be acknowledged and received graciously." She replied with a warm smile, "Thank you, Austen."

"You're welcome. Can I ask you a question?"

Merritt leaned over the table, raising an eyebrow. "Is it personal?"

"No," Austen answered with a laugh. "You said you liked cooking. I'd love to hear about your best dishes."

"Ah…my favorite topic," replied Merritt unable to stop her wide smile. She launched into stories about her culinary experiments from her travels, describing the exotic and sometimes very unusual recipes that she'd picked up from various countries.

When she finally trailed off, Austen exclaimed. "It all sounds fantastic. I don't suppose you bake cookies?"

"I have a few good recipes. I could make you some if you like so you'll have a supply in your room. What are your favorites?"

Austen stared into her glass dreamily. "Cherry and chocolate chip cookie delights. Sophie cooked me a batch and I've never forgotten how good they tasted."

Merritt perked up her ears. She hadn't heard that name before. In spite of herself, she felt a tiny stab of jealousy. "Sophie? Is she a chef?" she asked.

"No, no. Just a friend." Austen cleared her throat. "Actually, she's engaged to Eleanor Godwin."

"The famous movie star? You know her? I saw her in *Wings of the Hawk*. She was fabulous." Her eyes widened as it sank in. "She's gay?"

Austen laughed. "You didn't know? So much for Ellie worrying about coming out."

"I don't bother with social media. Most of it is made up crap," said Merritt, feeling stupid. She was probably the only lesbian on earth who didn't know. She'd never been interested in the tabloids and had only followed Austen's career. Then it hit her. "That night at college when Ellie rang. She's *that* Ellie, isn't she?"

Austen inhaled sharply, looking like a cornered rabbit. "Um…yes."

"You and *Eleanor Godwin* were lovers? Wow!"

"We weren't," said Austen, flinching. "We became close when I went to America. Being both Australian, we had the same set of friends. Expat Aussies tend to stick together. I read more into our friendship than she did."

"But why did—" Merritt bit off the sentence just in time. To ask Austen why she'd been trying to seduce her when she was in love with Eleanor, would have been a giant date killer.

In the following silence, Austen avoided her eye as if she had sensed what she had been about to say. Finally, she said gruffly, "I was young and fucking full of myself. I played hard in those days. I couldn't even spell monogamy. When I did something to save her career, it was only years later that she forgave me."

"What did you do?"

Austen stiffened, regret and some distress evident on her face. "Even though it was for the best intentions, I broke her trust. When we were in Rome, she had an affair with a married woman. A very high-profile woman. I can't tell you who it was, but if it had ever become public, Ellie's career would have been down the tube. But she was head-over-heels and couldn't see the woman was a player. So I...I went after her and cut Ellie out."

"Oh," murmured Merritt, understanding why Eleanor would hate Austen. Friends didn't do those things to each other. "Did you try to explain why you did it?"

"I tried, but she wouldn't speak to me. She left Rome immediately and wiped me completely. We ran into each other a couple of years ago on an island resort, which was the first time I'd seen her since." Austen gave her an anguished look. "She was the first woman I'd ever really loved, but she never ever saw me waiting in the wings."

Merritt gazed at her, wondering what on earth to say. Her family didn't *do* emotions well. But seeing Austen upset, stirred something in her she'd only ever felt at work. Her protective instinct rose, and she had an inexplicable urge to shield her from more hurt. "Hey," she said gently. "I'm not judging you. It just sounds like you were both too young for a commitment. And there's nothing worse than pining after someone who doesn't know you're crazy about them and who doesn't share the same feelings."

Austen colored slightly. "You're too soft on me. Sure, we were young, but I still behaved like a shit. For a long moment she fiddled with her glass before her eyes flicked to Merritt's face. "You sound like you've had experience with heartbreak. Who was she?"

Merritt brushed her hair back with a nervous flip. She could hardly say Austen was the only woman who'd ever set her blood on fire. How pathetic—and odd—it would sound. "Just a woman I knew. I was enamored with her. She convinced me love should come with whistles and fireworks. She left me hankering for something I've never found," she said, silently echoing the last two words, *since you.*

"Damn, babe. You're deep. What's wrong with a good ol' shag for the sake of it?" Austen said with a chuckle.

Merritt felt herself blush again. "Touché! But I can't divorce emotional involvement from sex. I wish I could be like you and just go for it without overanalyzing everything."

Austen was quiet for a moment, staring at her face. "I hope I'm around when you stop analyzing," she murmured.

Merritt dropped her gaze to Austen's lips. They were slightly pursed as if ready for a kiss. "You do?" she managed to say through the drumming of her heart. She gave a shy smile. "I have no idea why you're interested in me. I'm sure you've known lots of women sexier than me."

"Hmmm…but still waters can run deep." Austen's voice lowered to a purr. "Very deep."

Merritt blinked, it wasn't just her pulse that was thrumming now, it was her whole body. Suddenly, she was conscious that they were both leaning over the table, their lips inches apart. She straightened and gulped down the last of her drink. Things were moving way too fast. She glanced at her watch and said overly brightly. "We'd better go or we'll be late for our dinner reservation."

Austen relaxed back, finished her drink and pushed up from her chair. "I'll get reception to call a cab."

At Sage, a waiter took them through to a quiet table overlooking the gardens. A perfect romantic setting.

"I've taken the liberty of ordering this month's seven-course degustation with wine pairings," said Austen. "I thought you would enjoy the chef's creations."

"That sounds fabulous. I love tasting menus," said Merritt enthusiastically. "They always bring out the best in chefs. They can have the biggest egos and like showcasing their menus."

It was a magical night for Merritt. The staff were attentive and friendly, the atmosphere warm, the food excellent. The wines were so superb that she guessed Austen had instructed they had to be the cellar's best offerings. They chatted easily throughout the meal, discussing a range of topics. Eventually, she opened up and told Austin about her experience in Peru and the post-trauma she had been experiencing. Every so often through her recital, Austen reached over to touch her arm or hand for support. By the end of dinner, Merritt knew that she would have to find some very strong self-control to be able to leave Austen at the door.

After they strolled out of the restaurant, they stopped and faced each other under the streetlamp. The night breeze ruffled Austen's hair, her eyes glimmered in the soft glow. Merritt caught her breath—she looked absolutely stunning. Austen gave her a lopsided grin that sent goosebumps rippling across her skin. Moving closer, Austen leaned in and gently kissed her. The feel of those soft lips sent a sizzle of desire through Merritt to her very toes.

But Austen didn't linger. She shifted her head and murmured huskily in her ear, "Would you like to come to my room at the Hyatt for coffee?"

Merritt shivered as she felt the warm breath on her skin. Lightheaded from the wine, it took all her will power to ignore the flush of arousal. She touched Austen's cheek lightly in a gesture of apology. "Not tonight, Austen. It's late and I've had a little too much to drink."

"Oh…okay, of course you're right," Austen answered, her voice tinged with regret. "I'll call a cab."

She dug in her pocket for her phone and it was only a few minutes before a yellow cab came up the street and pulled into the curb.

"What's your address, babe? We'll drop you off first," Austen asked as she opened the back door.

Merritt climbed in and called out the address to the driver before she sank back with a sigh into the leather seat. Austen slid along until their thighs touched, then wrapped her arm around her shoulders. Merritt closed her eyes, relieved. For a moment, she thought she'd offended Austen. They snuggled together as the taxi sped through the city until they pulled up outside her driveway. Austen got out with her and asked the cabbie to wait. She grasped Merritt's hand, pulling her off the driveway into the garden out of sight from the driver.

She leaned close with a soft, "Goodnight," sliding her arms around Merritt's waist and pulling her close.

The kiss wasn't a light brush like before. This was sizzling and demanding. Merritt's legs buckled and all she could do was hang on while her mouth was being devoured. Without a second thought, she opened her lips to Austen. When her tongue entered and teased, it was as if something within Merritt was unleashed. She clutched a fistful of Austen's hair to hold her tightly in place and responded with abandon. Soft moans and ragged breaths swirled in the air. She didn't know who they were coming from, nor did she care. All she wanted was for Austen not to stop. She slid her hand down her back and grasped Austen's bottom, pulling her tight against her.

But then Merritt came to her senses. God, she was acting completely out of character.

With an effort, she dropped her hands and eased out of Austen's embrace. Placing her hands on her shoulders, she planted a chaste kiss on her forehead. "Goodnight."

"Would you like to come with me for a drive tomorrow?" Austen asked, her voice husky and low.

Merritt nodded mutely.

"I'll pick you up at eight. I guess it would be better if you waited for me on the street."

"Yes," Merritt said, finding her voice, "that'd be wise. Text me when you're on your way. I guess I better go in, the cab's meter is ticking. Sleep well."

"You too. And babe?"

"Yes, Austen?"

"I'm looking forward to it."

And she disappeared to the street, whistling as she went.

Merritt turned to go inside, the heady taste of Austen's mouth lingering on her lips.

CHAPTER FIFTEEN

Austen caught her breath when she saw the familiar turnoff ahead. The yellow road sign stenciled with the image of a kangaroo and the words NEXT 35 KM, was still there at the entrance. Involuntarily, she eased off the accelerator as she neared. Though her instincts screamed to keep going, that it would only bring heartache to drag up the past, she pulled over and glided to a stop.

Merritt tilted her head to look at her from the passenger seat. "Is something the matter?"

Austen sat quietly, scanning the narrow gravel road opposite. She closed her eyes, pushing her fingers over her temples to try to blot out the memories. What the hell was she doing here? She'd moved on, said her goodbyes. She'd never ever intended to come back. That part of her life was over.

Until now it seemed.

"My old home is down that road," she said finally, flatly.

Merritt turned to gaze over at it. "Really? Wow! I'd love to see where you grew up."

Austen couldn't ignore the enthusiasm in Merritt's voice, or her expectant look. She shrugged. Why not? She was no longer that scared kid getting on the bus. Maybe subconsciously, she'd intended this all along when she'd asked Merritt on the drive. Perhaps she needed final closure. Nineteen years ago, she'd just scooted out of town.

But why now and why with Merritt? Later, in a quiet place she'd figure that one out. The woman did something to her. Brought out feelings that had been long since buried.

"Okay," she said, barely breathing out the word, and turned the Range Rover onto the gravel road.

Time and miles flew by.

In from the highway, the countryside changed. It was no longer so flat but undulated gently as the road headed further into the bush. It weaved around bends and across small gullies, while tall eucalypts and grasses crowded the gravel edges. She slowed down to take it all in, stuck in the past. Nothing had changed. It remained a backwoods, but strangely now that didn't bother her. Compared to her frenetic life in New York, it seemed a haven—dependable and peaceful.

Fifteen kilometers along, it all became a reality. She was back home.

Trailing a cloud of dust, she pulled up at the familiar old iron gate. "This is it," she said, killing the engine. When she stepped out of the vehicle's air-conditioning, heat wrapped around her like a blanket. But despite that, she shivered.

She walked to the gate, and then shaded her eyes with her hand to gaze at the cattle in the distance. The black and white Friesians looked like polka dots on a green and brown tapestry. She stood frozen as the flashbacks flooded in. Long-suppressed emotions welled up and she bit back a gulp.

At the light touch on her arm, she turned to find Merritt beside her. "You miss it?" she asked, her voice soft and caring.

"I never thought I'd say this, but I do. Strange, for all I ever wanted in my teens was to get out. I never wanted to stay in the country. I longed to see the world…to be with interesting people who had more to talk about than milk prices and the weather. Play my music."

"But you had a happy childhood?"

"Yeah. I did. The farm was a great place to raise a family." She gave a chuckle. "I was the skinny little kid who was always in trouble."

"Noooo. I don't believe *that*."

Austen winked. "Now I'm a skinny *big* kid, always in trouble."

Merritt openly appraised her with a light in her eye. "Oh, I wouldn't say you're too skinny. Not from where I'm standing."

"Why, Dr. Harrington honey child, ah do believes ya flirtin'."

Merritt laughed. "You're rubbing off on me."

"You're a fast learner."

Merritt's smile faded. "What happened to make you leave home?"

Austen gripped the top rail of the gate and let out a long breath. "By the time I reached high school, money had become tight, and the laughter had disappeared. All we did was work. No vacations. No trips to town just for fun." Moisture suddenly filled Austen's eyes as she remembered the arguments. Always about money. *Fucking money.* She had vowed if she ever got out of the place, she'd never be poor again.

Shaking off the painful memories, she pointed at the shed next to a set of yards. "Our house was over there. You can see the stumps where it used to be. The milking shed must be still in use though—it looks like it's been recently painted."

She could understand why the new owners had dismantled the old house. Built after the First World War, she could only ever remember it as dilapidated, neither attractive nor functional. But it had been her home where there had been happy times as well as hard ones.

"Who bought it?" asked Merritt. "I don't see a house."

"One of our neighbors, over that rise. There are no small farms left. The supermarkets cut prices until anyone wanting to stay in the industry had to get bigger or go under."

Merritt regarded her, her eyes shining with sympathy. "Is this the first time you've been back?"

"Yep. Never wanted to before. As soon as I became successful, I set the folks up financially so they could get out. Dad took some convincing to move, but Mum was just happy their money worries were over. My brother and sister were still studying."

"Where are they all now?"

"Tom's in telecommunications in Melbourne, and Helen's a primary school teacher in Newcastle. I'll catch up with Helen when I drive up the coast to visit my parents. They live further north in Port Macquarie. Though knowing my mother, she would have already organized a family get-together when I'm there." She shot a look at Merritt. "A bit different from your childhood."

"Very. But in a way, not so dissimilar. We might have been wealthy, but there were not many choices for a kid growing up with a dogmatic, strict father."

Austen didn't say anything, just put an arm around her shoulder and drew her close. For a moment Merritt nestled against her, then said in an undertone, "Do you want to go in?"

"Nah. I've seen enough. Now the old house is gone, there's nothing of interest left." Austen gave a humorless laugh. "And I'm not going into the milking shed again."

Merritt gave her a dig in the ribs. "I was hoping for a demo."

"You wish. The only milk I drink now comes in a carton," Austen replied. When Merritt planted a kiss on her cheek, all her old ghosts seemed to melt away. She felt light-hearted and free. "Come on. I'll show you Cowra. And afterward, we'll have lunch in the Japanese Gardens."

* * *

Austen hardly recognized the place. The main street had had a major facelift, no longer the sleepy little town she remembered. She was pleased to see, though, that the historical buildings remained as they were.

"It's pretty," Merritt commented as she stared out the window. "What's there to do?"

"There are a few wineries, but tourists usually visit for its history. Cowra has a Japanese Garden and a World Peace Bell."

Merritt raised an eyebrow. "World Peace? Here?"

Austen chuckled. "Yep. Believe it or not. The bell is made up of melted coins from all over the world."

"Why on earth would they have a peace symbol in a small rural town?"

Austen turned the car left at the traffic lights before she continued. "It's an interesting story. During the war, there was a Japanese Prisoner of War camp here. In 1944, a thousand prisoners attempted to escape. It was the largest POW prison escape in the Second World War, and the bloodiest. My grandfather's brother was the quartermaster stationed in the compound. He was shot in the arm in the riot," she chuckled, "taking cover in the outdoor dunny."

"Dunny?"

"Outdoor toilet."

Merritt laughed. "Not an auspicious place to be caught."

"Poor bugger never lived it down. Twenty years later, the town built a Japanese Garden and planted a line of cherry blossoms linking the Japanese cemetery to the gardens."

"I can't wait to see it," Merritt said. "I love the cherry blossoms in DC."

Austen drove the Rover into the café carpark and climbed out. "How about we walk around after lunch?" The five hectares of Japanese Gardens looked as impressive as ever, with an expanse of lawn, shaped trees and shrubs and a meandering stream that cascaded over rocks in a succession of little waterfalls.

"Wonderful," murmured Merritt as they gazed over the railing.

"It is," Austen said wistfully, and reached over and took her hand. "Come on. Let's eat."

The café was far more upscale than she remembered. No curious glances were thrown her way. It didn't surprise her. Even though she had donned a cap and a shirt to cover her tats, the patrons were older tourists. They probably wouldn't have recognized rock singers if they fell over them. The younger backpacker fraternity tended to stick to places with more nightlife and exciting things to do, and the press was nonexistent in a place like this.

"Oh my God. Meg McRoberts. Is that really you?"

Austen looked up quickly from the menu, finding a pretty woman with curly blond hair staring down at her. Even though she was older with a fuller figure, there was no mistaking the face. Her best friend at school, Penny Humphries. Austen's smile faltered, uncertain of the reception. She hadn't attempted to contact anyone from the school or the town. It hadn't been deliberate, just not high on the agenda as she fought to make ends meet. When she had finally made her way in the music industry, too much time had passed to reconnect with old friendships. Too much water under the bridge. She had become Austen Farleigh, someone else entirely.

As she rose in greeting, a flood of nostalgia rushed through her. "Hi, Penny. How have you been?"

Penny studied her closely for a moment, then with a delighted smile, moved forward to pull her into a hug. "I'm so glad to see you, Meg. I'd given up hoping you'd ever come back. You look great."

"So do you."

"I missed you a lot when you left. I wish you'd kept in contact."

"I know, but it was hard at first just living in Sydney. Then I guess…" Austen fidgeted self-consciously, "well…I got too wrapped up in my new life."

"I can't say I blame you. You were always too talented to stay around in a place like this." Penny flashed her a proud smile. "Now look at you…Austen Farleigh, Rock Star."

"Huh! It's not as glamorous as it sounds. What did you do after school?"

"Went to work for an accountant. Got married. Usual stuff."

"Any kids?"

"Two. A girl and a boy…Emma and Jack." Penny smiled. "I married the accountant."

"I'd like to hear all about your family. Why don't you join us for lunch? We can talk."

She introduced Merritt.

"Hi, Merritt," Penny said and politely shook her hand. "I've just finished helping with the café's bookkeeping, so I'd love to join you. It'll be nice to catch up, though I have to warn you my life hasn't been nearly as exciting as Austen's."

For the next hour they reminisced over old times. And as they talked, the years fell away. They were teenagers again, bickering and laughing as if they hadn't been apart for nearly twenty years. When Penny looked at her watch and declared she had to go back to work, Austen stood up reluctantly. "I'm seeing my folks before I go back to the States, so maybe on the way, we can get together again. I'd love to meet your family."

"That would be wonderful. I might even persuade Adrian to take a holiday to America."

"I'd love that."

"Let's swap phone numbers before I go."

When the phones were back in their pockets, they hugged again, this time tighter. Penny said tearfully into her shoulder, "You look after yourself, Meg."

A lump formed in Austen's throat as she watched her walk out the door. She felt Merritt squeeze her arm. "She's a sweetie, Austen."

"Yes, she is."

"Why your guilty expression?"

Austen met her eyes, then looked away. "I feel like a shit for not letting her know I was all right. We were best mates."

"Hey. Don't be so hard on yourself. You were only sixteen. Come on, let's go for a walk and you can tell me all the adventures you two got up to."

"Okay," said Austen, lacing their fingers together, "but this isn't a one-way street. I expect to hear some of the things *you* did as a kid too."

"I was a model child," Merritt said primly.

"Bullshit. I bet you got up to as much mischief as I did."

Merritt chuckled. "Maybe I wasn't as pure as I make myself out to be."

Austen smiled as they strolled along. For the first time in years, she felt true contentment.

* * *

Austen glanced sideways at Merritt, wondering what she was thinking. She had chatted on all day but tapered into silence as they drove into Canberra.

"Would you like to come up to my suite for dinner? We could order room service. I don't feel like going out," she asked softly, careful not to sound insistent. She didn't want Merritt taking the invitation to her room the wrong way and become skittish again.

Merritt turned to look at her, her eyes searching her face. Austen shifted nervously under the scrutiny and added, "I don't want the day to end yet, babe. I had a great time today."

"Me too."

"Are your parents expecting you home for dinner?"

"No. I told Mom I wouldn't be joining them tonight." She eyed Austen thoughtfully. "So, what do you intend to order?"

"What do you feel like?"

"Pizza," announced Merritt emphatically. "With beer."

Austen laughed delightedly. "Great choice. The works with extra cheese."

"Yum."

Feeling buoyant, Austen turned the car into the hotel driveway. After she tossed the keys to the parking valet, she took Merritt's hand and led her into the hotel.

"Wow!" said Merritt as they entered her suite. "This is swanky."

"It's one of the executive suites. There're extra towels in the bathroom if you want to tidy up. You go first, and I'll get a couple of beers."

When Merritt disappeared, Austen went into the bedroom where she kicked off her shoes and shrugged out of her shirt, exposing the white tank top underneath. She went to the bar to pour two glasses of beer and pulled out the plate of nibbles from the fridge. Satisfied, she ordered the pizza, then she waited her turn for the bathroom.

Merritt was settled in a lounge chair when Austen returned, her shoes on the floor, her feet tucked under her, a beer in her hand.

Austen reached for the other glass and raised it in the air. "Cheers!"

"Proscht!" Merritt said. When Austen lifted her eyebrows, she added, "I work with a Swiss doctor."

"I'm glad you came, babe. Upmarket or not, a hotel room can be a lonely place."

"I know. Do you spend much time on the road?"

"We travel a lot. I've been thinking of cutting back on the tours." Although Austen had made that statement often in the last few years, she realized she meant it this time. The thought of making a real home for herself had far more appeal lately than it used to. With a dreamy smile she looked over at Merritt. It would be nice to have someone waiting at home. As the thought sank in, she abruptly took a gulp of beer. *Crap! Where did that come from?* She straightened, concentrating on what Merritt was saying.

"I'm looking forward to staying in one place again. After nearly three years flying all over the world, I'm ready for a more settled life."

Austen forced herself not to look at the glimpse of cleavage as Merritt stretched an arm over the back of the chair. It was hard to ignore. She gestured to Merritt's empty glass. "Another?"

"Yes please."

As Austen rose, the doorbell rang. "That'll be dinner," she called out.

"Good. I'm starved!"

They ate the pizza with their hands. After she'd dispatched the last slice, Merritt wiped her fingers clean, and cocked her head to study Austen. "Can I tell you something?"

Austen looked at her curiously. "Of course."

"You've got," Merritt said, delicately dabbing the side of Austen's chin with her napkin, "a piece of tomato topping here." She pulled her hand away with a satisfied hum. "There, that's better."

Austen rolled her eyes. "Very funny."

Merritt gave a tinkling laugh. "I don't give my secrets away that easily."

"Then I'll have to work harder to get them out of you," Austen said, giving a grin.

"You're not that good."

"Don't you bet on it. Would you like to watch a movie?"

"That sounds great."

Austen moved up to make room on the couch as Merritt slipped in beside her. They decided on *Captain Marvel*, Merritt declaring she liked women who kicked ass. Content just to be in her company, Austen couldn't have cared what she watched. Sitting close together was wonderful, intoxicating. Austen told herself she'd better watch out. It felt entirely *too* comfortable. But when Merritt snuggled closer, those cautionary thoughts vanished as desire took over. She kept herself in check, only allowing herself to put her arm around Merritt's shoulders.

It was Merritt who initiated the kiss. It was so light that it felt like a butterfly had brushed her lips. Austen's heart tripped. She leaned into her, the musky perfume mixed with Merritt's salty, yet sweet skin smelled so good. Craving more, she deepened the kiss. When she slipped her tongue between the lips, Merritt opened her mouth to welcome it in. Austen pulled back, running her fingers through Merritt's lush brown hair. Arousal brightened Merritt's eyes, her lips eagerly claiming Austen's again. Austen balanced on the edge of the couch to take her in her arms. Merritt's nails scraped down her back as they kissed, with just the right pressure to send Austen's libido skyrocketing.

She groaned. Merritt was so sexy.

But then Merritt slowly dropped her arms and slid away. "I guess I'd better go…it's getting late. I had a wonderful time, Austen."

Austen gulped down a ragged breath, gathering her wits. "Oh…right…of course." Ignoring the aching throb, she climbed to her feet. "Hang on. I'll get my keys and drive you home."

"No, no. I'll get a cab."

"It's no trouble."

"You've had a few beers, Austen. June said they're very strict about drinking and driving in Australia."

She grimaced. "Yeah, you're right. I'll ring reception to order a taxi."

Merritt didn't linger, collecting her things and heading for the door as soon as Austen put down the phone. As they walked to the lobby, Austen looked over at her. "Um…would you like to do something tomorrow?" she asked hopefully.

"Love to. I promised Mom I'd go to a dinner with them at seven, but I'm free all day."

"Fantastic. Shall I pick you up?"

"No, it'll be easier if I meet you here. You can tell me what you've planned in the morning. It can be a surprise."

"Shall we have breakfast here so we can make a full day of it? I'll get room service and we can eat out on the balcony. Just the two of us."

Merritt touched her arm lightly. "Sounds delightful."

"A quarter to seven not too early?"

"No. That's fine. I'm an early riser. Till tomorrow," Austen murmured.

As she watched the taxi's lights disappear down the road, Austen just shook her head. She was so messed up—tomorrow couldn't come fast enough.

CHAPTER SIXTEEN

Merritt floated on cloud nine as she entered the Hyatt. At this early hour, except for two elderly women at reception, the lobby was deserted. With a spring in her step, she gave the receptionists a cheery wave as she walked past the desk. They acknowledged her with friendly smiles. As she turned the corner, an elevator door slid open. When she caught sight of the tall man in a dark-gray suit who stepped into the corridor, she stopped dead in her tracks and her stomach gave an anxious lurch. *Oh crap!* There was no mistaking that familiar figure.

Her father.

It was too late to backtrack as he turned her way. When he caught sight of her, he halted abruptly, and his eyes widened. "Merritt!"

It took Merritt a concerted effort to pull herself together. Finally, she blurted out, "Dad. What are you doing here?"

To her surprise, he appeared equally as alarmed. "I had an early appointment with the Japanese Trade Minister," he replied gruffly. Inexplicably, he didn't ask what she was doing at the hotel at this hour, instead went on quickly, "I'll see you tonight," and hurried off to the front lobby.

As she watched him disappear, her whole body sagged with relief. Feeling she'd escaped a bullet, she entered the lift. Once her nerves had settled, it occurred to her that it was entirely out of character for him not to ask what she was doing here. She concluded he must have been conducting some delicate business and needed to get out of the hotel before it became busy. She knew she'd gotten off lightly, but that didn't mean he wasn't going to cross-examine her about it later. That was a given. She'd just have to come up with some credible explanation, though she didn't have a clue what. That one would require some thought.

More subdued, she knocked on Austen's door. When it opened, all thoughts of her father vanished. Casually dressed and hair tousled, Austen looked so irresistible that it seemed the most natural thing in the world to pull her into a hug.

When they moved out of the embrace, Austen draped an arm around her shoulders and led her over the threshold. "Come on in. I'll make you a cup of coffee while you choose what you want to eat."

Merritt took the menu, feeling utter contentment. "A croissant and the Spanish omelet, please. And an orange juice."

"I'll have the same," Austen said, handing her a steaming cup topped with creamy froth. "After I order, let's sit on the balcony. It's too beautiful a morning to be inside."

Merritt quietly studied her as they sat sipping their coffee. Austen was nothing like how she was portrayed in the media, but unfortunately, the public generally believed what they read. She had herself. It was the oldest trick in the book—if people were told something often enough, they'd start to believe it was true. And the simple truth was, Austen's bad-girl image sold magazines. Now she was getting to know her, Merritt realized that underneath the swaggering was a sensitive woman who cared about others.

Catching her scrutiny, Austen raised an eyebrow. "What?"

She gave her a grin. "Just tell the paparazzi where to go."

"Hell, I'd like to, but can you imagine how the trolls would react to that tidbit? They'd have a field day." She gave a shrug. "Everything in life has a price. Even success."

"How true. Politicians can be harassed too. My father can attest to that." Merritt made a face. "And speaking of the good senator, I met him coming out of the elevator this morning."

"Here in the Hyatt?"

"Yes."

"Did he ask you what you were doing here?"

"No, thank goodness. He was in an almighty hurry to get out of the place. I presume his business had to be kept secret. But without a doubt, he'll give me the third degree when I get home." Merritt looked at Austen anxiously. "I'll have to come up with some explanation. I don't honestly know how he'll react to me dating you."

"Come on, Merritt. You're in your thirties. Who you choose to go out with is your own business."

"It should be, but it's not so black and white when it comes to him. He knows how to hurt." Merritt grimaced. "According to my mother, he has political aspirations for me."

Austen gave a mocking chuckle. "And I certainly wouldn't fit the mold of a politician's partner."

"Hell no," said Merritt, unable to suppress an answering smile.

Austen looked at her curiously. "Do you want to go into politics?"

"No way. I like medicine."

"And I bet you're a terrific doctor. So fob him off when he asks. Just say you were going sightseeing with a friend you'd met at a party."

"You make it sound so easy, but you're right. I'll have to stand up to him eventually." Merritt waved a hand between them. "Not just about this. I can't let him run my life when I get a position back home."

"If I know you, you'll work something out." Austen paused, rising to her feet at the knock on the door. "That'll be breakfast."

She arrived back pushing a room service trolley. For the next twenty minutes, they engaged in small talk while they ate.

Merritt placed her knife and fork on the empty plate and said with a satisfied moan, "That was delicious."

"Can I make you another coffee?"

"I've had enough thanks. What's on the agenda today?"

"We're going truffle hunting. I've organized a special tour for just the two of us, so there won't be any annoying fans. Afterward, we'll be served a gourmet truffle lunch."

"Really?" Merritt asked, feeling a stir of excitement. Tasting truffles was something she had yet to experience. "Sounds great."

Austen met her eyes with a wide smile. "I figured with you being fond of cooking, it would be right up your alley."

* * *

Truffle hunting wasn't at all what Merritt expected. She knew very little about the subject and imagined they would be taken to a cultivated spot and given a spade to dig in ploughed earth. Instead, after a brief history on his truffle-farming enterprise, Colin, the proprietor, gave them gumboots and led them into the yard. At his whistle, a big black Labrador ran out from the shed and trotted by his side as they headed out into a paddock lined with trees.

"This here's Sam," he said, pointing to the dog. "Truffles are hard to find. And I mean really hard. They only grow on the roots of certain trees—hazel, poplar, and beech. That's why they're so expensive. And if they didn't stink, we'd never find 'em. Not that humans can pick up the scent under the earth. Dogs can. In some countries they use pigs, though they're more inclined to eat them as soon as they find 'em." Clearly very fond of the Labrador, Colin bent to run his hands slowly across his silky back. "Sam is a whiz at tracking them down."

Merritt looked on with interest and some amusement as the dog ran. Immediately, he weaved around, lifting his leg to pee often as he sniffed around the tree trunks. After much snuffling, he stopped still and dug frantically. Colin pushed him aside, knelt down and dug a little deeper. He sniffed audibly. "This one has a very sweet smell. Extra grade for sure."

He dusted back the soil carefully with a gloved hand, uncovering a small ping-pong size clump. With a satisfied grin, he turned to them. "This little jewel is worth about three hundred dollars."

"I'm in the wrong business," quipped Austen. "How long do they take to grow?"

"Seven to eight years. The truffle is actually a tree root fungus. This beauty is a black Périgord."

Intrigued, Merritt examined it. The truffle was imperfectly round, with a dense black covering that was firm to the touch like a potato. She bent down to smell it. At the first whiff, her senses exploded. It had a pungent aroma, slightly off and highly complex. Because the truffles had such a strong odor, she imagined they were an acquired taste. "What's it like inside?" she asked.

"A lighter black with white veins, and a firm texture. We slice them up." He popped the truffle into a bag then signaled to the dog. It ran off enthusiastically again. "We'll move on. This is only the start."

After three hours' hunting, Colin gave a whistle and Sam ran back to his side, disheveled and panting. "That's enough for the day, folks. We've done very well. Time for lunch."

As they strolled after the man and the dog, Austen took Merritt's hand and squeezed it gently. "Having fun?"

Merritt glanced across at her, relishing the feel of her warm palm and the intimacy of the clasp. "It's fascinating," she said, "though I'll be pleased to get off my feet. Following that dog was a marathon."

Austen gave a soft chuckle. "He reminded me of Mick. Dashing around and marking his territory."

"I hope he doesn't pee everywhere too," said Merritt with a giggle.

After tidying themselves and shedding the gumboots, they were shown to a private alcove overlooking the gardens. Accompanied by a relaxing glass of wine, they were served a gourmet truffle feast: soup with freshly pickled-truffle sourdough, truffle pork terrine with cranberry jam and goat's cheese, truffle panna cotta and lastly truffle honey hazelnuts with their coffee.

Merritt found she loved the taste. Earthy, musty and sweet and addictive.

Pleasantly tired and full, she was sitting back enjoying her coffee when Austen's phone rang. She glanced at the caller ID. "Sorry, babe, I've got to take this. Excuse me for a minute," she said and wandered off down the stairs into the garden.

As Merritt watched her go, she thought how much like a truffle Austen was. A hidden gem. Tough on the exterior, but underneath something special and unique. She wondered what it would be like to be her partner, her exclusive lover. Her nipples tightened at the thought. Austen was fast becoming very important in her life. And sexual desire aside, the more she got to know her, the more she liked her as a person. Merritt knew she was going to get hurt when her vacation ended. When the dating was over, would there be no hope of being happy again?

She snapped out of her thoughts when Austen reappeared. Before taking a seat, she leaned over Merritt and lowered her mouth to gently kiss her. Immediately, the soft moist pressure of the lips enveloped Merritt in such a cocoon of want she could only manage a weak smile.

"That was Katie," Austen said, screwing up her nose. "She wants me to fly to Melbourne tonight to meet with the CEO of our marketing studio in Australia."

"But it's Sunday."

"I know, but the appointment's early Monday morning. I haven't a choice."

"As your business manager, isn't that her responsibility?"

"Yeah, usually. But apparently, he wants to meet me in person since I'm over here. One plus if I have to go…my brother, Tom, lives in Melbourne so it will be an opportunity to catch up with him." She reached over and took Merritt's hand. "I was hoping to see you again tomorrow."

"Me too. But at least you'll be able to see your brother. What does he do?"

"He's a marketing director for Telstra."

"Married?"

"Nope. He's a bit of a party animal like me."

"When will you be back?" murmured Merritt.

"Monday night. Maybe we can do something Tuesday?"

Merritt shook her head regretfully. "I'm tied up completely. I've an appointment with the therapist in the morning and the hairdresser in the afternoon. I promised Mom I'd help entertain the Arts Council people at dinner. Sorry."

"Okay. Tuesday's out. I'll stay another day in Melbourne and have a night out with Tom." Austen lifted her hand and brushed a kiss over the back. "What about a getaway on Wednesday to check out Sydney for a couple of days? Longer if you like."

Merritt's heart gave a flutter. Going away with Austen would mean sleeping with her. There was no turning back after that. But she knew that there was no momentous decision to be made. She already knew her answer. Her body would have it no other way.

"I'd love to," she whispered.

CHAPTER SEVENTEEN

With more trepidation this time, Merritt stepped into the psychologist's waiting room. Since she'd made that stupid slip last session, she knew it was going to be difficult avoiding a conversation about her father. Therapists had a way of digging out secrets.

The redheaded receptionist looked up with such a bright welcoming smile that Merritt at once felt more at ease. She mentally gave Angelica Turner a big tick for choosing her staff well.

"Please take a seat Dr. Harrington. Dr. Turner won't be too long."

After settling into a chair, Merritt took the phone out of her handbag to look at her messages. She was pleased to see notes from both Terry and Rose. From the attached photos of Terry and Jordan white-water rafting and hang gliding, the girls were having a wild time. Jordan seemed to be having as much fun as Terry. There was also a picture of Alice with her arm around Terry. The sisters looked very alike.

In contrast, Rose's vacation was more sedate, taken up with family gatherings. She'd sent a snap of her standing next to an old, white-headed Asian woman, who was slighter and even shorter than Rose. Merritt was chuckling over the description of the first "date" her grandmother had organized, when Angelica Turner appeared at the door.

"Come on in, Merritt," she called out, and stood to the side as she ushered her into the office.

With a soft slap the door closed behind them.

The décor didn't seem as austere as the week before, with an elaborate dreamcatcher now hanging on the wall behind the desk. Merritt sat on the edge of the chair and regarded the therapist as she shuffled through her notes. She didn't have the dangling earrings on today. Instead, a colorful scarf confined her curls, which made her look even more like a gypsy.

Angelica looked up with a friendly smile. "How have you been, Merritt? Any more episodes?"

"No. None, Angelica." With a jolt of surprise, it occurred to Merritt that it was quite true. The bad memories had faded into the background since dating Austen. If she hadn't been so upset, she would have laughed. Her anxiety at seeing the therapist was centered solely on her father not her flashbacks.

"Wonderful. You've been keeping busy?"

Merritt felt the warmth seeping into her cheeks. "Um…yes. I'm having a great vacation."

"Tell me what you've been up to."

Pleased to be on an innocuous subject, Merritt described the places she'd visited with Rose, though couldn't help more animation creeping into her voice as she talked about her trips with Austen. She didn't volunteer their names. That, she figured, was her business.

"I gather from your enthusiasm there is a man involved?"

Her lips twitched into a little half smile, Merritt met her eyes with no embarrassment. "A woman."

Angelica acknowledged this with a nod and continued smoothly, "She's obviously become special. I'm happy you've found someone to share your time with here. Have you told her about your last assignment?"

"Yes. She's a good listener and it helped enormously to have her support."

"Any nightmares?"

"No."

"Good. Talking things over with a friend is good therapy." Angelica looked at her intently. "Have you discussed this problem with your mother?"

"No. I have no wish to upset her."

"And your father?"

Merritt shrugged. "He wouldn't be interested."

"No? Why exactly?"

"He's a busy man," Merritt replied, hunching back a little in the chair. She cursed that whenever he was mentioned, she couldn't help becoming prickly. "My father despises weakness, *especially* from me."

Angelica tapped her teeth with her pen as she regarded her thoughtfully. "Those are strong words, Merritt. What did he think about you joining Doctors Without Borders? Was he proud of you?"

"He was annoyed when I signed up, but now he sees me as a diplomatic point scorer. Senator Harrington's daughter is a doctor with the esteemed Médecins Sans Frontières. He's been using that often enough," Merritt replied, unable to keep the bitterness out of her voice.

"You said he was annoyed. Did he tried to talk you out of it?"

"Actually, I didn't tell him until after I'd signed up. It was entirely my decision." Noticing Angelica's expression, she added defensively, "For heaven's sake, I'd left home years ago. It's my life."

"But it did give you an opportunity to get well away from his control, didn't it?"

Merritt took a deep breath, knowing where this was heading. "I suppose so. He likes to run my life."

"And your mother's as well?"

Merritt stared at her hands. It was difficult talking openly to a stranger about her parents. She'd always been taught family business was to be kept hidden away. Like rats in a basement. "Yes. Mom's too."

Then the therapist asked the question she'd been dreading. "Was he ever violent toward you and your mother?"

Merritt felt her throat tighten with unshed tears. "Yes. Hard smacks when I was young, but it was more degrading than that. It was the nasty verbal abuse and he was continuously putting me down. He was a bully and still is. 'His way or the highway.' I worry about Mom now."

"You think he abuses her?"

Merritt slid her eyes away, twisted the dress ring on her finger. "Nothing physical. Or I don't think so. He's emotionally controlling. Being a senator's wife, she's expected to look and act a certain way. I can see it's becoming more of a strain as she gets older."

"But you got the brunt of his anger when you were growing up?"

"Yes. His expectations went beyond reason. I always thought it was because he had wanted a son not a daughter. My mother couldn't have any more children after me." She looked helplessly at Angelica and said bitterly, "What's the point of dragging all this up?"

"Look, Merritt," Angelica said in a warm, caring voice. "Sometimes we do something for all the wrong reasons. And we stay too long because we feel we have to. I imagine you felt months before the Peruvian disaster that these traumatic rescues were getting harder and harder on your nerves. There's no shame in that. But you didn't want to let down your team, especially your friend Terry, and you definitely didn't want to give your father any more reason to deride you."

Merritt slumped back in her chair. "I'm not as resilient as Terry. She seems to be able to shrug it off. I've worked in an ER for years, but this pressure is entirely different. The work environment is so nerve-wracking."

"Have you given thought to finding less stressful work?"

"Yes. I've already made my decision. My three-year contract will be up in four months and I'm not renewing it. Not even for part-time assignments. I've been thinking I would like to work in a burns rehab unit."

"That's good news," Angelica said with a smile. "If you'd like, I'm prepared to write a letter to your management, recommending the rest of your time be spent in a safe zone." She held up her hand when Merritt leaned forward to protest. "I want you to go home and seriously think about it. I would like to have another session with you next week if you're able to make it. Same time if that suits. We can work out some strategies to keep your mind healthy."

"Do you work Saturdays?"

"Yes. Make the appointment with my receptionist on your way out," said Angelica, rising to her feet. "and Merritt—"

Merritt met her eyes inquiringly.

"Go home and forget about all this. Have a wonderful time with your friend."

For the first time in the session, Merritt flashed a genuine smile. "Will do."

* * *

"Hey, babe. How did your session go with the shrink?"

Merritt happily smiled into the phone, warmth bubbling inside her like champagne. They had been talking every night, and the sound of Austen's voice was the best medicine of all. "A bit confronting, though she helped me get everything into perspective. I'll tell you all about it when I see you tomorrow. Tonight though, I'm just going to try forget about it."

"That bad, eh? What are you doing tonight?"

"We're dining here. Our four guests are from the city's Arts Council, so it should be more interesting than the usual dry diplomatic conversation. My father's Senate Committee fosters connections in the arts as well. Where are you now?"

"Just got back to my hotel room…"

They chatted on, until nearly an hour later Merritt reluctantly looked at the time. "I guess I'd better get ready. Predinner drinks are at six thirty. What time tomorrow?"

"I'll pick you up at eight on the street." A wistful note crept into Austen's voice. "I'd prefer to come to the front door."

"I know, honey, but I plan to do something about that. See you tomorrow." When the phone clicked off, Merritt stretched back into the pillow, focusing on her thoughts. How easily that "honey" had slipped out. She knew she was becoming possessive of Austen and had no right to be. She wasn't even her girlfriend and she doubted Austen would ever want to be monogamous. That sounded awfully harsh, but she had to be realistic. Hot sex was one thing but falling in love was quite another. Caution was essential.

After putting the final touches to her makeup, Merritt went downstairs. An idea had formed in her mind while she was dressing. If she could persuade her father to throw a party for the arts, it would be realistic that Austen could be invited. During the course of the evening, she could make it clear to her parents that Austen and she were more than friends. Now all she had to do was select the best candidate from the Arts Council guests to influence.

They were a diverse bunch, well known in their fields: a painter, a sculptor, a ballet teacher and a songwriter. As they gathered on the terrace for drinks, she sized them up. The painter was a tallish man in his early fifties, with bad posture and thinning hair. He didn't look like he'd care for entertaining.

The ballet teacher was a striking woman, with an upright slender figure and a long swan neck. She was dressed immaculately in a pale lavender suit, and her fingers dripped with diamonds. Merritt dismissed her—too upscale.

The sculptor was a swarthy man with a solid muscular body and dressed in jeans and a slightly worn sports coat. He would probably welcome a free party, but it was Simon, the cool songwriter, who caught Merritt's interest. He would be ideal. Being from the music industry and young, he would most likely be an Austen and the Black Heat fan.

When the chef announced dinner, she made sure she took the seat next to the songwriter. During their conversation, she let drop that Austen Farleigh was in town.

His reaction was everything she hoped for. "Wow? She's awesome. I've heard she writes most of their songs." He eyed her enthusiastically behind his Harry Potter glasses. "You've actually met her?"

Merritt beamed at him. "I know her quite well. What a coup it'd be if she could be persuaded to come along to a function. Not to sing, but as an ambassador. After all, she was born in Australia."

His eyes turned as owlish as the spectacles. "You reckon you could swing it?"

She nodded. "She's pretty good-natured. If your group can organize something, I'll make sure she comes."

"What would you propose?"

"Well," said Merritt, slipping on a casual smile. "It doesn't have to be anything big. Finger food and drinks somewhere. A hotel function room perhaps, that way they can do the catering. She's only here for two and a half weeks more." She touched his arm lightly. "If you ask my father, the US might foot the bill. Try to make it seem like it's his idea. I wouldn't mention Austen though to him. Let that be a surprise."

"Yeah, that sounds like a plan. Will you back me up?"

"Absolutely. I'm a great advocate for the arts."

"Senator," Simon called out, when there was a lull. "What do you think of having a party with members of our arts community and the trade delegates?"

Her father looked him over thoughtfully. "That's not a bad idea, son. The arts can bridge a lot of cultural gaps. It's as much a part of the fabric of our individual societies as trade. It's something everyone can relate to, whatever their language."

At once the conversation at the table veered down that path, and Merritt watched with delight as they began discussing the idea in earnest. Her father was in a good mood, which made things a lot easier. And she had to give him credit, for he did support the arts. He was a patron of the Richmond Performing Arts Alliance, and she knew he made large private donations to the Virginia Ballet Company. As she watched him laugh and joke with the guests, she thought how much this appointment suited him. She'd never seen him so amiable for such a long period.

By dessert, the project had the green light and was to be funded by the US Government.

Simon leaned over and whispered smugly, "How's that?"

"Well done," she murmured back.

"Now it's up to you to persuade Austen to come."

"That'll be no problem," she replied with a secret smile.

CHAPTER EIGHTEEN

Canberra was awash with sunlight. A Rihanna song was softly playing on the stereo and Merritt was sitting beside her in the car. Life couldn't get any better.

"How long will it take us to get to Sydney?" Merritt asked when they joined the freeway.

"It'll depend on the traffic. This time of day about four hours," Austen replied. "Did your mother ask who you were going away with?"

"Of course. I said you were just a friend I'd met at a party."

Austen threw her a quick glance. "Did she want to know my name?"

"She merely asked if my father would approve. When I said it wasn't likely, she didn't persist."

"Hell, my mother would never have given up. She'd be like a dog with a bone until I cracked," Austen said, feeling a little hurt. She had been dismissed as no one. Suddenly, she was aware of the differences in their families. Merritt's were top of the tree, hers working class. The more they got to know each other, the wider the gap seemed. She'd never worried about all that crap when she was in bed with someone. Women were women. But somehow now it was beginning to matter.

Wishing she could ask if Merritt had ever brought anyone home to meet her parents, she said instead, "Has your father asked yet what you were doing at the Hyatt?"

"He still hasn't mentioned it."

Austen reached over and squeezed her thigh. "All your worrying was for nothing. Though I can't understand why you don't tell him to go to hell when he tries to manipulate your life."

"Yes…well…I'm getting close to it. Come on, let's not talk about him. Tell me where we're staying in Sydney and what you have planned."

"I've booked a room at the Park Hyatt. It's right on the harbor and has great views of the Harbour Bridge and the Opera House." Austen cleared her throat. "If you want a separate room, they're holding another for me."

There was a heartbeat's silence before Merritt replied, "One will be just fine."

Austen let out the breath she was holding. "I'll let them know when we pull up for a break. I was hoping you'd say that."

"You doubted I wouldn't?"

"I didn't presume. Not with you."

"Why?"

"You really mean something to me. I don't want you to feel pressured," said Austen, flicking her another glance. Merritt was staring through the windscreen, her face inscrutable.

"You might've forgotten, but I remember vividly that time we first met," Merritt began, her voice pensive. "Every look you gave, every word you spoke, every kiss, every touch. They're etched into my mind. You did something to me that I've never forgotten. No other woman I've known has come close to what you made me feel. And I've cursed you for years over it. Not just because of the unforgiveable way you treated me, but because you left me wanting something I've never found again."

Austen's smile faded. "Hey, babe, you're getting a bit serious."

"Sorry. That must have sounded rather odd."

"Nah. I get what you meant." Austen didn't add that her own attitude toward sex had been much shallower. It had been always just about pleasure.

"You've never become attached to anyone?"

Austen could hear the empathy in the curiosity and flinched. Now, as much as she tried to concentrate on the highway, her past seemed to be reflected back at her. In her mid-thirties and what did she have to show for it emotionally? A string of sexual partners she barely could recall. Geez, Merritt even had the capacity to make her feel ashamed. Time to change the subject. She had no desire to dwell on her past.

"I was in love with Ellie," she replied, offering nothing else.

"But you said you were never lovers."

"We weren't."

Merritt patted her knee, then slid her fingers up until their hands were touching. "That's sad, Austen."

Austen frowned. The last thing she wanted was to be an object of pity. "I got over it. I certainly was never lonely," she said brusquely.

"Now I've upset you," murmured Merritt.

Austen took her fingers in her hand and tightened her grip. "It'll take a hell of a lot more than that to upset me."

There was a long pause before Merritt muttered, "Just ignore me. Overanalyzing things is one of my greatest failings. You're the most self-possessed person I've ever met. Anything I have to say should hardly worry you." She slipped her hand free and continued in a lighter voice. "Let's change the subject. It's very picturesque countryside we're traveling through."

As soon as her hand was pulled away, Austen acutely felt the loss of the warm skin. She sighed and launched into a running commentary of the landscape.

* * *

Austen slipped the key card into the hotel door. Excited, she pushed open the door. She was in a vibrant city with a lovely woman. Nothing could beat that. With a satisfied hum, she threw her bag down next to the king bed covered by a plump duvet, and watched Merritt explore the suite. She did it with delight, making little murmurs of approval at the breath-taking view.

"This is absolutely gorgeous." She turned and beamed at Austen. "The places I've had to stay in the last few years make me appreciate luxury."

Austen smiled back at her—the room paled in comparison. With her hair swept back casually, her lips curved enticingly and eyes eager and shining, Merritt was the epitome of a desirable woman. When their gazes locked, Austen couldn't help herself. She took Merritt's hand, slowly brought it to her lips and pressed an open-mouthed kiss on her palm. Merritt gave a little mewing sound, which sent a tingle through Austen. She moved closer and trailed the tip of her tongue over the soft inside of her wrist.

"Austen," Merritt murmured, slightly breathless. "I need to go to the bathroom."

Austen blinked up at her. She gave a teasing smile. "You go first. After we tidy up, we'll have lunch and afterward I'll show you the sights. Wear shoes you can walk in."

"Sounds like a plan," Merritt said softly.

When Austen emerged from the bathroom in a shoulder-length blond wig, a long-sleeved shirt and a pair of blue-tinted glasses, Merritt quirked an eyebrow. Normally Austen wouldn't have bothered, but she knew Merritt would be uncomfortable if she was approached by fans or pestered by photographers.

"You like?" she asked.

"You don't look half bad as a blonde."

"You think?" Austen said, coyly flicking a lock of hair.

Merritt looked amused. "Come on, Diva. let's go eat."

Five minutes later, they were seated in the hotel restaurant with a waiter taking their orders. Though the lobster salad was delicious, Austen didn't remember much about the lunch. She was too absorbed with Merritt. It had been years since she'd seriously talked to a woman and listened to her dreams and ambitions. The more she got to know her, the more she realized what a caring person she was. An honorable, dedicated doctor. Not only a consummate professional, she had an innate charm and easy grace.

Austen knew she was fascinated by her but was powerless to stop the feelings. Everything about her appealed: her quiet manner, her expressive intelligent eyes, her stubborn chin and even the sprinkle of freckles across her nose. Merritt looked fresh and natural, her makeup understated. Her hands were strong and capable, the nails filed neatly short. A doctor's hands. She had a habit of nibbling her lower lip when concentrating and twisting a curl around her finger when pensive, endearing little idiosyncrasies.

When the waiter appeared with their coffee, Austen glanced at her watch. Over an hour since they'd sat down. Incredible. She hadn't noticed the time passing.

Merritt poured milk into her cup and stirred it absently. "You're a good listener, Austen. I guess I did most of the talking. I haven't spoken about my life and career like that for a very long time. It was nice to be able to do it."

"I enjoyed listening, babe. Very much. But it made me realize what I do isn't very important."

"Nonsense. Entertaining people is wonderful. It would be a sad old world without music. I can't imagine life without it. And in the places and situations I've been in, it was the best stress relief."

"You have a way of making me feel important," said Austen with a smile. "Drink up and we'd better get going. I thought we'd walk up through the Mall and then back down to Circular Quay. The best way to see the harbor is from a boat, so we'll take the ferry to Manly."

They strolled through Pitt Street Mall, window-shopping as they went. It was one of Australia's busiest and most cosmopolitan shopping precincts. What struck Austen the most as she walked through the crowds, was how much more multicultural the city had become since she had left for the States. And the urban sprawl had certainly accelerated, new housing estates had popped up on the outskirts of the city. She took Merritt's hand as they walked, pleased she didn't pull it away. Not that anyone looked or cared about same-sex relationships in a progressive city like Sydney.

Eventually, they made their way down to the Quay to catch the iconic ferry for the thirty-minute trip. The newer boats were faster, but the old ferry was the touristy way to go. They made their way to the front top deck. It was a perfect day to be on the harbor, the water sapphire blue, the air crisp and clear. Shortly, the hum of engines churned the water as the boat eased backward from its moorings. She sat back to watch Merritt as she enthusiastically snapped photos. They leaned against the rail close together, savoring the view as the ferry crossed the heads and sailed into Manly.

They spent a pleasant afternoon walking along the beach and riding electric bikes along the promenade fronting the long surf beach. They then walked around to Shelley Beach, a secluded inlet with aquamarine water. By the time they sailed back past the Opera House it was dusk, the Harbour Bridge starkly silhouetted against the orange sky. Merritt exclaimed approval at the sight, which Austen had to agree looked spectacular. She had forgotten just how picturesque this part of Sydney was.

On their way out of the Quay, she lightly tugged Merritt's hand. "Would you like a drink? I know a terrific bar in the heart of the Rocks."

Merritt tilted her head to look at her. "The Rocks?"

"It's the area over to the right, near our hotel. The first white settlement in Australia, in fact. It used to be the seedy side of the city, but now it's ultra-touristy."

"A drink sounds just what this doctor ordered."

"Come on then," Austen said with a laugh.

By Sydney standards the spring night was a trifle chilly, so Austen draped her arm around Merritt's shoulders as they crossed into the Rocks district. She led the way through the narrow cobblestoned streets until she saw the familiar set of stairs tucked away under a storefront. At the bottom was The Doss House, a whiskey joint in a sandstone basement. She was hit by a wave of nostalgia. It was just as she remembered: dimly lit, cozy, and very olde-worlde. The vintage bar was still stocked with an amazing whiskey selection.

"This is really something," Merritt whispered in her ear with a shiver. "It's heavy, like a cavern in a stone catacomb. I can nearly feel the ghosts around us."

Austen glanced at her with amusement. "You've got an overactive imagination. But it does have a dodgy history. The place used to be a Chinese gambling and opium den."

"Were there a lot of Chinese people in Sydney in those early days?"

"They were brought over for cheap labor. When gold was discovered out west, there was an influx to the fields. A lot of them moved to work in the city when the gold petered out." She turned to Merritt when they reached the bar. "What'll you have? They specialize in whiskey, but if that's not your thing, there's a good cocktail and wine menu."

"What the heck," said Merritt, eyeing the array of bottles. "When in Rome. I'll have a whiskey sour, please."

"Right. I'll have an Irishman single malt on the rocks. Smoothest whiskey you can buy."

Merritt raised an eyebrow. "You're a connoisseur?"

Austen gave a laugh. "Hell no. Mick tells me it's the best."

After the bartender had their drinks plus a charcuterie and cheese platter ready, they adjourned to an intimate corner booth. "Thanks for the day," Merritt murmured, running a fingertip over the back of Austen's hand. "I had a great time."

"It's not over yet," whispered Austen in return. She moved closer and feathered her lips across her earlobe. "There's a very exclusive private club I know in the city. A friend of mine owns it. I'd love to take you there. We could dance."

Merritt sank into her. "Tomorrow night. Let's just sit here a while and then…" she paused to lightly kiss Austen on her mouth, "then I want to take you to bed. To make love to you, to make you forget all those other women."

Austen swallowed. Her libido had been on edge for days in anticipation, though it still was surprising how fiercely her body responded to the whispered words. *Fuck!* It was a complete turn-on. She was always the one who took charge, the one who set the pace. Yet when Merritt uttered those words, instinctively she wanted to put herself completely in this woman's power, to be consumed by her. She knew it was going to be something that she would never forget. But beneath the anticipation, an awareness niggled that perhaps it wasn't going to be the best thing. She wouldn't want to be left like Merritt, pining for something she couldn't find.

But those thoughts soon faded into a hormonal haze. Every sense seemed to be heightened. Every smell, touch, and sound were like tiny electric shocks.

Austen only went through the motions: she sipped her drink, talked convivially and helped herself to an occasional nibble. But underneath she was a seething mess. Merritt's scent wafting in the air was an aphrodisiac over which she had no control. The moisture between her legs was becoming uncomfortable.

Finally, after the third drink and the plate of food had been demolished, it was Merritt who made the move. With a light of promised passion in her eyes, she stood up and stretched out her hand. "Come on. Let's go home."

Smiling foolishly, Austen took the outstretched hand. She was so worked up she would have walked across a bed of hot coals with her.

CHAPTER NINETEEN

They were mostly silent as they walked back to the hotel. It no longer seemed necessary to talk, their clasped hands all the communication needed. Austen's calloused thumb was rhythmically stroking Merritt's palm, and every so often she squeezed her hand lightly. It seemed incredible to Merritt that such simple acts could be so erotic. By the time they reached the entrance, she was nearly bursting with want.

Inside the elevator, Merritt could hardly contain herself. If they had been alone, she would have kissed Austen to relieve some of her pent-up arousal. Instead she had to be content to press closely against her in the back corner while passengers got on and off.

As soon as they slipped inside the room, Austen tossed her wig onto a chair with a "Thank the stars I can take that thing off."

A second later, she had Merritt in her arms, kissing her fiercely.

With an effort, Merritt gently pushed her away and caught her breath before she murmured, "Wait…wait. Let's get into bed." When Austen pulled impatiently at the buttons on her shirt, she grasped her hand. "I want our first time to be special."

Austen groaned softly. "Me too. But at the moment all I want to do is rip those clothes off and lose myself in you."

At those words, the pulsating ache between Merritt's thighs became so insistent that she could no longer ignore it. "Let me, honey." Without hesitation, she pulled Austen over to the bed, stripped the duvet aside and pushed her down onto the sheet. Hurriedly, she hauled off Austen's top. After a few deft twists to remove the bra, she cupped the curve of her breast.

The breath caught in Merritt's throat. Tempting firm nipples protruded from the puckered brown areolas, and she wanted them in her mouth. She looked up at Austen. Her parted lips glistened, her hair was mussed up in cute disarray, her gaze pure sex.

Ignoring the blood roaring in her ears, Merritt delicately flicked her tongue over a nipple. It tightened further, wrenching a groan from Austen. Encouraged, Merritt settled over her and rubbed her thumbs over the hardening tip until it was like a little stone. She could feel Austen's muscles contracting as she shuddered with pleasure.

"You like that?" asked Merritt. She gently took the nipple into her mouth.

Austen grasped her by the shoulders. "Shit yes, babe."

"Good," Merritt murmured, then sucked much harder. She massaged the breast as she alternately rolled the nipple with her tongue and nipped it lightly.

Austen worked her fingers through Merritt's hair, while she twisted and arched her pelvis against her with unspoken demand.

"Be still," Merritt admonished gently, moving her head to lavish the other breast. "This one has to have attention too."

Her lips suckled and nibbled, until the pressure in her own groin became too intense to ignore. With a quick roll, she slid off the bed. "Now, off with those pants," Merritt demanded in a stern voice.

Austen gave a gasp of raw desire. "You're so hot when you're in command." She hastily slipped her pants down until she was clad only in a pair of Victoria's Secret boy shorts.

When Merritt drew back to rake her eyes down Austen's body, her lips parted in a soundless pant of desire. The briefs were so sexy. Her nipples tightened, sending tingles of arousal south. She took off her top and bra, wrapped her arms around Austen's neck and pressed her body on top of hers. Their breasts crushed together felt like heaven. She lowered her head to kiss her. When their lips touched, Austen claimed her mouth like a starved woman. She twirled her tongue with Merritt's as she undulated against her in a steady rhythm.

In a fluid movement, Austen slipped her mouth to her neck and trailed wet kisses to the soft hollow at the base of her throat. When her teeth scraped the sensitive skin, shivers cascaded through Merritt. She puffed in excitement as her sex lit up and her toes curled.

She felt a hand skate down her stomach and slip beneath the waistband of her pants. Before she could react, a fingertip hit her clitoris through the thin lace of her panties. Merritt gave an involuntary squeal of pleasure.

"Get these off," Austen growled as her fingers caressed her with light strokes.

Ignoring her body's pitiful cries of protest, Merritt grasped Austen's wrist and pulled it over her head. "Oh no you don't. I'm in charge."

This elicited a loud hiss from Austen, but she allowed her arm to be pressed into the pillow. Merritt nuzzled her collarbone and slid down until she was settled between Austen's legs. Immediately, her thighs opened wide to accommodate her. Merritt raised her head to look up. Dark eyes met hers, their depths filled with arousal and trust. A small smile played over the full lips. Merritt's insides melted as she knew this was an Austen few women had ever seen. She was putting herself completely in Merritt's power.

Merritt lowered her head and swirled her tongue. The intensity of her desire frightened her. She'd never wanted anyone so much in all her life. Each gasp, each moan, every jerk were aphrodisiacs she couldn't get enough of. And though Merritt lacked experience, she was a quick learner. All her performance anxiety fled as she learned to read how the body underneath responded, and she brought Austen slowly, and thoroughly, to her climax. She didn't hurry—this was her chance and she wasn't going to blow it. She wanted to twist her in knots and make her beg.

Soon Austen began bunching the sheets in her fists, squirming in frustration as Merritt applied just enough pressure to hold her teetering on the edge. Finally, she growled and tugged Merritt's hair. "Please, babe. Please. No more teasing. I really need to come."

With a breathy hum, Merritt lowered her head. After one last stroke of her tongue, she closed her lips on the nub and sucked hard. Austen's entire body stiffened, and her release came with a drawn-out guttural cry. "*Merrittttt! So fucking good!*"

Her own sex burning with arousal, Merritt dragged out Austen's pleasure with soothing flicks of her tongue. As the aftershocks spaced out, she reveled in her essence.

When she raised her head, Austen caressed her hair languidly. "Come up here, you."

Merritt crawled back up until she was nestled in her arms. Austen's hot breath fanned over her earlobe as she pulled her close. "That was something. And here I was thinking you were inexperienced."

Merritt chuckled. "We doctors know all about anatomy. And besides…" She ran a finger across the tip of her shoulder. "…I've been dreaming about doing that for a long time."

Austen grabbed the finger to suck it into her warm mouth. "Me too. Now…it's time I take off those pants and make you cry out *my* name."

Merritt's heart hitched. Austen's eyes had turned darker, promising hidden passions and delights. Then she was on her knees, pulling Merritt's pants down her thighs and over her ankles. She took a long moment to sweep her gaze over her. Merritt kept still, not uncomfortable under the scrutiny. She couldn't be, not with the arousal on Austen's face. The dark eyes lingered on the cropped curls between her thighs and Merritt knew they would be glistening.

"Lovely," murmured Austen, bending to suck a nipple into her mouth. Merritt arched into her to urge her on. But Austen didn't hurry, sucking the soft skin in all the tender little hollows up her arms. When she stroked under her armpits, it was a real turn-on. Merritt had no idea she could be so super sensitive there. She moved down over her breasts and abdomen, nipping and kissing, while palming her mound and pressing down firmly. Merritt felt herself moving closer to the edge at each press.

When one long finger slipped between her thighs, sighs and murmurs tumbled from her lips.

"Shhhhh," Austen whispered against her breast.

"Please, hon, please," she begged. "I need to come. I—"

"Not yet, babe. I haven't finished yet."

This time she circled the clitoris lightly. Merritt's sex clenched. It felt glorious, but she wanted harder, faster. Her hips writhed, seeking to relieve the pressure. "Please, Austen, I'm ready to explode."

Austen's fingers stilled. "Hold on, babe. This is going to make you feel really good." She moved down to the vagina and massaged the outer rim. Slowly she slipped inside, continuing until she hit the g-spot. She worked across it with increasing pressure. For a timeless moment Merritt floated on the brink, breathless, possessed. Spots floated in front of her eyes. Her orgasm rose in an exquisite rush and she came apart with strong, wrenching convulsions. She had never felt anything so wonderful in all her life.

She squeezed her eyes shut, letting the waves wash through her. They seemed endless. When she at last flopped back onto the bed, she could only gasp out the words, "That was... wonderful. Sublime."

Austen smiled with satisfaction and slid down to stroke Merritt's clitoris with her tongue. Her body responded almost immediately. This time Austen wasn't slow or gentle. She relentlessly drove Merritt to her climax with tongue, mouth, and teeth.

The second orgasm seemed to start somewhere deep inside, rumbling every fiber of her body as it shattered into an implosion of mind-blowing intense pleasure. Somewhere in her subconscious as she screamed out her pleasure, she was dimly aware Austen had climaxed with her.

Merritt fell back completely spent. After a long languid pause, Austen moved up, took her in her arms, and rubbed her jaw against Merritt's cheek as she held her tenderly. Merritt hadn't expected anything so incredible. What she had imagined making love to Austen would be like, hadn't come anywhere close to the real thing. They had completely meshed—she had never been so in tune with another woman's body. Intuitively, she knew that on some level it had affected Austen as well, even though she had been with lots of other women.

Merritt didn't know what it had been, but it sure as hell hadn't been just sex. There had been a much deeper connection, an emotional bonding.

Love?

Too soon for that, but something had shifted within her. Life changing. She was Austen's completely—if she wanted her.

A heavy weight lodged in Merritt's chest.

Austen wouldn't want her in that way. She was a free spirit, used to playing the field.

Austen's voice scattered her internal monologue. "You wanna take a shower with me?"

Merritt's insecurities vanished in a twinkle. She bit her lip to hide her smile and asked solemnly, "Does that include sex?"

"Fuck, yes." She smoothed a hand over Merritt's tummy and ran her finger round the navel in a slow circle. "I haven't half finished with you yet."

"You haven't?" Merritt squeaked. She squeezed her thighs together as a dull throb began. *Wow!* She was ready again. Rarely did she come more than twice in a night. But then again, she'd never been with anyone like Austen.

"Let's just lie here a minute," Merritt said shyly, brushing a thumb across Austen's bottom lip. "I just had the best orgasms of my life and I'd like to cuddle for a little while longer."

"You wouldn't want to come again? Your body's telling me you do."

"I do," Merritt said with a laugh. "You've woken up my libido. But…I guess what I'm saying…I want real intimacy too."

Austen pulled her closer and kissed the top of her head. "I know. I'm not used to being really close to someone."

"You weren't in the habit of staying all night?"

Austen cleared her throat. "Not really."

"Hmmm. Interesting. I could never be like that."

"Not the love 'em and leave 'em type?"

Merritt chuckled. "Sometimes I think I should have been. It would have solved a few of my stress issues. Terry always told me I should lose my inhibitions." She glanced at Austen slyly. "But I would have stayed for breakfast."

Austen shrugged. "Yeah…well, I'm not a breakfast-type gal."

"Oh, you're incorrigible." She extracted herself from Austen's arms. "Okay. Let's take that shower. And Austen."

"Yes?"

"It's my turn first."

CHAPTER TWENTY

The stream of light through the window was the first thing Austen saw when she opened her eyes. Blearily, she looked across at the clock on the side table. 9:20 a.m.

She propped herself on her elbows. A smile touched her lips when she remembered how little sleep they'd had. It had been a night to remember, sheer exhaustion the only thing that had brought it to an end.

After blinking several times to clear her eyes, she gazed around the room. Merritt was nowhere in sight, though clearly, she'd been up for a while. The curtains had been pulled back, yesterday's clothes were folded in a neat pile on the chair and the towel was gone from the floor.

The sound of off-key singing in the bathroom brought a wide smile. She snuggled back under the covers to relive the night. Though she had sensed that they would be good together in bed, never in her wildest dreams could she have imagined just how easily and completely they would fit. It was as if their bodies had been made for each other. Merritt just seemed to know intuitively the right pressure in the right spots that turned Austen on. And Merritt had been so responsive to her every touch.

Passionate and romantic.

The perfect lover.

Austen swallowed hard, knowing she was in unfamiliar territory. The depth of her feelings had been heady and deep. It hadn't been just sex—it had been lovemaking. *Sonofabitch*. She might be screwed. She could crash and burn after the affair was over. And worse. It could fuck her up for anyone else.

At the sound of the door opening, her anxiety fled in a wave of tenderness and longing. Wearing a fluffy white towel Merritt exited the bathroom. She looked adorable.

"Hello there, sleepyhead," Merritt said, and bent to kiss her lightly on the lips.

Austen drew a sharp breath as an acute rush of emotions flooded her. She wanted her under her, to taste her, to consume her again. "Morning, babe." She pulled back the sheet and patted the space beside her.

Without a word, Merritt dropped the towel and slid onto the bed. Her sultry look under lowered lids fueled the heat in Austen's belly. She trailed her mouth over Merritt's shoulder and down to her breast to claim a nipple, pleased to feel her tremble. "God, you smell wonderful," Austen murmured. "But I have to go to the toilet, and I'd better have a shower before we go any further."

Ignoring Merritt's low moan as she left the nipple, she threw her legs over the side of the bed. She stood up, pleased to see Merritt avidly eyeing her naked body.

When she caught Austen's amused gaze, she blushed. "I'm ogling your tats. They're beautiful in the light. Shall I order something to eat?"

"Good idea. I'll have whatever you're having."

"Okay. Ham and cheese croissants and fruit." She tilted her head, twitching her eyebrows at her with a seductive smile. "We could eat in bed."

Austen's stomach gave a little flip. From that look, she doubted they would be eating breakfast anytime soon.

She took her time in the shower, letting the water sluice over her body to wash away the lingering fatigue. After she toweled dry, she cleaned her teeth and tidied her hair. Not being one to worry about nudity, she didn't bother with the robe.

Refreshed, she emerged from the bathroom to find Merritt wheeling a covered trolley into the room. She swept her eyes over Austen, parked the trolley and crooked a finger. "Come here, lover girl."

Raspy with want, Austen needed no second urging. In a heartbeat, they were joined, her hands cupping Merritt's ass. Austen sniffed appreciatively. The creamy skin smelled of lavender soap mixed with her unique spicy essence.

Heady, addictive.

She ran her tongue down her neck. Merritt's arousal seemed to be emanating from her pores.

"You taste divine," she murmured, and clasped her harder, grinding their pelvises together.

"I want you so much," Merritt said huskily, her breath hot against Austen's ear.

Her own need rising rapidly, Austen wrapped her arms around Merritt's waist and guided her backward to the bed. Stilling her with a hand, Merritt whispered urgently in her ear, "No. Take me against the wall. Don't be gentle. Fuck me."

A wave of pure lust swept through Austen. The woman knew how to hit her buttons. She pressed Merritt against the wall, massaging her breasts firmly as she pushed her tongue into her mouth. When she slid her hand between her thighs to stroke her, Merritt gave little squawks of encouragement. She opened her legs and Austen pushed two fingers into her depths. It was warm and slippery inside, overwhelmingly erotic. Their bodies dampened with perspiration as Merritt met her thrusts, grinding against her fingers, her hands tangled in her hair. When she burst into her climax, she scraped her fingernails hard down Austen's back as she screamed out her pleasure.

"That was just incredible," Merritt said, slumping against her in post-orgasmic bliss.

Her back stinging pleasantly, Austen propped Merritt up and ran her tongue over her neck. The skin tasted salty. "You're so fucking sexy."

Merritt gave a little gurgling chuckle through her heightened breathing. "That was one of my persistent fantasies. Being taken by you against the wall."

"Really? That's hot."

"Yep. And what do you think about when you're tucked up alone in your bed in the dark?" asked Merritt, giving her bottom a squeeze.

Recalling her heated dreams, Austen felt desire reignite deep in her groin. "It's a bit embarrassing."

Merritt laughed and kissed her nose. "Oh, Austen. I didn't think anything about sex would faze you."

"Okay. I fantasize I'm your patient. When I walk into your office, you're at your desk, wearing nothing but a frown and your stethoscope. You tell me to get up on the table, then start palpating me. And I mean every part of my body. It ends with the pelvic examination. I'm not allowed to move while you put on gloves, squirt gel on your fingers and slide three into me. Then the exam really begins."

Merritt studied her for a long moment. She disentangled herself and walked over to her bag. She turned back to Austen, waving a stethoscope. "I always carry it with me."

Austen's pulse gave a jump.

Merritt's expression changed as soon as she hooked the stethoscope into her ears. She morphed into a doctor: caring and professional. Her brows furrowed when she placed the stainless-steel chest piece over Austen's heart. "Hmmm. Your heart rate is far too fast. This requires more investigation."

Austen shuddered in excitement. Of course her bloody heart was racing. She could barely contain herself.

"Get on that bed, Ms. Farleigh," Merritt ordered sternly. "Lie flat and don't move while I examine you thoroughly."

Austen's muscles tensed in anticipation.

* * *

"This is so indulgent," Merritt said with a satisfied hum and popped a cherry into her mouth.

Breakfast had become brunch in bed.

Austen reached for her coffee cup. "Yeah, but we can't stay in bed all day."

"I'm happy just lounging about here looking at a movie until we go out to dinner tonight. Maybe a massage as well?"

"Good thinking. I'll organize with the management to send a masseur to our suite at four. That'll give us plenty of time for a predinner drink."

"Are we dining here?"

"I know you like seafood," replied Austen, "so I booked a table for seven thirty at the Boathouse on Blackwattle Bay. Our hotel has a first-class menu, but I think you'll enjoy a different view of the water while you eat."

"Sounds delightful."

Austen turned her head to smile at her. It was so easy with Merritt. She never played the diva. She eyed her thoughtfully—were their dreams for the future anywhere near the same?

Merritt caught her gaze and raised her eyebrows. "What?"

"Just wondering what you want in the future?"

"Oh. I wasn't expecting you to ask that question quite so soon."

"Why?"

"It's a loaded question. Do you want me to be serious or flippant?" Merritt asked evenly.

Disconcerted, Austen studied her. "I was only trying to get to know you better. But okay…be serious."

Merritt slid her eyes away and picked at the sheet with her fingertips. "I've met many terrific people in my life, Austen, many who have remained my friends, and a few I consider dear friends." She paused to take a long breath. "But it isn't enough anymore. I want someone who cares about me as much as I care about them. Someone prepared to give me love and support when I need it. Without counting the cost. A partner who is there for *me*."

"We all want that."

"I know, but I want someone to make a life with. And that relationship will have to be built on trust." Merritt looked at her a little sadly. "I want it all…the white picket fence, kids, maybe a pet."

Even though she'd given up sugar, Austen lowered her head and stirred her coffee. Hell, what could she say? She should never have opened her big fat mouth, not with her track record. She picked her words carefully when she replied, "My perspective on life has changed in the last few years, but to be honest, I've never given a life like that any thought."

"And why should you? You're at the peak of your career. You're talented, wealthy, and popular. I envy you. You know exactly who you are and you're perfectly happy."

Austen frowned. Why did those words grate so much and why did Merritt look relieved? Her response was a little too loud. "Yeah…well. Of course I'm happy. And why are we making such a big deal of this? It's a bit early for that."

"The length of time you date doesn't mean everything. How deep the attraction is more important in my book," Merritt said primly. She gave her a sweet smile. "Actually, I'm relieved we got that out of the way. Now we can enjoy ourselves, with no expectations that this is anything but a holiday romance."

Austen returned the smile half-heartedly, unable to shake the feeling she was missing something. "Okay," she said gruffly. "Pick a movie you'd like to see."

Merritt perused the list. "What about *Bombshell?*"

"That'll do. At least it's about women kicking ass."

Merritt smiled, but didn't comment. She climbed out of bed and stacked the dirty dishes onto the trolley. While she pushed it out the door into the corridor, Austen rang reception. By the time she'd organized the masseur, the bed was neatly made with hospital precision. Austen looked at it longingly. No hope of going back for a cuddle. A dressed Merritt already had the TV on, scrolling through for the in-house movie channel. With a sigh, Austen pulled on her jeans and a fresh tank top and joined her.

They settled down together on the sofa. Though Merritt was lounging against her, everything seemed off. The intimacy they'd enjoyed earlier had somehow faded. Austen covertly watched her, trying to work out what she was thinking. Her face was a mask. She threw an arm around her shoulder and pulled her closer, but Merritt seemed too absorbed in the movie to notice. When Austen kissed the top of her head, she absently patted her hand without looking away from the screen.

Austen felt a spurt of hurt and winced. When had she become so needy? This was all crap. She should be pleased they'd worked out what this was between them. There would be no expectations when she went back to the States. Strictly no strings.

Annoyed, she lifted her arm off the shoulder, then caught her breath when Merritt pulled it firmly back in place. She closed her eyes, relishing the closeness. Everything was back on an even keel. Soon her head was drooping onto Merritt's shoulder.

She woke disoriented and stiff, to the sound of a voice, "Wake up, honey. The movie's over."

Slowly, she opened her eyes to find Merritt looking at her. To Austen's horror, there was a little wet patch on her shoulder. "Um…sorry. I didn't mean to nod off. Um…or drool."

A chuckle burst from Merritt. "I've had far worse on me." She tucked a strand of hair away from Austen's eye. "You must have needed the sleep. Feeling better?"

"Apart from a twinge in my neck, I'm good."

Merritt kissed her tenderly. "The massage will get that out of you. She'll be here in an hour and I'd like to shower beforehand." Without another word, she rose and headed to the bathroom.

Austen leaned on the wall outside, listening to the sound of the shower. The thought of Merritt naked under the water got to be too much. What was the point of torturing herself when she could be in there with her? Impatiently, she stripped and hurried to the bathroom. On the threshold, she forced herself to slow down. She wasn't a stupid teenager with a crush. She was a mature woman, always in control. But she didn't feel like that at the moment, especially now that she could see the outline of the luscious body in the fog of steam.

Merritt was standing with her head thrown back, washing her breasts. It was enough to send Austen's libido soaring even more.

She slipped into the shower recess and pressed her body firmly against her. The slippery wet skin felt fantastic. With a hitch in her voice, she whispered in her ear, "Hi, babe."

A sultry smile on her lips, Merritt turned to face her. "What kept you?"

CHAPTER TWENTY-ONE

It was just after ten o'clock when they entered the Darling Harbour club.

Austen took Merritt's hand, and with her characteristic swinging stride, led her past the ground floor nightclub. Merritt peered into the massive room as they went by. It was choked with screaming dancers, blaring electronic music bounced off its walls and gaudy disco lights flashed brightly amidst bursts of blue techno smoke. It looked wild and far too energetic for her. She hoped they were going somewhere quieter, more intimate. Dining at the marina overlooking the water had put her in a romantic mood.

When they reached the second level she looked expectantly at Austen, who shook her head. "The drag show is on this floor." She jerked her thumb upward. "Ours is on the next."

On the third level, a woman in a dark tailored suit was guarding a red door down the end of the hallway. She had clearly been told to expect them, for when Austen appeared, she gave her a wink and ushered them into the room.

Merritt paused on the threshold to take it all in.

This club was another place entirely from the frenetic discotheque downstairs. It was much smaller and very classy. The velvet chairs and drapes were a rich deep purple, the carpet lush and thick, the bar a polished wood and a series of small chandeliers lit the room with an intimate glow. Renoir, Dali, and Picasso lithographs decorated the walls, while a print of Lefebvre's famous nude, *Chloé*, took center place behind the bar.

Jazz echoed quietly through the room. Expensive French perfumes wafted in the air. It wasn't crowded, sixty or seventy people, all women. Some sat around on the comfortable chairs, while others danced on a small space at the back.

Plenty of money here, Merritt noted. Exclusive, but with a tad of decadence as well.

"Cool, huh," Austen whispered in her ear. "The owner is an old friend."

Before she could reply, a throaty female voice sounded to their right. "Austen Farleigh. Well I'll be. What a surprise."

Merritt turned her head to watch the woman approach. She was striking, with auburn hair cascading in silky waves over her shoulders, perfectly proportioned facial features and a curvy hourglass figure. Her black cocktail dress was cut very low and the split up the side showed plenty of thigh.

Austen gave her a tight hug. "Petra. Long time no see. You look freaking terrific, babe."

"So do you," Petra replied, her dark brandy eyes wandering over her. "How long has it been? Seven…eight years? You look even better than I remember."

"Eight. It's good to be back."

"We've missed you. A few of the old crowd are here tonight."

"Great. I can't wait to catch up." Austen tugged Merritt forward. "This is a friend of mine…Merritt Harrington."

The woman studied her with undisguised interest before she nodded. "Petra Vandenburg. Pleased to meet you, Merritt."

"Hi," she replied, forcing a mechanical smile. The proprietary way Petra had eyed Austen rankled immediately.

The look Petra turned on Merritt was friendly enough but there was a measuring light in her eye. A sizing-up-the-competition gleam. "Welcome to the club," she said, and turned her attention back to Austen.

After standing back politely while they reminisced for a few minutes over old times, Merritt felt like the third wheel. She decided to leave them to it. "I'll get the drinks while you two catch up. What will you have?" she said, patting Austen on the arm.

"You go ahead and get yours. I'll join you in a minute."

"Okay," she said and wandered off to the bar. By the curious glances cast her way, Merritt guessed the club was definitely as exclusive as she first thought. Few would be strangers to each other in a place like this. Much like her parents' country club back in Virginia, catering to the wealthy.

The bartender was a cute young woman in her mid-twenties, dressed in a sassy black and white uniform. Judging by the efficiency with which she was mixing a cocktail, she was more than just eye candy for the patrons.

After she handed the glass to a waiting customer, she slipped over to Merritt. "What'll you have, ma'am?"

Merritt eyed the array of bottles lined up on the shelf behind the bar. "Can you recommend a nice cocktail?"

The bargirl flashed a white toothy smile. "You're in a hot club, so what about a Cosmo?"

"I've never had one of those."

"You know…Sex in the City."

"Oh. Right."

A chuckle puffed in Merritt's ear. She swiveled round to find a tall fit woman standing beside her. "You've never seen the show, have you?"

"Not really," Merritt replied. She cocked her head and quirked an eyebrow. "Does that mean my education is sorely lacking?"

"God, no. Its just fluff. Entertaining, but still fluff," the woman said with a grin and took a seat. She thrust out her hand. "Olivia Mendes. I haven't seen you here before. From your accent I'm guessing American."

"Virginian born and bred," Merritt replied. She shook the offered hand. "Merritt Harrington."

"Any relation to Senator John Harrington?"

Merritt glanced at her in surprise. "He's my father. You know him?"

"Only *of* him. I'm a photographer. I've done a number of shoots for political magazines amongst other things."

"You have?" Merritt studied her, noting with approval the handsome, slightly weather-beaten face and eyes crinkled with laughter lines. She radiated confidence, despite being dressed more casually than the rest of the patrons. A down-to-earth woman thought Merritt approvingly, so much more appealing than fashion-plate Petra. And something about her looked familiar. A second later it clicked. "Oh, of course. You're Ollie M. I saw your photos of the Afghan women. And the Syrian refugee camp in Turkey. Wonderful."

Olivia looked pleased. "Thanks. It's always a pleasure to meet someone who's seen my work."

At the bartender's discreet cough, Merritt swiped her card and with a "Thanks" collected her drink. Smiling, she turned her attention back to Olivia. "I'm a great fan. You must be very busy following the political arena as well as field trips to war-torn countries."

"I'm interested in politics and it pays the bills," Olivia replied. "I also do celebrity portraiture." She winked. "Now *that* is the top of the money tree."

"I bet. With your talent, I imagine you'd be sought after. Do you do many?"

"A couple a year max. After some of the horrendous places I've been in, it seems a little superficial."

Out of the blue, the words triggered something in Merritt. She was back on Mount Huascaran, back in the rain. Nervously, she stroked her finger on the stem of the frosty glass. She watched the condensation form into a drop and trickle down to the base before she raised her head to look again at the photographer. "I know exactly what you mean," she said quietly.

Olivia searched her face. "Where did you work?"

"Peru. I'm working with Médecins Sans Frontières and my last assignment was in the Andes. Now all of a sudden, all this," she waved her hand in the air, "seems so…so trivial."

"I know," murmured Olivia, placing a hand gently on her knee. For a moment, her eyes held a faraway look of someone who had seen things no one should. "But it's important to relax too. More so for people like us who've seen unimaginable things."

"Yes," said Merritt, the images fading as the comforting warmth seeped into her skin. "Sorry. Getting too serious. It's a bit raw yet. Sometimes I can't help it getting to me."

"Don't I know it. It took me a while, but I learned to switch off."

"I'm interested to hear how you managed that?"

"Definitely not by heavy drinking. I tried that for a year," Olivia said with a self-deprecating shrug. "Now it's yoga, dancing, and friends."

"Dancing?"

"A friend persuaded me to try. Jazz, swing, and even some ballroom. I'm still learning but I'm wrapped. It's a terrific way to keep fit and a great way to meet people."

"Good for you."

"It's surprising how many people take lessons," Olivia said, and added in a more serious tone, "I found I had to value recreation time more and leave all the nasty stuff at the door."

"I appreciate the advice. Tell me about some of your celebrity shots. There are power women here tonight. Have you photographed any of them?"

When Olivia swept her eyes casually around the room, she gave a sudden intake of breath. "Hey. Well, I'll be. There actually is someone here. She was a fantastic subject too."

Merritt followed her gaze. "Austen Farleigh?" she muttered.

"Yes. It was for one of her earlier albums. The camera loved her." She gave an amused glance. "Judging by the way Petra is flirting with her, she does too."

Merritt narrowed her eyes. "Is that so. You know Petra well?"

"Oh, yes. Very. I fell under her charms for a brief dalliance. *Brief* being the optimum word. She spits out lovers like orange pips."

"That must have hurt."

Olivia laughed. "After our passionate night in the sack, I got out first. She certainly didn't like being the one given the brush-off."

"Who is she?"

"Her father's the major shareholder of a multinational construction firm and she's the CEO of their operations in Australia. Being his only child, she's also his heir apparent. She's hard as nails and used to getting what she wants. Believe me, when that woman goes after someone, she's relentless."

"Huh!" Merritt snorted out. She tried not to look over but couldn't help herself. She flicked a quick sidelong glance their way. Much to her relief, Austen wasn't hanging on Petra's every word. Instead, she was staring over at them, her eyes locked on Olivia's hand on her knee.

"She won't get anywhere with Austen," Merritt stated emphatically.

"You think? I knew Austen years ago… She won't say no."

"That was then…this is now."

"She still has a reputation."

"Rubbishy gossip."

"You think?"

"Yep."

"Wanna bet?"

"Okay. You're on."

Olivia gave a smug smile. "Right. I'll buy the most expensive bottle of champagne in the place if Petra hasn't got her out into the back room in the next fifteen minutes. If she does, you buy. Agreed?"

"It's a bet." She glared over at Petra. "Is that her seduction ploy?"

"Let's just say the room is much more intimate for a tête-à-tête. It works all the time."

Merritt finished the last of her cocktail in one gulp. "Right, Twinkle Toes. Would you like to show me some of your dance moves?"

"I'd love to," Olivia replied, her eyes crinkling with laughter. "Just remember the champagne will be around the four-hundred-dollar mark. This place isn't cheap."

"I don't imagine it is," Merritt shot back as she led her to the floor. "I'll enjoy drinking your bottle."

"You wish. Victory will never taste so sweet," Olivia replied promptly.

To her delight, Olivia hadn't been kidding about the dancing. Ignoring the others on the floor who were energetically bouncing to the fast tune, she swept Merritt into her arms and launched into a complicated swing step. She led her with a grace so smooth and effortless that Merritt felt as if she was floating. Even though her mother had insisted her education wasn't complete without dance lessons, Merritt had never had a partner quite so accomplished.

She laughed delightedly, forgetting everything except the exhilarating dance.

When a love song began, Olivia began to slow dance. When she pulled Merritt even closer, a figure in black materialized beside them.

"I'm cutting in, Ollie," said Austen with a firm tap on the shoulder.

Olivia immediately loosened her grip, her expression showing how completely she had been caught off guard.

Austen gave her a dismissive glance before she held Merritt captive with her bewitching gray-green eyes. She held out the hand. "Shall we?"

Merritt took it without a word, though unable to resist a wink at Olivia before sinking into Austen's arms. "See you later for that champagne," she gurgled out.

Left flatfooted in the middle of the floor, Olivia stared blankly at the two of them. Then she smiled. "Con artist," she called out as she turned to leave the floor.

"What was that about?" Austen said with a possessive growl.

"Nothing." Merritt leaned in, her face tilted to hers. She brushed her lips over Austen's mouth. "Jealous, huh?"

"You think?"

"She's a wonderful dancer."

"Terrific. But can she sing like this?" Austen murmured. Without missing a beat, she softly crooned in her ear.

Soon Merritt found herself melting as the husky voice wove its spell. The singing called to her, stirred her blood. The love song had a lilting melody, poignant and sweet. The powerfully controlled voice gently picked out the notes, sweeping waves of sensation through Merritt.

Their dancing slowed to a shuffle. Entwined, Merritt wasn't even conscious of the music anymore. She could only hear Austin's voice in her head.

She came down to earth suddenly enough though, when someone murmured nearby, "Get a room."

Embarrassed, she laughed a little shakily. "I think we better go back to the bar."

Austen gave her hand a squeeze. "I guess we should."

Olivia was sitting on a stool, a bottle and three flutes on the bar, watching them interestedly as they approached. "Shall we find somewhere to sit in comfort?" she asked.

When they were relaxed back into the velvet armchairs, Olivia poured the champagne. "Enjoy. It's a 2008 vintage Dom Perignon." She eyed them with a twinkle. "This is a surprise. I'm glad for you both. Staying in Sydney long?"

"Back to Canberra tomorrow."

"So then let's make this a night to remember," Olivia said, raising her glass in a salute. "Was this Australia trip a holiday or working gig, Austen?"

"I played at a diplomatic ball put on by the US Government for the Asia-Pacific Trade Summit in Canberra."

"That was where you met?"

"More or less," said Austen vaguely.

Merritt took a sip, not commenting.

Olivia chuckled. "Me thinks there's more to this story."

"We're lucky that you're a photographer and not a reporter," Austen said with a gleam in her eye.

"You are, my friend. Now tell me what's been happening since we last met."

As they talked on through the next hours, Merritt found herself enjoying the night tremendously. Austen's old friends came to say hello, and Olivia kept them entertained with anecdotes of some of her weirder subjects and places she'd visited. Mostly though, she was relieved to see Austen was far more relaxed now she wasn't the focus. And without the wig, she could be herself.

Petra came over to join them after a while, deliberately ignoring Olivia's good-natured ribbing. Intrigued, Merritt watched them interact. It seemed Petra wasn't so immune to Olivia's charm. Nor, she suspected, was Olivia so oblivious to her as she would like everyone to think. When Austen asked if she was ready to go, she wondered if the two of them would ever get together. But that was a story she would probably never know. A pity, for she liked the photographer and hoped she'd find happiness.

As they walked out of the club, she prayed her own prospects in the love department were a lot brighter.

CHAPTER TWENTY-TWO

It was nearly six the next evening when they pulled up at the footpath fronting the entrance to the Harrington house.

"Bye, babe," Austen whispered. She pulled her into a lingering hug and gently stroked her back.

Merritt pressed her lips against her cheek. "I don't want to go, but I have to."

"I know. See you tomorrow night."

Merritt watched the car disappear around the corner before she walked up the driveway.

When her mother answered the door, Merritt gave her a quick peck on the cheek with a "Hi, Mom," before dashing upstairs to get ready for dinner. She hoped they weren't entertaining. The last thing she wanted was to have to engage in small talk with strangers, not after her great time away. And the disappointed look on Austen's face when she had to refuse her invitation to eat at the Hyatt, made her decision infinitely worse. But she had promised her mother and she hated disappointing her.

When Merritt entered the lounge for their predinner drink, Gloria was alone in the room. She waved absently toward the bar. "There's a bottle of sauvignon blanc opened if you would like a glass, dear."

Merritt poured herself a small glass and took a seat. "How's everything, Mom?"

"I had a quiet few days. John was away most of the time with meetings, so I took the opportunity to catch up with my correspondence. Did you have a good time in Sydney?"

Merritt couldn't help breaking out into a happy grin. "Wonderful."

Her smile disappeared when John Harrington's voice boomed out from the doorway. "So you're back. Who did you go off with?"

Wincing, Merritt turned to face him.

An inquisition was coming. And it wasn't going to be pleasant.

Already she was regretting not staying with Austen. Judging by his expression, her father was in a particularly foul mood. She glanced over at her mother for a clue to what was wrong. Something clearly was, for by the way she was refusing to look at him, he must have already given her a few licks of his temper.

"Just a friend," Merritt answered cautiously.

"You expect me to believe that you went away with *just a friend*? Who is the dyke?"

Merritt's temper rose. "There's no need to speak like that."

"I call it how I see it. Who are you mixed up with?"

"That's my business."

"You're here at my invitation, Merritt, and I expect you to conduct yourself with some semblance of respectability. I asked you a question and I expect a fucking answer."

Furious, Merritt gritted her teeth. Enough was enough. She'd be damned if she would continue to be his whipping board. "Get over yourself, Father. You're a bigot and a prude, living in the past. What I do is entirely my business. As for sullying the family name, that's a lot of outdated crap too."

"Don't you dare speak to me like that."

"Then treat me like an adult," she snapped. "You will meet her when I'm good and ready. And you will treat her with the respect she deserves."

When his expression turned uglier, she waited for the tsunami of toxic words. Though this time, if he thought she was going to take it, he had another think coming. She was no longer young or impressionable. She glared at him, ready for battle. Austen meant too much to her to back down now. For once in her life she was going to fight for her happiness and damn the consequences.

She stiffened, waiting.

But his response never came. Her mother rose suddenly from the chair and said in an icy voice, "That's quite enough, John. Apologize to Merritt, or so help me God, I'll be on the first plane home. And I'm not joking."

Merritt stared at her nonplussed. Wow! Her mother had suddenly grown a set of balls. She amended that to ovaries.

Her father's mouth sagged open. His teeth clicked sharply as he snapped it shut.

Silence fell in a suffocating pall over the room.

Moments later, it shattered like brittle glass when the housekeeper called out from the doorway, "Dinner is served, Mrs. Harrington."

They filed into the dining room and took their places wordlessly. Fortunately they were alone, the tension palpable.

The meal was one of the most uncomfortable Merritt had ever sat through. Her father ignored them, her mother picked at her food, and Merritt kept her head down as best she could. When her father got up abruptly after the main course and retired to his office, she breathed a sigh of relief.

"Just the two of us for dessert, thanks Janice," Gloria said when the housekeeper appeared to take away the plates.

Merritt studied her mother closely. Though paler than normal, she seemed to have herself under control. "Sorry, Mom. He got to me tonight."

"His bad temper had nothing to do with you. He's been like that all day." Pensively, Gloria twirled her wineglass round. "I think your father is having an affair."

Taken aback at the bald statement, Merritt blinked at her. "How did you find out?"

Gloria looked at her sadly. "I notice you didn't question that it was true."

"Well…um…I'm not surprised. I've seen the way he treats the young women on his staff." She'd often suspected he was having it off with other women. It wasn't in his nature to be faithful to anyone or anything. That was why he was such an astute politician. It was a cutthroat game, an environment in which he thrived.

Gloria's shoulders sagged, seeming suddenly defeated. "I've turned a blind eye to a lot of things over the years. He's a powerful man and has become used to certain liberties. Unfortunately, power does corrupt in some instances. It's turned him into a tyrant."

"Sorry, Mom," Merritt said gently, reaching over the table to take her hand. "I haven't done much to help you."

"Don't be silly, Merritt. I've failed *you*. I should have stopped him picking on you right from the start."

"I got over it," Merritt said with a shrug. "He hasn't the capacity to hurt me anymore." She eyed her mother curiously. "Who do you think he's having an affair with?"

"It's probably that beautiful press secretary in the Japanese contingent. He's been paying particular attention to her at every function." Gloria paused while dessert was served, then continued when they were alone again. "I found a pair of women's earrings in his coat pocket when I sent it to the drycleaners. They weren't mine."

"What a bastard," Merritt exclaimed. "What are you going to do?"

"I haven't decided, but I will see this assignment out for the Committee's sake. A scandal would do irreparable damage."

"You're a trooper. I'd tell him to go to hell."

Gloria's smile looked more like a grimace. "I may eventually. You know, dear, that I've always been extremely proud of you. I would like very much to meet your girlfriend."

"I'll bring her to the Arts Council party." She cleared her throat. "Father is so not going to approve."

Gloria gave a satisfied smile. "Good."

* * *

Rain had been hanging around since daybreak. The city looked dull and gray, but it didn't dampen Merritt's feeling of contentment. Her mother had at last stood up for herself, which was a relief. Though she hadn't said so in as many words, Merritt knew she'd leave her father when they got back to Virginia. And she was pleased. The asshole didn't deserve her mother's love or loyalty. But the best thing to come out of the confrontation, he had lost the capacity to hurt or influence her anymore.

Those times were gone.

The psychologist's receptionist flashed a bright smile. "You may go straight in, Dr. Harrington."

She threw a welcoming grin back, pleased to see her cheery face. Noting the vibrant red hair was now a bright blue, Merritt called out as she passed the desk, "Love the hair."

Angelica Turner pushed the computer to the side and stood to greet her. "Welcome, Merritt. Please…take a seat."

Seated in the armchair, Merritt fiddled with her silver bracelets. A nervous habit she hnever been able to shed. Therapists always made her a little uneasy, especially Dr. Turner. She seemed to read her mind, or at least preempt what she was thinking. She nodded to her. "Hi, Angelica."

"So…how have you been?"

"Great thanks," replied Merritt, relaxing a little more into the seat.

"Any episodes this week. Nightmares?"

"I've been sleeping soundly. One brief flashback."

Angelica studied her over the rim of her glasses. "Tell me about it. What brought it on?"

"I was chatting to a woman at a club. We were discussing her photography shoots in shitty hotspots around the world, when an image of that godawful mountain flashed into my mind. It only lasted a second or two, but it spaced me out long enough for her to notice."

"What did she do?"

Merritt thought back to how Olivia had been so calming. "Gave me a few tips how to handle the trauma."

"And what did you think of her advice?"

"I thought it made good sense. She was a down-to-earth person who'd had plenty of experience in the stuff I was going through. She advised me to learn to switch off, value recreation time, and get an interest away from work. Oh…and don't try to fix myself with copious amounts of alcohol."

Angelica chuckled. "Wise woman."

"She's Ollie M."

"Really? I think her photography is marvelous."

"I do too," agreed Merritt. "And she's an extremely likeable person with it."

"You look blooming, by the way," Angelica said with a twinkle in her eye. "I'm guessing your social life must be going well."

"Yes," Merritt said, feeling her cheeks glow warmly. She was blushing like an adolescent with a crush. "I've been seeing someone a lot. She's become special."

"I'm very glad for you, Merritt. Becoming emotionally involved with someone is just what this doctor orders. People always tend to separate sex and love into a pigeonhole, but it's an important part of our physical and mental well-being. It'll certainly make you heal faster." Angelica paused, then prodded, "How's it going with your father?"

Merritt cleared her throat. "Things have come to a head. I stood up to him last night."

"And how did you feel about that?" asked Angelica softly.

"Great actually. My mother took my side as well." Merritt didn't elaborate on the argument, or her father's cheating. It would have been disloyal to her mother.

"Good for you." Angelica studied her thoughtfully. "I can see by the way you talk about him, his hold on you has diminished. Part of getting a healthy mind is facing your demons."

They chatted on for the rest of the session, toward the end of which Merritt declared, "I'm in a much better headspace now, thanks to you."

"I'm sure of it, Merritt. Glad I was able to help," replied Angelica. "There will be no need to see me anymore. I'm hoping you won't have any further repercussions from the assignment. Your mind needs rest, and I advise you to ask to serve out the remainder of your contract in a low-key place. I'm prepared to recommend that to your boss. Shall I go ahead and write the letter?"

Merritt knitted her brows, grappling with her dilemma. It would certainly be easier, and probably sensible if she accepted the therapist's advice. There were plenty of less stressful places where doctors were needed for humanitarian help. But then she thought about Terry and Karl. They were her colleagues, her friends. They had formed a well-oiled medical machine and knew they could depend on each other in times of crisis. Times when lives depended on how well they worked together. To desert them would be a cop-out. Regretfully, she shook her head. "No. Sorry. I can't let my team down."

"I had a feeling you'd say that," Angelica said with a nod. "I respect your decision, and although I wish you'd take my advice, I applaud your loyalty." She steepled her fingers and peered over the desk at Merritt. "The next best thing is to give you a few ways to cope in tight situations. Humor is the best medicine. Wisecrack, make jokes."

"I wish," groaned Merritt. "But I invariably forget the punchline."

Angelica laughed. "Okay." She went on in a more serious voice. "The most important point to remember, try not to blame yourself for everything that happens. You have to differentiate between those things you can prevent and those you have absolutely no control over."

Merritt irritably tapped a finger on the arm of the chair. "That wasn't the problem in Peru. I was always conscious that the mountain could bury us at any time. I was afraid. It was the reason my nerves were shot."

"Your nerves were already stretched to breaking point trying to save those who were unable to be saved. Everything was interwoven." Angelica shifted forward in her chair. "When you feel you're at a point when it's hard to cope, there are a few things you can do. If there is only time to snatch a few moments, a quick series of breathing exercises will help. I'll give you a printout of some techniques to get your mind in the right zone." She rifled in her desk and handed over three pages stapled together. "Here. Make this your survival bible in the field."

"Thanks," said Merritt gratefully. "I appreciate all you've done for me."

"You're welcome," Angelica said with a smile. She glanced at her watch. "I guess that finishes us for the day." She rose from her chair and came round the desk. "I'll walk you out the door. You're an incredibly caring doctor, Merritt. Look after yourself and if you ever want any help, just give me a ring."

The clouds had cleared, the sun shining brightly when Merritt exited the office block. Feeling on a high now the therapy was over, she wondered how she was going to fill in the rest of the day. A book or a movie didn't appeal. She supposed she could experiment with a new recipe. The Alfajore, a Peruvian cookie filled with sweet caramel cream and dusted with icing, sounded interesting. Austen may like a batch. She sighed. It was a no-brainer what she wished to do. But she didn't want to seem too clingy, she was seeing her tonight.

She hailed a cab, calling out as she stepped into the backseat, "The Hyatt, please." Realizing her mistake, she opened her mouth to amend the address but shut it again. There would be no harm in seeing if Austen was free to have lunch, would there? By the time she wrestled with herself whether she should text or not, the cabbie had pulled up outside the hotel. Not stopping to second-guess herself, she hurried into the lobby.

By the time Merritt reached the door of the suite, she was on tenterhooks. Was she making a complete fool of herself? Austen may want some downtime. Or she mayn't even be home. Ignoring her doubts, she tapped on the door.

It swung open. Dressed in old jeans, a T-shirt with the slogan *Best Pants are No Pants*, and flip-flops on her feet, Austen had never looked so appealing.

"Hi," said Merritt shyly.

With a quick step forward, Austen pulled her into a hug. "I missed you," she murmured into Merritt's hair.

Merritt sighed, relishing the warmth of the body pressed against her. "Me too. I just wanted to see you. I hope that's all right."

"You're kidding. I was just sitting here feeling sorry for myself. How did you go with the shrink?"

"All good. I got the okay to go back to work," Merritt replied. She saw no point in telling Austen that Dr. Turner would have preferred her to see out her time with DWB in less stressful places.

"Come on in. Shall I order some lunch?"

Merritt gave her a quizzical look. "You want to eat?"

"Hell no. I've got something better to do with you."

"Umm. Does it involve a certain type of exercise?"

"Most definitely," replied Austen, dropping her hands to squeeze her hips. "And there could be a little workout for these love handles."

"Oh, my. Lead the way, honey."

CHAPTER TWENTY-THREE

Time flew by to the eve of the Arts Council party. Austen was seated at the piano in her suite, finishing off a new composition when her phone beeped. She reluctantly put her pen aside to read the text.

Hey, Austen. If you're not busy, could you come to my suite? I've finished the itinerary for you guys.

Annoyed at the interruption when she was on a roll, with a curse Austen put her work-in-progress into the drawer. She didn't want to think about going back, didn't want to leave Merritt. They had seen each other nearly every day since their trip to Sydney, and she couldn't remember ever feeling so at home with anyone. But now this text from Katie made the end of her vacation real.

After a quick message to Merritt to go right in when she arrived, Austen made her way down the hallway. She'd barely seen her manager for the last fortnight, which had been a relief. Since Katie had made it quite clear she disapproved of their dating, Austen wasn't prepared for Merritt to suffer any censure from her often waspish-tongued friend.

She knew she shouldn't be getting so protective of Merritt, but she couldn't help it. Somewhere along the line, her feelings had slipped into something far beyond enjoyable company and great sex. She had become the center of Austen's world. And though they had avoided discussing the future again, it was plain that the holiday romance was becoming so much more. Austen knew she had better yank her head out of the clouds pretty soon or she'd be totally screwed. She was getting dangerously close to losing her heart.

She rapped on Katie's door, and she beckoned her in. Austen eyed the silk top and pants. Even at home the woman was a regular fashion hound. She gave a grin as she glanced down at her own comfortable old jeans and T-shirt.

"I'm having wine," Katie said, waving her glass. "Would you like a drink?"

"A beer, thanks."

Katie rummaged in the bar fridge. "A local brew or a Heineken?"

"I'll have a VB," Austen replied. With a satisfied hum, she swallowed a mouthful. Aussie beer—just like old times.

"I'd like to go through the bookings. If you're not happy with anything, let me know now so there's time to change things."

Austen followed her into the lounge area and took a seat opposite in one of the leather armchairs. "What have you lined up?"

"Ellen's interview is scheduled the first Thursday you get back, then Jimmy Fallon the following week. You're booked for three concerts in New York, and after that, you and the boys will go on tour for a month in Canada."

"So the rat race begins again," Austen muttered.

Katie looked at her sharply. "I thought you'd be glad to get back. You've had quite a break. This place is a provincial backwater after New York."

Austen bit back the retort on the tip of her tongue, instead said mildly, "It's a pretty place. Not wildly exciting but has a certain charm."

"To each her own I guess. I'll enjoy getting back to some decent shopping."

"That's not a priority for me."

Katie swept her eyes over her. "I don't know how you do it, but even in those old clothes you manage to look good."

"Why, Ms. Bell, is that a compliment?"

Katie laughed. "Most of us have to work at it, Austen. Back to business." She handed her a sheet of paper. "Here's the timeline. After Canada, I've managed to snag you a Vegas stint at Caesar's Palace. Any problems?"

Austen perused the schedule. "No, that'll be fine. We'll appreciate playing in the States for a while." She folded the paper into her pocket, then eyed her thoughtfully. "Would you like to come to a cocktail party tomorrow night? The City Arts Council has asked me along as their special guest and you're far better at PR networking than I am."

Katie made a face. "Do I have to? Those things can be a dead bore."

"No, but I'd appreciate it if you did," Austen said, injecting authority into her voice. It wouldn't hurt Katie to do a bit more to earn her money. The Black Heat was making her millions. "Senator Harrington is funding the show to foster the arts between countries, and I imagine there will be quite a few of the visiting trade delegates attending."

Katie must have caught her pleading tone, for she acquiesced immediately with a smile. "I'd love to come. Want to go together?"

Austen hesitated. She didn't know if Merritt wanted a lift. If she did it might be awkward. "I've a couple of things to do, so I'll meet you there if that's okay."

"That's fine. You know me. I like to be fashionably late."

Austen swallowed the last of her beer and got to her feet. "I'd better be off. I'm trying to finish a song I've been working on for ages."

"I'll see you tomorrow night then. Where's it being held?"

"At a private venue, Lakeside Gardens. Seven p.m. I'll text the address."

With a spring in her step Austen walked back down the corridor, pleased she'd thought to ask Katie. Having her at the do would take the pressure off. Not only did she know how to handle business people, a friend could come in handy if the senator turned nasty.

When she opened the door of her suite, Merritt appeared in a pink apron and a pair of cute shorts. Austen ran appreciative eyes over the long, athletic legs. "Beautiful," she murmured.

A slight blush spread across Merritt's neck. "Hi, honey." She kissed her softly on the lips. Merritt's mouth tasted spicy: a mixture of peppers, herbs, and tart lemon.

"Hmm. Whatever you're cooking smells delish." She was getting used to Merritt coming up with some unusual concoctions from weird places. The aroma was mouth-watering.

"It's a recipe I picked up in Guatemala. Their national dish called Pulique, which translates to a thick meat and vegetable stew. I'm serving it with that crusty loaf you bought at the artisan bakers."

Austen chuckled. "You're trying to fatten me up."

"Can't fatten a thoroughbred," Merritt said with a wink. "Shall we sit on the balcony to have a drink before we eat? It's too lovely an evening to sit inside."

"Sounds good." Austen fetched the drinks and followed Merritt outside. Once settled on the deck chair, she twisted the top off her beer. "Tell me. What were you doing in Guatemala?"

Merritt stared out over the gardens. "There was an eruption, which isn't a rare occurrence there. The country has thirty-seven volcanoes, four of them active. All the villages had been evacuated, even those considered safe enough, which was lucky because the mountain spewed out far more lava than the scientists expected. There were rivers of the stuff. We were stationed in Antigua, and mostly helped the local medics with ash burns and smoke inhalation."

"I've never been in that part of the world."

"It's the most populous country in Central America," Merritt said. "Great scenery…very pretty beaches. Karl, Terry, and

I took a trip to the Tikal National Park after we left Antigua. Since the country was a dangerous place for unmarried women without an escort, Karl went with us. The region was the center of the Mayan civilization, the main tourist attraction is their ancient city and pyramid ruins."

"Tell me about the most interesting places you've seen," Austen said and sat back happily to listen to Merritt launch into her adventures.

She idly took stock how the two of them were lounging in the deck chairs. When had she become so freaking domesticated? Since Merritt loved cooking, she'd begun to make dinner in the kitchen in Austen's suite. Which pleased Austen no end. After so many years of restaurant meals, nothing beat home cooking. And she hadn't been joking when she said she was fattening up. She'd had to squeeze into her jeans today.

After relating her stories for half an hour, Merritt got up from the chair and collected the empties. "If you set the table, I'll serve."

"Sure," Austen replied, knowing if Mick could see her now, he'd be astounded and the ribbing would start. Not that she would give a flying fig. He could tease her 'til the cows came home. She was having a ball with Merritt.

Soon Merritt appeared with a hotpot and carefully put it on a placemat. After she ladled out the stew onto a plate, she passed it over together with a thick slice of bread. "Dig in."

One bite and Austen said delightedly, "Scrumptious."

"Thanks," Merritt said, looking pleased. "You're so easy to cook for, Austen. I've never seen anyone enjoy food so much."

"I know. I'm a food junkie and you're the best cook." She waved her fork in the air. "I'm going to miss all this."

When Merritt's smile vanished and she ducked her head, Austen cursed herself for ruining the moment. "Sorry. I didn't mean to say that. We've still got the five days in Port Macquarie. My family's going to love you."

Merritt raised her head to study her. "Then let's enjoy what time we have left."

Austen wriggled uncomfortably under the scrutiny. Detecting sadness and a hint of recrimination in the blue eyes, she hastily changed the subject. "What time are they expecting me to turn up to this do tomorrow night?"

"Six thirty. Umm…I thought we might go in holding hands."

"Like you're my date?"

"Yes."

"But your father will be there."

Merritt placed her fork firmly down on the plate. "Of course he will. That's the point. I'd like to introduce you to my parents, and the world, as my girlfriend."

"Wow! That's a big step for you."

Merritt gazed at her anxiously. "You're fine with it, aren't you?"

"Of course. I'd like nothing better. But won't he go ballistic?"

"No. He won't make a fuss in public. That'll be bad for his image. Believe me, he knows which side his bread is buttered on…he was voted in by young liberals and the artistic community. It's mostly right-wing conservatives who are the homophobes."

"What about your mother?"

Merritt laughed. "She's dying to meet you. She's been consumed with curiosity."

Austen eyed her skeptically. "Maybe, but will she *approve* of me?"

"All she wants is me to be happy, and she should be aware by now I'm very much so. I can't help smiling all the time."

"I hope so. I don't want you to feel awkward."

"Hey," Merritt murmured, reaching over to run her fingers down her cheek. "I think you're wonderful. You're talented, kind, and considerate, and I'm so proud you want to be with me."

For one of the very few times in her life, Austen felt completely humbled. "Thank you for saying that. I don't deserve you."

"Of course you do. And don't worry about Mom. She wasn't a society lady when she met Father. She was a contestant in the Miss Delaware beauty pageant competition and won the crown."

"No kidding. She's still a stunner. Did she know your father before that?"

Merritt chuckled. "Not likely. The Harrington name dates back to a pre-Civil War tobacco plantation. My mother's family were seafood merchants from Delaware."

"Was the marriage frowned upon by the Harrington family?" asked Austen curiously.

"Hardly. They were struggling financially, and my maternal Grandpa Leo had loads of money. It was Mom's inheritance that set up my father's electronics business." With a gleam in her eyes she eyed Austen. "Mom owns the controlling shares in the company, so it's going to be a big blow when she leaves him."

"Will she go?"

"I think so. Time will tell though. He's as slippery as an eel."

Austen finished the last of her stew with a sigh. "That was awesome. I'm so full."

"That's a pity," said Merritt, as she gathered up the plates. "I baked some Guatemalan cream pastries for dessert."

Austen straightened in her chair. "Well. Not that full."

* * *

It was just after seven when Austen booked a Silver Service taxi to take them to Lakeside Gardens. She'd chosen one of the two special ensembles she'd packed, a black double-breasted blazer with a red pocket hanky, black tailored slacks and black dress boots. She was a little nervous, though mainly for Merritt's sake. For all her assurances, the senator might behave poorly if provoked enough. And he certainly wasn't going to like his daughter being tied up with her. Though, she silently vowed, if the bastard thought he could tyrannize Merritt, he'd have her to contend with this time.

She texted Merritt she was on her way.

A message came straight back. *Parents have left. Come to front door.*

Austen smiled as she sank back to watch the city whizz by. When they pulled up at the Harrington house, Merritt was standing on the front porch, wearing a silver cocktail dress, and her hair in a loosely braided updo style. As the porch light bathed her face in a rich glow, a lump caught in Austen's throat. The woman looked breathtaking and incredibly sensual.

When she stepped out to open the door of the BMW for Merritt, she was rewarded with an intimate smile.

"You're dazzling," whispered Austen as she moved in beside her.

Merritt's eyes settled softly on hers. "You've scrubbed up pretty well yourself."

When they stopped outside the venue, the driver held the door open. Austen firmly took hold of her hand. "Ready, babe?"

"Oh, yes," Merritt muttered back. "As ready as I'll ever be. Just don't let go of my hand."

"I won't," Austen said with an encouraging grin. "Shall we go ruffle a few feathers?"

They could hear laughter echoing from the building as they walked up the three steps to the wide veranda. A good sign, Austen figured. Not a stodgy show.

Merritt grasped her hand more tightly. The huge room was decorated in a rustic style, with a long timber bar, solid wooden stools, wine barrels and strings of festoon lights.

"Cool," murmured Merritt.

Austen flicked her glance. She seemed composed as she surveyed the crowd. No one appeared to notice them initially, but soon the room gradually fell quiet. Austen silently cursed that she was so well known. There was no slipping in unnoticed—they were obviously waiting for her, even though she wasn't going to perform.

"I'd say the word got around you'd be here too," whispered Merritt.

"Yeah," muttered Austen ruefully.

And then she saw him. Senator Harrington was standing at the corner of the bar, his back to them. As the chatter ceased, he swiveled around. When his eyes flicked down to their joined hands, he looked like he'd just swallowed something rotten. His eyes narrowed, his expression hardened.

Abruptly, he left the woman he was engaging in conversation and pushed through the crowd toward them.

The look on his face was pure fury.

CHAPTER TWENTY-FOUR

Everything suddenly morphed into a nightmare for Merritt. She felt Austen freeze beside her, and she turned her head to follow her gaze. Her breath caught at the sight of her father bearing down on them. *Oh crap!* By his expression, he wasn't going to hold back. He looked like Lucifer ready to deliver her straight to the fires of hell. Try as she might, she couldn't look away, his eyes had her pinned like a Prufrock butterfly to a corkboard. Panic flooded through her. She had miscalculated badly—no way this wouldn't end without a nasty public scene.

She tilted her head defiantly and waited for the onslaught. When Austen moved to shield her, she tugged her back. "No," she muttered hoarsely. "This is *my* fight."

Help came from an unexpected quarter. Gloria Harrington appeared in a flurry of blue chiffon, slipped in front of the senator and caught Merritt in a firm hug. Taken by surprise, Merritt sank gratefully into the embrace. As she breathed in the familiar loving scent, her tightly coiled body slowly unwound.

"Well, my dear," her mother whispered in her ear, "aren't you a surprise." She turned to Austen with a gracious nod. "How nice to see you again, Austen."

Austen's face broke into a smile. "Hi, Mrs. Harrington."

"Please...do call me Gloria." She turned to her husband and said in a quiet, even voice. "It seems Merritt has brought a special friend for us to see again, John."

Her smile never wavering, Austen replied in a clear voice, "Hello, Senator." Merritt hoped she felt as confident as she sounded.

Conflicted emotions flitted across his face. Caution won out. He gave a grudging nod. "Hello, Austen. I didn't know you were still in Canberra."

She casually placed an arm around Merritt's shoulders. "I found a great reason to stay."

Merritt smiled brightly, but inwardly groaned. *Don't poke the tiger.*

"Well, I'm delighted that you're keeping my daughter so well entertained," Gloria interrupted, her lips curved into a satisfied smile. Merritt glanced at her sharply, catching the gleam in her eye. Her mother was actually enjoying this. The worm had definitely turned. Gloria was no longer content to be a puppet on her husband's string.

"She's showing me a super time," murmured Merritt. This was rewarded with a radiant look from her mother and a dark frown from her father. Seeing his lips tighten as if he was on the tip of venting his anger, she desperately searched for a way to close him down.

It was her mother who saved her again. "I see Mr. Ji Zhang is here. He told me how much he enjoyed talking to you at the gala dinner, Austen. Take her over to say hello, dear," Gloria said, blithely ignoring her husband.

Merritt squeezed her hand gratefully. "Okay. See you later, Mom." Without another glance at her father, she shepherded Austen over to the Chinese Ambassador for Trade.

After reacquainting themselves with Zhang, they moved through the diplomats, politely chatting with each. When Katie

Bell, in a sleek red cocktail dress, joined them twenty minutes later, relief flitted across Austen's face. Her reaction didn't surprise Merritt. Though Austen showed no outward sign she wasn't relaxed, she had said often enough that politics weren't her thing. Katie, on the other hand, seemed completely at home. The smile she turned on the Vietnamese couple, was both charming and practiced. The consummate professional woman.

But when Merritt leaned against Austen affectionately, Kate's smile faltered. She threw a disbelieving glance at them. Austen caught the look and immediately put her arm around Merritt's waist. Katie glared in disapproval. Austen winked in defiance.

Fearing a spat looming, Merritt quickly stepped into the breach. "If you'll excuse us, General Nguyen, Ms. Nguyen, we must move on. It was lovely meeting you both," she said with a bow.

Katie was ominously silent and without a word, abruptly headed off in the other direction. With some misgiving, Merritt watched her go.

"Don't worry about her," whispered Austen in her ear. "She's just pissed I didn't tell her I was still seeing you."

"It's none of her business," Merritt said sharply.

"That's what I told her."

"So, what's her problem?"

"Beats me."

Merritt raised an eyebrow at her. "Maybe she fancies you."

"Huh! Are you jealous?"

"Hardly." Merritt took a glass of wine from a passing waiter and said haughtily, "And I'm not going to lose sleep over her. Let's go see Simon, the songwriter, now that we've done the diplomatic rounds. He's been waving at me for ages. He organized the function and is dying to meet you." She led Austen to a group of brightly dressed people standing near one of the big windows. They immediately folded them into their circle.

Simon was bursting at the seams when he saw Austen, his Adam's apple bobbing erratically in his excitement. The others swarming around them seemed just as keen to meet the night's biggest drawcard. Merritt was pleased to see that Austen was a great deal more relaxed in this company. Helped along by constant refills delivered by circling waiters, laughter and jokes were pouring out as fast as the alcohol flowed in. Merritt was swept along by their enthusiasm.

She washed down the finger food with some really good red wine, very conscious that with a few subtle gestures, Austen was making it clear they were a couple.

Initially, Merritt had scanned the room intermittently for her father, but as the night wore on, she found she didn't give a damn. Her attention was focused on Austen, in scintillating form. She had the artistic crowd hanging off her every word.

When finally the guests were distracted by the arrival of delectable sweets, Austen leaned over and whispered in Merritt's ear, "You've been staring at me with a goofy expression for ages."

Merritt murmured back, only half joking. "Either I've had too much wine or you're making me dizzy."

"Come with me," Austen replied, and added in a louder voice, "excuse us for a few minutes, folks. We won't be long." She took her hand and led her to a side door.

"Where are we going?" Merritt asked, happily following.

"For a little walk in the gardens. I want to have you to myself for a while."

Merritt didn't argue—she wanted the same thing. Austen led her away from the main lights, through colorful flower beds, past a Grecian fountain to stop further down amongst a stand of trees.

A three-quarter moon hung in the sky, a lover's moon casting a soft glow over the foliage. It seemed just magical to Merritt. Perfect.

Austen slipped behind a large red gum, reeled her into her arms and pressed her against the smooth bark. "No prying eyes here," she murmured.

With a touch as tender as the night, she stroked her hair, her cheeks, her neck. Merritt yielded herself completely, floating on the sensations. The brush of Austen's fingertips, the warmth of her lips, the slide of her tongue, pulled her into an erotic whirlpool. When Austen cupped her breast, she pressed urgently against her thigh.

Suddenly, a crunch of leaves sounded in the night.

Austen immediately put two fingers onto Merritt's lips. "Shush," she whispered into her ear.

Merritt bit back a giggle.

A male voice echoed faintly on the light breeze, "For Christ sake, sit down on the bench and discuss this rationally." The muffled tone was distorted, as though he was deliberately trying to keep his voice low.

"I thought I made myself quite clear when you left my bed last. It's either her or me. I didn't come all this way just so you could have your fucks," a woman hissed back.

Merritt felt Austen stiffen. She peered at her, to find her intently listening. "Katie," she breathed out in a voice so soft that Merritt wondered if she'd heard her correctly.

"I told you I was going to leave her. Just have patience." Now Merritt cocked her own head to hear better as well. The male voice had a very familiar ring.

"I've had years of patience. Now it's run out."

"Come on, sweetheart, don't be like that. I promised I'd divorce her when this assignment is over."

It took all Merritt's willpower to stop the gasp. Tears leaked over her eyes and she frantically blinked them back. Her legs wobbled. It was only Austen's iron grip around her waist that prevented her from collapsing.

"In the meantime," John Harrington continued, "get that dyke tramp Austen Farleigh away from my daughter."

That was enough for Merritt. Anger flamed through her like a hot poker. She wrenched free from Austen and stalked round the tree.

Her father was sitting on the bench seat, one arm around Katie's waist, the other rubbing her inner thigh.

At the sound of her approach, he looked up. His eyes widened and he jerked his hands away. When he began to rise, Merritt snapped, "Don't bother getting up, Father. I've heard enough. I'll be speaking with Mom tomorrow."

His jaw clenched. "Now see here, Merritt—"

Merritt furiously cut him off. "No, you won't silence me this time. You're just a disgusting fraud," she spat out. "I've spent my whole life trying to live up to your expectations. And for what? For someone who has no honor or integrity. You know what? I don't give a shit about you now, which takes away any capacity you have to hurt me." She swung abruptly to Katie, who was staring at her with tightly pinched lips. "As for you...you're not worthy to be in the same room as my mother."

Her father lurched to his feet, his hands balled into fists. "Don't you dare speak to us like that."

"And what will you do? Hit me? You did enough of that when I was young." She moved closer, daring him. "And don't you ever speak like that about Austen again. She's worth ten of you."

A snort erupted from Katie. "That's a joke."

Merritt's temper flared even more. But when she opened her mouth to retaliate, Austen gripped her arm and said firmly, "Let it be, babe. You're too upset and angry to think about what you're saying. You'll only say things you'll regret. Tomorrow when you're calmer, you can have a talk with your mother."

Katie interrupted with a sneer. "What's with your holier than thou attitude, Austen? Since when did you acquire scruples?"

"I've always had them. You've just seen what you've wanted to see. Denigrating people is your way of manipulating them. You've made millions out of the band with very little effort on your part." Austen poked a finger at her. "You're fired. I'll organize Rose to terminate your contract tomorrow."

"God damn you, Austen. You can't do that."

"Just watch me."

As she stood by as Austen dismissed her business manager, Merritt's body trembled. Everything was spiraling out of control. She swallowed back bile and tugged at Austen's sleeve. "Please...please take me home, honey. I really need to get away."

"Of course, babe," she said, giving her a gentle squeeze.

Without waiting, Merritt stumbled off along the path toward the bright lights of the building. Austen reached her side and grabbed her hand. "I'll order a cab. You wait out front while

I run in and tell your mother you're not feeling well and I'm taking you home."

Merritt dashed away the tears trickling down her cheeks. "Okay. Can I spend the night with you? I can't go home tonight and face her...not yet."

Austen wiped a tear away with her thumb. "Sure you can stay with me. We can pick up your suitcase for our trip to my parents in the morning."

* * *

Without saying a word, Austen led her into the bedroom. "Let's have a shower," she said, already shedding her clothes as she walked.

Austen lathered her with soap while softly crooning a love song in her ear. To Merritt, it brought another meaning entirely to singing in the shower. The melody floated in the steamy recess with perfect harmony and pitch, a far cry from her own out-of-tune warbling. Austen made no attempt to initiate sex but treated her like a delicate piece of porcelain. Merritt had never felt so cherished. After soaping her thoroughly, Austen gently washed her clean, then toweled her dry.

Once she led her onto the bed, she crawled under the sheet beside her. Merritt watched her, savoring the moment—not speaking, not doing anything, just being with someone who cared about her. The hotel was dead quiet this time of night—no footsteps, no rattle of doors, no voices, nothing to break the close mood.

"Are you tired?" Austen asked.

"A little."

"What are you thinking?"

Merritt took her hand. "Just that people think intimacy is about sex. But it's really about being honest with each other."

"Ah, but truth can come at a price. Do you intend to tell your mother who your father's sleeping with?"

"I don't honestly know. It would really hurt her to find out he's had a mistress for years, but she needs to leave him." She wiped away an errant teardrop. "It's such a mess. He's been a liar to his wife *and* his mistress. Since Katie's trying to force him to divorce, I'd say she hasn't a clue Mom holds the purse strings."

"Do her good. She really is a slimy piece of work. She made out she was doing us a big fucking favor by organizing the gig at the ball, when all the time it was just an excuse for her to be over here with her lover."

"No wonder Father didn't say anything about me being at the Hyatt that morning. He was coming home after spending a night with Katie."

Austen grunted. "Let's forget about both those assholes. You want to go to sleep?"

"No."

"Good." She ran her fingertip down her arm, smiling as Merritt's skin blossomed into goosebumps. She nuzzled her neck and kissed the sweet spot behind her jaw. Her lips traveled over her upper body, stopped to lavish each nipple which stood up immediately for attention. When she traveled lower to her navel, Merritt breathed out a shaky sigh.

And with her teeth, tongue, and fingers, she brought Merritt slowly and lovingly to her climax. All Merritt's pent-up emotions exploded in a scream of ecstasy as she crested into the most intense orgasm she had yet to experience. Each glorious aftershock battered her until her body wept with the pleasure of it.

Spent, she flopped back on the bed with the realization that she was stupidly and helplessly in love with Austen.

She snuggled in close, gathering the courage. "Honey, I…I—" *Come on, just say the words.* "I love…um…being with you."

"Me too, babe. Now, it's really late…we'd better get some sleep."

"Sweet dreams."

Tomorrow I'll tell her.

* * *

Persistent buzzing from her phone woke Merritt from a deep sleep. Disoriented, she opened her eyes. The room was in darkness. Groggily, she glanced at the clock on the side table. 4:20 a.m. A wave of anxiety hit. A call at this time could only mean something was wrong. Or someone hurt. Mom? Terry? Karl? The displayed number wasn't one she recognized.

She padded to the lounge so as not to wake Austen. "Merritt speaking," she said, trying to keep the panic under control.

An unfamiliar woman's voice replied. "Dr. Merritt Harrington?"

"Yes."

"This is Lois Miller from Doctors Without Borders' head office in Sydney."

Merritt grasped the phone tighter. "What can I do for you, Lois?"

"Sorry to ring you so early, Merritt, but this call can't wait. We've been coordinating with the Army Medical Unit in Townsville to bring medical teams as soon as possible to Papua New Guinea. At midnight, a series of severe earthquakes rocked the Highlands and there have been large aftershocks periodically ever since. PNG has sent Australia an SOS. The army is sending medical supplies and personnel, but we need more experienced field doctors."

"You want me to go?"

She cleared her throat. "I know this is short notice, but you're in Australia and have extensive field trauma experience."

Merritt's belly lurched. It was the last thing she wanted to do, but there wasn't a choice. "Certainly I'll go. What do I need to do?"

"The RAAF has a base at Canberra Airport. They'll have a jet waiting at six a.m. for you and two other M.O.s. They'll take you to Townsville and you can all catch a lift from there on the cargo plane to Port Moresby. The rest of the response crew will be flying out of Townsville and Cairns at first light. A Royal Navy hospital ship has already left."

"I'm on my way, Lois."

"Good. And thanks very much, Merritt."

Her emotions raw, Merritt called a cab before jamming the phone back in her purse.

Son-of-a-bitch! Why now?

She pulled herself together and quickly slipped on last night's clothes. There was no time to dawdle. She'd be flat out making it—she had to get back to her parents' place, change into her fatigues, pack a backpack and get out to the airport.

After hurriedly dressing, she turned to the bed. Austen was sound asleep, her face soft as silk in the muted light. Merritt bent down and kissed her gently on the lips. With a little sigh, Austen stirred and her eyes fluttered open. "Good morning, babe. What time is it?"

"Half past four."

Austen propped herself up on her elbows, running her gaze over Merritt's clothes with a puzzled look. "Are you going home already? It's not even light."

Taking a long breath, Merritt sat down on the edge of the bed and took hold of her fingers. "I've been called to work, honey. There's a crisis in Papua New Guinea, earthquakes, and they need experienced doctors immediately. I'm in Australia, so they've asked me."

Austen's expression tightened. "When do you have to go?"

Merritt winced. This was so hard. "Now."

"Bloody hell! Fucking *now*!" Austen exclaimed. She shot over the side of the bed. "Wait and I'll take you."

Merritt put a restraining hand on her arm. "No, honey. I've already ordered a cab." She took her in her arms, unable to stop a sob escaping. "Just hold me for a moment. I'm going to miss you so much."

They rocked together without a word. Summoning all her willpower, Merritt pulled out of the embrace and walked to the door. On the threshold, she paused to take one last look at the woman she had to leave behind.

Her heart breaking, she ran out into the corridor.

CHAPTER TWENTY-FIVE

Merritt grasped a firm hold on the armrests as the huge Hercules began its descent through the heavy clouds blanketing Port Moresby airport. As the cumbersome plane lurched in the turbulence, she wished they'd sent her in a more comfortable aircraft. Even though she tried to relax, her body remained tense until they were finally through the clouds and the wheels were screeching on the runway. Only after they rolled to a stop beside a smaller Air Niugini jet parked on the tarmac, did she fully let out the breath she was holding.

Christ, how she hated rough landings.

"Right to disembark, folks," the pilot's voice echoed over the intercom.

Folks meant Merritt and three other passengers—the doctors from Canberra and an army nurse. The rest of the enormous belly of the plane was taken up with cargo.

She collected her backpack and followed the nurse to the exit door. A solid wall of heat and humidity hit like a sauna. Panting in the stifling air, she grasped the thin cord along the fuselage to balance herself to walk down the ramp. Perspiration immediately beaded over her skin, darkening the shirt under her armpits. She grimaced. At this rate, she'd better keep a deodorant in her pocket. Irritably she brushed back the sticky strands of her now-frizzy hair, wishing she'd at least had the sense to wear a lighter top. She'd known this was the tropics, not like Canberra that had still been a bit chilly in the spring mornings.

"Bloody hot, isn't it?" muttered the nurse, fanning herself with the magazine she'd been reading.

"It's awful," said Merritt, using her PNG information booklet as a fan. "You've been here before?"

"We did inoculations in the villages last year. Port Moresby is the pits in the wet season…the humidity will kill you. It's much cooler in the Highlands, but it rains most of the time so you're perpetually damp."

"I imagine that's where I'll be heading." Merritt waved the booklet. "I've been reading up about the place. It says the population of PNG is eight million?"

The nurse raised her eyebrows. "Don't believe all you read. Those figures were from the census ten years ago. It was deemed a failure, so no one knows if they're were actually true. There's a census due next year. It'll be no surprise if the population has exploded. Most women have at least five children, and demand for health services have had a forty percent rise just in the last three years."

"Birth control not widely used?"

"Not much. Most women have to get permission from their husbands to go on contraception."

Merritt snorted. "Typical. Men would take it if they had to have the babies. I've been to other third-world countries like that. Constant childbirth wears the women out by the time they're forty."

"In PNG, children are incredibly important because land is passed down through family lines. The women remain under intense pressure to have babies." She eyed Merritt solemnly. "Port Moresby is a very dangerous place for women, so don't go wandering off alone. And keep your valuables on your person. It also has a very high crime rate."

Merritt winced. "In the Highlands too?"

"Things are different in the mountains but still can be dangerous for women in some places. More tribal, with lots of very remote communities. Extremely pretty scenery…crazy-high mountains and endless waterfalls."

"Have you heard much about the earthquake?"

"A friend texted me before I boarded. Reports coming in suggest it could be pretty grim in the more isolated villages." She pointed to a dark man in a stained orange jumpsuit and earmuffs, who was waving at them. "We'd better go. He wants us to follow him."

Merritt hitched her pack onto her back. "Right oh."

Once in the terminal, they joined the line going through customs. Merritt had barely made it out the other side, when a harassed-looking woman appeared with a clipboard. "Drs. Marlo, Jackson, and Harrington?"

"I'm Harrington," Merritt said, reluctantly slipping her phone back in her pocket. She'd have to ring Austen later when she was afforded more time.

The woman put a tick on the list. "Come with me please, Doctors."

"Best of luck," called out the nurse. "We may catch up again at the hospital."

Merritt tossed her a quick goodbye, then hurried to follow the clipboard woman heading through the terminal at a fast trot. She directed them into a room where a group of men and women—she presumed medical personnel—sat in white plastic chairs facing a board covered with a large map. After finding a seat, she focused her attention on the two men running the session. The taller of the pair was a sturdy fit army officer in a camouflage uniform. The other, a plumper shorter man, she recognized as a doctor she'd met at a DWB function in Brussels a year ago.

In a commanding voice, the Australian army officer stood to address them. "Welcome to Port Moresby. I'm Major Jim Carter.

Dr. Doug Fredricks and I are coordinating this operation. The army will be organizing transport for all personnel, supplies, and evacuations. We need to get medical staff into the field as soon as possible. It won't be easy. Have any of you have firsthand knowledge of the terrain?"

Two hands went up.

He nodded to them. "You'll appreciate how difficult this operation is going to be. In the torrential rain, some places will be impossible to reach by air. Communication has been lost in a lot of the harder hit areas, so we'll be going in blind. To put it bluntly, we haven't a clue what we're going to find up there. Your group will be issued Defence Force high-band portable transmitters to ensure you can be in contact with us, though in some remote mountainous areas they may not work. Evacuation procedures will be explained by the emergency personnel already on the ground up there. Now I'll hand you over to Doug who's organizing the medical staff. He is also familiar with most of the country."

Fredericks nodded to the Major and said with a hint of a Scottish accent, "Thanks, Jim. Now listen up everyone. I'll keep this brief as I can." He pulled the detailed map of PNG forward and pointed at a spot. "Here is Hela in the Southern Highlands, the epicenter of the first quake. It registered six-point-five on the Richter scale. The place is very remote and most of the population in the region is scattered over the mountains. This is the same area that suffered a severe quake in 2018, so you can expect landslides."

Merritt went cold at the mention of landslides. *Great!* Another Peru.

"A second and much stronger quake last night hit the Mount Hagen area an hour later. As the crow flies, Mount Hagen is a hundred and forty kilometers from Tari, but two hundred and ninety-three by road. A very rugged mountain range lies between them. There have been a series of aftershocks as well, which I imagine added significantly to the damage. Wet weather is going to make it infinitely worse in the mountains."

After pushing his glasses more firmly up his nose, he shuffled through the papers on the desk. "The PNG government has already dispatched their Emergency Services, local medics and soldiers out at first light, but their health system is woefully understaffed. Mount Hagen is the most populated—the town has a hundred and fifty thousand people—so I'm sending most of you there. You will be joining the local teams." He tapped the map. "Three of you will be sent to Tari, where you'll be working with the local hospital staff. Tari is one of the least developed places in the country, and apart from a police station, airstrip, and hospital, there's not much there, only one tourist lodge and a few trade stores. Most of the Papuans live in the mountains." He looked around the room. "Which one of you is the American?"

Merritt called out, "Here."

He squinted his eyes at her. "Ah, Merritt. Good to have you on board. I've put you with Doctors Elliot Garside and James Freemont. You'll do well together. You three have the most experience, so you're going to Tari. You'll be on your own with the local guys." He passed around sheets of paper. "These are the lists of medical supplies, survival kits, and the protocol when interacting with the indigenous people. Just remember the terrain will be difficult, the air will be a lot thinner up there and it's going to rain constantly. Humidity will be a killer. Don't ignore your personal health, even the smallest scratch will ulcerate in this climate. Take magnesium tablets and drink plenty of water. Now find your team and get acquainted over a quick cuppa. You'll be directed shortly to where you're going."

Not believing her luck, Merritt looked around for Elliot. He was a friend she'd worked with a year ago in Africa. He was a great guy and a very capable surgeon.

Wearing a grin, he appeared at her elbow. "Well blow me down. Merritt Harrington."

"This is a really nice surprise, Elliot." She grasped his hand tightly, gazing at him fondly. The Australian surgeon was still as handsome as ever, with a footballer's body, a mop of wavy black hair and a cheeky grin. He was also a favorite with the ladies.

"How have you been? Where's that mad mate of yours?"

Merritt made a face. "Terry's in New Zealand, not contactable because she's hiking the Milford Track with friends. She'll be sorry she missed this…*ha ha!*"

"Yeah. Poor bugger. You grab us a cup of that black tar they call coffee here while I find James."

He appeared a minute later accompanied by a short man with a round cheery face. Dressed in brown cargo pants and a white and red Médecins Sans Frontières T-shirt, he looked to be pushing forty.

"Hi, James. I'm Merritt." She handed out the coffees. "It's not very hot. Milk and sugar are on the table."

James smiled, answering with a slightly nasal accent. "Hello, Merritt. You're a Yank?"

"I am. The DC area. You're an Aussie?"

"Kiwi. I was visiting over here."

"Like me. I was on vacation."

"Doctors Garson, Freemont and Harrington," the clipboard lady interrupted. "You've been assigned to Tari. Come with me please."

Merritt gulped down the rest of her lukewarm coffee and followed the others out. From there, everything moved quickly. They were shuffled into a minibus at the passenger entrance and driven out to a light aircraft with a tourism logo painted on its tail. Cargo was still being loaded through a rear door.

"I hope it's sturdier than it looks," Elliot muttered.

Merritt felt for him. She knew he hated flying in a small plane even more than she did.

The pilot, a grizzled man in his fifties, poked his head out of the door of the plane. "The ground crew will be finished shortly and then you can board. Make whatever calls you have to now. Your phones won't work where we're going."

"Where are you taking us?" Elliot called out.

"Mendi. It'll be road transport from there 'cause the Tari airport's damaged." He disappeared back into the cabin.

"Handy to fucking know," said Elliot testily.

"It's all in our briefing papers," piped in James. "I went through it on the bus. You were too busy gawking around."

Merritt smiled, knowing Elliot was just venting what they all felt. Apprehension. But she knew there was nothing any of them could do now, except wait for what was coming.

Retreating some distance away for privacy, she dialed Austen, who answered almost immediately. Worry crackled her voice. "Where are you, babe? I've been waiting for you to call for hours."

Merritt bit back the sudden urge to cry. She'd only had time to send off a quick text in Townsville and her phone had to be turned off in the Hercules. She had been dying to speak to Austen, but now hearing her, it made the separation infinitely worse. "I'm at Port Moresby Airport. We fly out to Mendi in a minute."

"Where the hell is Mendi?"

"In the Southern Highlands. We go on from there by road to Tari."

"Is it safe?"

Merritt rolled her eyes. Austen sounded more anxious than her mother. "It'll be safe enough. There's been no aftershocks for a few hours. The local crews are already up there."

"Be careful." There was a pause before Austen spoke again. "I wish you hadn't agreed to go. You've just got over that last crappy mission."

"Yes, honey. But you know I couldn't refuse. That's what I signed up for."

"I'm aware of that, but I don't have to like it."

"I'll be back before you know it," Merritt said, then stopped as the realization hit. At the end of the week Austen would be back in New York. Back to her real life. She had to face facts. Their vacation romance had been over as soon as she had stepped on the plane this morning in Canberra. And she had no idea if their attachment was strong enough to survive being away from each other. The future was tenuous at best, they had been denied time to discuss what they wanted in the future. "Will you—"

A shout from the pilot made her pause. "Get aboard, guys. We're ready to go."

"I gotta go, Austen. The plane's ready to take off."

"Ring me when you get there," Austen shouted into the phone.

"There's no service. Will you go and see my mother? Love you," Merritt babbled out, conscious the pilot was waiting impatiently to close the cabin door. She pocketed the phone and ran up the steps.

Once in the air, Merritt forced herself to refocus on the job at hand. Time enough in her lonely bed at night to miss Austen.

The one-hour-fifteen-minute flight to Mendi was in clouds all the way, and it was only when the aircraft began its descent that she could appreciate the truly magnificent scenery. The town was nestled in a valley, the hills on either side very impressive. As the plane threaded its way through them on its approach to the landing strip, she sucked in her breath.

Impressive but very scary.

If she thought the landing at Port Moresby was rough, this was twice as bad. It actually rattled her teeth. When they alighted she could see why. The runway was slightly buckled in places. They waited for the airport crew to load supplies in the back of the truck before they piled in.

Though a few buildings had partially collapsed, it looked as though the city of fifty thousand had escaped the worst of the quake. But it was evident from the stream of traumatized people walking down the littered asphalt road into town, that it had been much worse in the mountains. The men had what might be all their worldly goods in woven bags on their shoulders, while babies in carriers hung from their mothers' backs. The sick were being carried on basic stretchers by the more able-bodied.

"They'll be pleased to see us in Tari," James remarked as he stared out at them.

"We'll soon find out," said Elliot, as they pulled up outside the hospital. Waiting beside a Landcruiser were two men, a Papuan with distinctive Melanesian features and a thick black beard, and an Australian soldier with an assault rifle cradled in his arms. "I'm guessing that's our ride."

A doctor in a faded blue scrub top over a pair of khaki shorts, appeared and introduced himself while two Papuan orderlies unloaded boxes from the vehicle. "The hospital staff at Tari will be glad to see you guys. Half the supplies will be going with you. The road's still open, but the airstrip's closed. Isaac will be your driver and Corporal Dan Kennedy your escort. You've still time to get there before dark."

"We need a guard?" said Merritt, eyeing the rifle.

"You do," the doctor said sharply. "Tari is one of the most remote parts of PNG. Violence is commonplace, especially against women and children. Twenty-four people were killed in a brutal massacre only months ago."

Merritt gulped, viewing the rifle in a different light. Then she remembered how she had blithely told Austen that it was safe enough. She hoped she wouldn't look it up on the Internet.

"Up to a few years ago," the doctor went on, "the only way to get in was by air. The village is small and rainforest surrounds it as far as the eye can see. The people are scattered all over the mountains and most walk for days to get to the hospital."

"Which way to the toilet?" Merritt asked. Her bladder was bursting.

"On the left through the main door. Isaac wants to get going, so come straight back. It's only a seventy-five-mile trip, but it'll be slow going. A vehicle came through an hour ago and the driver said it was a hard slog. It's nearly two o'clock, so you'll need to get on the road if you want to make it before dark. It won't be any fun at night. The kitchen ladies have packed lunch boxes."

Merritt bolted into the building, envying the men who could just hang it out around the side of the vehicle. When she got back, they were already waiting in their seats.

And just like that they were on the road, driving into God knows where, and to God knows what.

CHAPTER TWENTY-SIX

The road was a highway from hell.

Merritt couldn't believe Tari was only seventy-five miles from Mendi. After well over an hour of grinding through mud and potholes, they were only a third of the way. The further they climbed into the mountains, the slushier and rougher the road. Huge cracks appeared, gaping evidence that they had entered the earthquake-affected area. On top of their having to battle deteriorating road conditions, the weather, which had been fine when they left Mendi, had burst into the predicted frequent torrential showers.

Heavy rain fell all year round in these mountains, but nothing could prepare her for just how heavy it was. It fell out of the low-hanging clouds in massive sheets, forcing the driver to slow to a crawl until it passed.

But despite the jerks, bumps, and unrelenting dampness, the mood in the vehicle was lighthearted. Elliot, a seasoned campaigner, kept them entertained with a stream of one-liners. James was no slouch in the jokes department either and

Dan, who was nursing his weapon in the front passenger seat, tossed over a few quips as well. Merritt didn't contribute much, content to listen to their prattle. The banter had the desired effect, soothing their nerves and keeping their minds off the hellish drive.

Merritt had to give Isaac full marks for the way he was handling the skids and slides, and for just keeping the four-wheel-drive truck on the road. The stoic Papuan was unreactive. It seemed to be all in a day's work for him. And maybe it just was. Tribal fighting was a way of life for the Highlanders. And he'd certainly have nerves of steel if he made his living driving on these dreadful roads.

She tried her best to rest, knowing it would be frantic when they got there. And she had been awake before dawn.

They climbed through the mountains for another two hours, a wall of vegetation on one side of the road and a sheer drop on the other. The views over the gorges were absolutely stunning, but also terrifying. There were few guardrails. Suddenly, around the next bend, the tropical green trees and lush underbrush were gone as if the earth had been slashed with a giant machete. The mountainside resembled a ski slope, not white with snow but dark with brown mud.

Their mood sobered immediately.

Aghast, Merritt stared out at the road in front of them. It was half gone, only a narrow strip barely wider than the truck.

"Landslide," muttered Isaac. "A big one."

"Fecking hell," exclaimed James, anxiety thickening his accent.

To Merritt's horror, Isaac didn't stop. He slowed to a crawl and inched his way through the thick slush. She closed her eyes, puffing out short breaths like Angelica Turner had taught her, all the while trying to ignore the mumbled commentaries of the men. She kept her lids squeezed tightly shut until she heard the tension in their voices ease. When she opened them again, they had left the mountainside and were making their way through the rainforest.

And they had begun to descend.

Going down was even worse, the tires fighting for traction. The truck slid and slipped in heart-stopping moments as it churned a path through the slick mud.

Finally, the incline flattened out as they neared the bottom of the mountain. They relaxed, the mood noticeably lighter when Isaac called out, "Soon be there."

But just when a fast-flowing stream with a wooden bridge came into view, it happened.

Vibrations began to rattle the floor of the truck. Merritt's pulse pounded. She'd felt this before—her worst nightmare was about to become real. She had jumped from a Peruvian frying pan into a New Guinea fire.

Suddenly, the whole countryside convulsed and with a roar, the earth ruptured.

A jagged crack sliced through the road at the water's edge, tearing through the underbrush and uprooting trees as it rushed down the ravine. The bridge disappeared into the torrent. Someone screamed, high-pitched, like material ripping into two shredded pieces. When Elliot clamped his hand on her knee, that scream, she realized, had come from *her*.

The truck spun out of control. As it careered wildly, Isaac urgently jerked the steering wheel to avoid plunging into the water. For a long excruciating moment, time seemed to slow as the vehicle hung balanced on its side. Finally, it righted itself with a jarring thud, shot off the road in a spray of mud and slammed against the roots of an enormous fig.

Moments later, the earthquake stopped as abruptly as it had begun.

Merritt flopped back in the seat, her chest pumping. She couldn't believe the quake had only lasted two minutes. It had seemed like two lifetimes.

With a muttered, "Holy bloody hell," Elliot turned to look at Merritt and James. "You two all right? That was a humdinger."

Merritt replied with a shaky, "I'm fine."

"Nothing broken," James said, and leaned over the seat in front. "Dan, how are you and Isaac?"

"Isaac's forehead is bleeding, and he looks half out of it. My foot's jammed against the door."

They hurried into action. Isaac was coherent again when they pulled him from the vehicle. Merritt attended to the cut on his forehead while the other two eased Dan out through the driver's side. Elliot diagnosed a sprained ankle rather than a break. Regardless, the soldier would have difficulty walking any distance. After they erected a tarp to keep dry, Dan used the transmitter to inform home base.

"The good news," he said as he packed the equipment back into its waterproof case, "by our coordinates, we're only five miles from Tari. The bad news, we'll have to camp here until they can get help out tomorrow. They just had word there's been further damage to the town from that latest aftershock. Considering we're on this side of the water and it's nearly dark, a rescue isn't practical until tomorrow. They told us to stay put."

"Right," said Elliot, assuming the leadership mantle. "We'd better make camp. We'll rig up the tents and you can sleep in the backseat of the truck, Merritt."

Dinner was subdued. They dined on army rations and leftover sandwiches. From his pouch, Isaac produced strips of Betel nuts covered in slaked lime. "You fellows wanna try some boo-eye." He smiled widely, showing his brilliant red-stained teeth and lips, having chewed it for years. The mild narcotic was commonly used throughout the population.

When the men enthusiastically took pieces, Merritt couldn't resist trying it as well. Their mood became noticeably merrier after that. Isaac showed them how to chew it into a wad and spit it out. No swallowing. They sat with legs crossed in a pleasant euphoric relaxed state while Isaac answered questions about the area. His English was passable, so she didn't need to decipher the commonly spoken Pigeon English, or Tok Pisen as it was colloquially known.

"I believe the Huli Wigmen are from this area," said James.

"All up in hills," said Isaac. "A few put on show for tourists, but them war-mongering bastards. They paint their faces with yellow and red paint so you can't miss 'em."

Curious, Merritt asked, "Why are they called Wigmen?"

"The men make wigs. They grow hair at bachelor school, winding it around bamboo sticks. When long enough, they clip hair off for wig master to make wig. They can't marry 'til have wig."

"Do they make the wig for their bride?"

Isaac looked amused. "Men wear wigs. Pay for bride with pigs."

Elliot burst out laughing. "I wonder how many you're worth, Merritt?"

Isaac gave a red-toothed grin. "Too tall for many pigs."

As Merritt chuckled with them, she felt a tightening cramp in her stomach. *Just peachy!* So not a good time to get her period. She rose to her feet and reached for her backpack. The tampons were at the bottom, so she'd have to take it with her. Thankfully, the rain had cleared away for the time being, which meant she could go into the trees for privacy. "I'm just going to duck into the bush for a minute," she said.

"Don't go too far away," said Isaac sharply. "Easy to get lost."

Merritt dug in her bag, pulling out a pair of Flybynite goggles with a confident, "My family makes these. Great for night vision so I'll be fine. They don't need batteries either."

Ignoring the Papuan's frown, she donned the goggles and left the campsite. As the undergrowth was thick, she had to push through a little way before she found a clear spot. After quickly attending to her toiletry, she'd zipped up her cargo pants and was washing her hands from her water bottle, when a rustle echoed behind her. A cold wave ran down her spine. Vaguely, she remembered there weren't any large predatory animals. She frantically tried to recall what wildlife was in PNG. Cassowaries. Wild dogs. Cats. Snakes.

God, she hoped it wasn't a snake. She hated the things.

A black pig suddenly dashed out of the ferns past her leg and she breathed out a long sigh.

But when she turned to go, she found herself staring straight at a short man in an enormous feathered round hat. She had no idea through the goggles what color was painted on his face, but it was obviously two-toned with some sort of plaster. He looked very scary. In a second, two more appeared. She opened her mouth to scream, but clamped it shut quickly. Her sixth sense warned her that to make any noise now would be signing her death warrant.

She stood still while they touched the night goggles, clearly fascinated. Another man appeared, this one older, with the most elaborate headdress sporting twice as many feathers. He stared at the goggles, and made a clicking sound with his tongue before plunging back into the brush. The others followed, dragging Merritt with them.

CHAPTER TWENTY-SEVEN

"What do you mean she's missing?" Austen asked in a strangled whisper. She grasped the phone tighter, her heart thumping as she fought for calm. Her half-finished song fluttered to the floor. She ignored it as she tried to get her head around the news, tried to process what she'd just heard.

Gloria Harrington replied calmly, though her voice sounded reedy and thin. "They were on their way to a remote place called Tari, when another earthquake hit the area yesterday evening. Because their truck was damaged, they were forced to wait the night on the road until help could get there in the morning."

"So how the fuck...sorry...how did she just vanish? Where are the others who were with her? The driver?" Austen hissed, now barely able to contain the panic.

Gloria sniffed. "Apparently, she...she went into the bushes for privacy. You know..." Her voice trailed off.

"I understand," said Austen testily, "but what happened to her?"

"She never came back."

"She just disappeared into the bushes?"

"Yes. Without a trace. No scream, nothing."

Austen relaxed a smidgen. At least that probably meant she was alive. She refused to even contemplate the alternative. "Why have they just notified you now if she disappeared last night?"

"They say it's bedlam up there. This last aftershock did a lot more damage to the road and the town. A lot of casualties. There wasn't the manpower for a search party until help arrived from Port Moresby. And they had to wait for the weather to lift before they could fly in a helicopter."

Austen had a lot more questions on the tip of her tongue but bit them back. Gloria needed help, not a grilling. "Would you mind if I came over? Merritt asked me to see you and … well…I think I should now." She hesitated then added, "If it's convenient."

A hint of something akin to amusement crept into Gloria's voice. "You mean is my husband here?"

Austen cleared her throat. "Well…yes."

"No. He stayed at his office to find out what he can. And yes, Austen, I would appreciate if you came over and kept me company. We'll both need support."

"I'm on my way."

Ten minutes later, she was knocking on the door of the house. Gloria opened it, her face as pale as the paint on the outside walls. "Come in, Austen. The three o'clock news is on shortly. There may be something about the earthquake."

Austen followed her into the lounge, taking one of the chairs in front of the TV. Though she had been riveted, she wished they hadn't watched. How anyone could survive in that jungle for even a day was beyond her. It was impenetrable rain forest.

The story showed old footage from the deadly 2018 earthquake that had devastated the region. A hundred killed and thousands missing or displaced. Huge landslides had torn through roads and collapsed bridges making rescue efforts nearly impossible. Apparently, this earthquake was nearly as bad. Austen couldn't imagine rescue teams could spend much time looking for just one person when there would be so many in need.

She searched for something to say as Gloria silently turned off the TV. Finally, she just said, "The press tends to sensationalize things."

Gloria gazed at her forlornly. "You know Austen, I hated it when Merritt joined Doctors Without Borders. Hated that she was going to dangerous places that had nothing to do with our way of life. But I was also proud that she wanted to help the less fortunate and I should have told her. Instead, I never mentioned it. I let her go on thinking I despised her choices, but in the end, it was *my* mettle that was in question. I made it about me not her." A tear trickled down her cheek. "And now I may never have the chance to tell her how much I admire her courage and dedication."

Austen gulped back a sob herself. Was she any different? She could have told Merritt how much she meant to her. Why hadn't she given her some sort of assurance that she was more than a holiday fling? That she had become very dear to her. When Merritt had ended their phone call from Port Moresby with *love you*, Austen's heart had given a flip. She'd known then for sure that Merritt was the one for her. Why the hell couldn't she have just said love you back? Quelling her own dark thoughts, she said as kindly as she could, "Merritt knows how you feel, Gloria. She hates causing you distress and she knows you worry about her."

Gloria gave her a wan smile. "I hope so." She rose from her chair, the empty look in her eyes replaced by determination. "Come into the kitchen for some afternoon tea and we'll talk. I'd like to get to know the woman who's put such a sparkle in my daughter's eye."

Seated at the table, Austen said with a shrug. "I imagine I'm not the person you'd envisaged she'd hook up with."

"On the contrary, I'm not at all surprised. Merritt was never happy with the mundane things of life. She's like her father in that respect." She produced the cups. "Coffee or tea?"

"Coffee please. Black. Was Merritt a model child?"

"Good heaven's no. She got into all the mischief under the sun…"

Austen sat back, listening as the stories of Merritt's childhood unfolded. And it was very clear that Gloria loved her daughter very much. When she mentioned her husband in one of the stories, Austen studied her thoughtfully. "The senator objects to Merritt dating me."

"Yes. Does that worry you?"

"Not in the least. Now Merritt's found out…" Austen stopped abruptly, horrified at herself. She'd nearly spilled the beans about the senator's affair.

Gloria looked at her keenly. "What happened last night?"

"Um…what do you mean?"

"I haven't been married to the man for thirty-five years, Austen, without knowing when something is wrong. I'm guessing you're aware what happened."

Austen fidgeted with her cup. "Merritt will want to tell you herself." Then she paused as the horror came rushing back. Gloria's face crumpled, mirroring her own misery. Merritt wasn't going to be able to tell her anything—she was missing in one of the most inhospitable, dangerous places on the planet. "I guess that was a stupid thing to say," she mumbled, feeling the prickling tears behind her lids.

"No, it wasn't. I know my daughter. She's very resourceful. She's had to be strong all her life. John hasn't been easy on her."

Austen felt a wave of compassion for Merritt. Her early life had been a dichotomy between motherly love and fatherly ruthlessness. "Well, he's got *me* to contend with now," she stated emphatically.

The sound of the front door slamming made them both turn toward the hallway.

A few seconds later, John Harrington appeared at the door of the kitchen. He stopped abruptly when he caught sight of Austen. "What the hell are you doing here?"

She flicked her eyes to Gloria. Her face was blank, the curtain had been drawn. "Austen is here at my invitation, John. I won't have her harassed. What have you found out?"

He sat down heavily. "There was a soggy tissue and her water bottle under a tree not far from the camp, but that's all. She has her backpack with her. As far as they could ascertain, there was no sign of a struggle. Their best guess, she went the wrong way and got lost. The rain washed out any footsteps, so it was too hard to tell what direction she took."

"But why leave her water bottle?" asked Austen

"They don't know," the senator said testily. "Three Australian Special Forces personnel have been flown in to search. If she's alive they'll find her." Then he added bluntly, "It's a dangerous lawless place. Prepare yourselves for the worst."

Austen got to her feet, her head reeling. The room had suddenly become claustrophobic and she couldn't stay in it a minute longer. "I'd better go."

"Of course." Gloria rose quickly and took her arm. "I'll walk you to the door." On the threshold, Austen cast a glance back at the senator. He slapped her with a look so angry it gave her the chills.

On the front porch, Gloria swept her into a warm hug. "Ring me tomorrow and I'll let you know what's happening. Thank you very much for coming. Your company was just what I needed. Take care now."

Austen waved to her before she climbed into the Range Rover. The woman looked lonely and forlorn, a mother on the cusp of losing her only child, and her marriage. Austen couldn't even begin to know how that felt.

* * *

Austen sat in the dark on her hotel veranda, misery clawing at her insides. Part of her wanted to scream, the other part wanted to cry. Three days since she'd disappeared, and Merritt still hadn't been located. Austen knew perfectly well that the longer someone was missing, the less likely they were going to be found alive, or worse still, not at all. Gloria had told her that the senator had pulled a lot of strings to get more men up there, yet they had found nothing. Hope was dwindling fast. She closed her eyes, hearing somewhere down below the sound of shoes clicking on the pavement. She winced. It sounded like a funeral procession passing by.

She lurched to her feet to get the unopened bottle of scotch. She poured three fingers, and downed half of it with a gulp. The initial burning was soon followed by a blessed warmth that spread through her body and dulled the ache. She emptied the glass with another swallow, then retired with the bottle back to the dark balcony. On the last of her second glass, her phone chirped in the lounge. She ignored the call, sick of having her hopes dashed every time she answered.

It went to voice mail. Then it began again, persistent and shrill. She sloshed more scotch into the glass, and ignoring the giddiness, weaved inside to answer it.

"Hello," she mumbled into the receiver.

"Austen. It's Terry."

It took a second to register that they'd only been talking that morning. She shook her head to clear the alcoholic fog. "Have you heard something?" she asked quickly.

"No. Have you?"

The fleeting touch of optimism gone, Austen replied morosely, "Nope."

"You're not sitting in your room drinking by yourself, are you?" asked Terry.

Austen licked her lips, which had suddenly become dry as chips. She took a peek at the amber liquid in the glass in her other hand. "Just one to settle the nerves."

"Bullshit. You're talking to an old pro here. Been there, done that…last night. I want you to sober up. I've found someone who could help you."

"Really? How did you manage that in New Zealand?"

A hint of excitement crept into Terry's voice. "My sister's husband, Ben, is a policeman. He did a bit of digging for me… rang a mate of his high up in the Australian Federal Police. Now listen carefully. There are covert operatives in Canberra who specialize in finding people. They're not in the phone book, and they're not cheap. He's given me a private telephone number and you're to ask for Claire or Vivian."

Austen straightened, put her glass on the coffee table and said, "They're experts?"

"Apparently the best. They find people judged unfindable. If Merritt's alive, they'll get her out."

Austen flicked a quick look at the wall clock. Eight p.m. "I'll ring now. Wait a second and I'll get a pen." After she jotted down the number, she said, the slur in her voice gone, "Thanks, babe. You're a champion."

A moan echoed in the phone. "I should have gone with her. We've always protected each other."

"Don't go blaming yourself. I've done enough of that too. It is what it is. Now we have to hope like hell she can be found."

Austen stood under a cold shower, letting the water pour over her until she felt reasonably clear-headed. Then she dialed the number.

A woman answered after four rings. "Claire Walker speaking."

"Hi, Ms. Walker," Austen began tentatively. "My name is Austen Farleigh. I was given your number by a friend. I understand you find missing people."

A note of incredulity echoed in the woman's voice. "Austen Farleigh, as in the rock singer Austen?"

"Yes," Austen said impatiently. "But this has nothing to do with who I am, it's about a friend who's disappeared, Ms. Walker."

"Of course. And it's Claire. May I call you Austen?"

"Well, no one's ever called me Ms. Farleigh."

Claire chuckled. "I don't imagine anyone has," she said, then added more seriously, "Have the police been notified? You do understand we offer a specific service and many of our clients seek anonymity. We specialize in difficult missing person cases, people that authorities haven't been able to find for whatever reason."

Austen cleared her throat. "There are people looking, but so far she hasn't been found. I hope you'll consider taking on the case. I'm desperate."

There was silence on the end of the phone for a moment, then Claire spoke softly. "I'll give you our address. Could you be here at six forty-five a.m. and we can discuss your problem? We do charge a substantial fee, half now and half on delivery. We'll discuss everything when you get here."

"I'll be there." After she jotted down the address, Austen tapped off the phone, feeling more buoyant than she had since Merritt had disappeared.

* * *

The address turned out to be a modern brick home in the suburbs, with a front deck and a spectacular garden. A tall woman with a solid athletic body opened the door. Her features were strong—high cheekbones, generous mouth and firm chin. She eyed Austen curiously, but there was no recognition in her keen gaze. Austen smiled at her, aware that the woman didn't have a clue who she was.

"Come on in." She thrust out her hand. "Vivian Andrews. Claire tells me you sing."

"Try to," quipped Austen. She followed her into the house, delighted not to be recognized. She liked her already.

Another woman appeared from the kitchen. She was attractive, with fine features, slender body and silvery white hair worn in a long braid. "Hi. I'm Claire. Come on in, Austen. We were just sitting down for breakfast, so I hope you'll join us."

"That'd be great," she said.

"So," said Vivian as she dished out bacon and eggs onto a plate. "You have a missing friend."

With a nod, Austen took the plate. "Her name is Merritt Harrington. She's working with Doctors Without Borders, on an assignment in Papua New Guinea to help with the earthquake."

Claire stared at her. "She's the relief doctor who disappeared on her way to Tari. It was on the news tonight."

"She's been missing for seventy-two hours. They've only released the particulars now."

"Why did they take so long?" asked Vivian.

"Because she's Senator John Harrington's daughter and he's had Defence special services searching for her."

"Ah," said Vivian. "I met the senator a couple of weeks ago at a Border Force meeting… about quarantine restrictions Australia has imposed on fish products imported from Vietnam. He was trying to push his Easy Asia free-trade agenda. He certainly likes to do things his way." She eyed Austen thoughtfully. "Where do you fit in all this?"

"Merritt and I are involved."

"Does Harrington know you're here?"

"No. He doesn't approve of me."

Vivian gave a ghost of a smile. "Must be your tats."

"That, as well as being a dyke and a rock singer," Austen said with a wide grin. "Bad combination in his book."

"This is a working breakfast, you two," interrupted Claire. "Tell us all you know about how Merritt disappeared, and the area searched. I presume you're privy to the information?"

Austen nodded. "Her mother keeps me informed." And she proceeded to tell them what she knew. After she finished, she looked from one to the other anxiously. "Will you take the assignment?"

Claire turned to Vivian. "It's up to you, sweetie. It's going to be a really tough one."

Vivian flipped Austen a wink. "That means she wants in. She knows I can't resist a challenge. Okay, we'll do it." She reached for the phone in her pocket and stood up. "While you two discuss the details, I'll ring Ross to come with me. We're in luck…he's in Canberra at the moment."

"You'll need someone in Port Moresby. I could stay there," Claire offered.

"Like hell. My pregnant wife won't be going anywhere near that place. It's the pits. I'll get Gaby to help out."

Claire scowled. "Next time, *you* have the baby."

Vivian chuckled. "Can you arrange to buy forty pigs in Mendi, please, and then see what flights are available." She put her hand on Austen's shoulder. "The sooner I get ready to go the better, so I'll say goodbye now. If she's alive, and I'd say there's a good chance she is, I'll find her. I'd like to hear some of your songs one day. I'm a country and western fan myself." And then she disappeared upstairs.

Claire watched her go, her face creased in amusement. "Viv's not up with the latest music."

"Believe it or not, it's actually refreshing to meet someone who's never heard of me." She dropped her eyes to Claire's stomach. "When's the baby due?"

"I'm only twenty-two weeks and already Viv's clucking around like an old mother hen." Her eyes misted, and she blinked away the moisture with a blush. "It's the hormones. If anyone can find your sweetheart, it'll be Viv."

"I'm beginning to think that," Austen said and meant it. The woman had radiated a certain devil-may-care competency. She wouldn't be afraid to bend the rules to get things done.

"By the way. What is she going to do with all those pigs?" she asked.

Claire smiled. "It's their currency up there. Pigs are worth much more than money in the PNG Highlands."

CHAPTER TWENTY-EIGHT

Merritt fanned herself with a palm frond. It wasn't to relieve the temperature—the thin mountain air was cool in the day and cold at night. The humidity was the killer. A permanent film of perspiration slicked her skin, making her clothes damp and uncomfortable. She had eventually abandoned her cargo pants for one of the grass skirts the native women wore. Or *arse grass* in Pigeon English. It allowed air to circulate up her legs. Though she drew a line at running around topless like the women.

She had no idea where she was, or in what direction Tari lay. All she could see in the distance were wild rugged mountains and an interminable canopy of rainforest.

Welcome to the jungle!

The village was clearly very remote. She hadn't heard a plane or helicopter since she'd arrived. And she had lost all sense of time. How many days had passed she could only hazard a guess. Fourteen? fifteen? Or maybe even sixteen? She wished she'd had the foresight to count. That had been the last thing on her mind.

She knew it was getting too long for the authorities to keep looking, not with so many people needing help after the earthquake. Her father would have sent a search party, but if they hadn't found her by now, they might never. She could be stuck here. Determinedly, she refused to dwell on that scenario. Angelica Turner had drummed into her not to abandon hope, and it could be worse. She had a roof over her head, and she wasn't being mistreated.

The Wigmen hadn't bothered to restrain her after the first day—they all knew it would be suicide for her to try to walk out alone. And fat chance the head Huli would take her back to civilization. He wasn't going to give up his personal witchdoctor.

Merritt knew she was lucky to be alive. If it hadn't been for the night goggles, she probably would have been knocked on the head, or worse, raped as well, and thrown into a gorge somewhere. But superstition was clearly rife in the tribes, for while they were fascinated by the goggles, they seemed very wary of her. She remembered reading that the indigenous tribes believed in witches and sorcery. Despite being thoroughly frightened, she had forced herself to maintain a stern demeanor and not utter a word.

It had paid off.

Once well away from the road, they'd made crude shelters with branches and palm fronds to shelter from the rain, tied her to a tree under one and left her alone. Beginning at daybreak, they had spent the next two days climbing into the mountains. It had been a grueling trek along mulchy mossy trails through thick rainforest, across deep gorges crisscrossed by vine bridges, and over rivers where waterfalls plunged in a display of pure power. She thanked God that her time on Mount Huascaran had toughened her up for such an arduous hike. Otherwise, she would never have kept up.

A cacophony of buzzing insects, croaking frogs, and a variety of birdsongs had accompanied them as they walked. Every so often, she would catch sight of a colorful bird of paradise. When they stopped for an occasional short break, she was able to forget her plight for a few minutes as she admired the splendor of the ancient forest. It was one of the remotest places on Earth, a last pristine frontier.

Midafternoon on the second day, they'd finally arrived at the Huli village. She gave a silent whoop—her face was on fire, her lips chapped, her bones aching, and skin red and lumpy from insect bites, but she had made it. The village was built in an upland basin and comprised a collection of huts with thatched roofs made from the strong, long-bladed grass that grew in abundance in the forest. She was claimed by two women who gave her a bowl of stew, which tasted like sweet potato with small chunks of chicken. Then one of the older women took her into a hut and pointed to a woven sleeping mat. Not caring she was filthy, Merritt took off her boots, lay down and fell asleep almost immediately.

Over the following days, she learned how the village functioned. It was a definite patriarchal society. Women were subservient to men, and once married, became their property. They were timid, happy, and very hardy. They went about their work, bent double under a huge load of firewood and never broke stride. When they were sitting, except for the old, most either had a child or a piglet hanging off their breasts. And the women were the gardeners, tending the sweet potato crops, called kau kau, their staple diet. Banana trees dotted the hillsides, a welcome relief to the constant kau kau cooked in huge clay pots or on a stick in the coals.

The men painted their faces and bodies with bright yellow and red clay, wore elaborate hair headdresses, and had cassowary quills piercing their noses. Although they looked fierce, Merritt found them surprisingly gentle people. The men were the hunters, killing mostly small animals to add to the stew. She realized quickly enough it wasn't chicken. On a couple of occasions, they'd cooked one of their precious pigs in an underground fire pit. They'd danced afterward and smoked a kind of leaf rolled up and stuck into the end of a hollow pipe.

Everyone in the village chewed betel nuts, and the dirt was littered with red wads.

The women and men slept in separate large group houses, even the married ones, which was a great relief to Merritt. One of her worst fears as she trudged along through the mountains, was being handed to one of the men as a trophy bride. The pigs shared the huts with the women and there was absolutely no romance with their husbands. Their sex life occurred in the fields standing up.

After Merritt recovered from the initial shock of her capture, she adjusted well enough to village life. There was a clear bubbling stream to bathe in and wash her clothes. It was remarkable how being clean eased living conditions. And the therapist's stress management tips proved a lifesaver.

The Huli hadn't touched her adversely in any way. On the contrary, she'd been treated well. She'd been elevated to some sort of deity, or perhaps just a witch, but whatever they thought she was, she was shown respect. Although the clan had their own dialect, most spoke Tok Pisen to her, and Merritt could work out some of what they said.

The only member of the tribe she didn't particularly like was the chief. He was a pompous little man, wearing a huge hair wig that made him look like a mushroom. It was decorated with an elaborate arrangement of bird-of-paradise feathers. He wore an extralong quill in his nose and a necklace made of knuckle bones. She hoped they weren't human. Merritt also knew he coveted the night goggles, but probably hesitated to take them in case of magical, or perhaps divine retribution. She made sure they didn't leave her person, wearing them around her neck even when sleeping.

It was on the second day that the chief realized that she was a healer as well as a witch. Three of the clan had returned home from a war party, one with an arrow buried in his side. One of the women informed her it was common for neighboring tribes to steal unmarried women and pigs, and the tribe would go off to war to get them back. Immediately, Merritt went into doctor mode. She asked for the man to be taken into a tent and fetched her backpack. She always carried a first aid kit, her stethoscope and a small suture pack. Thankfully, the arrow hadn't hit any vital organs, and after removing it, flushing the wound with boiled water and applying antibiotic cream, she dressed it.

From then on, she had a constant stream of people wanting a consultation, even some from other villages. The word had spread. She patched up the numerous parasitic lesions and attended to their health as best she could with such limited resources. On the fourth day, she even delivered a baby. The woman had promptly gone back to working in the garden with the baby in a sling. She was pleased to see that because of the isolation, they seemed to have avoided the HIV epidemic that plagued third-world nations.

While the days were full enough to keep her mind off her plight, it was the nights that were the worst. She missed her mother and Terry dreadfully, but it was Austen who was constantly on her mind as she lay on her pallet in the darkness. Where was she singing? Now she was in the States, back to her old life, did she think of her, or was it a case of out of sight, out of mind? Merritt ached to see her again, to touch her, to make love with her. Her thoughts became a simple plea, tumbling through her mind. *Please God, help me get back to her.* And every night she cried silently into the grass pillow before she went to sleep, "I love you, Austen."

Merritt threw away the palm fond and irritably squashed a bug on her arm. Time to go back to work. A pale ray of sunlight appeared through the constant blanket of cloud as she climbed to her feet. Her consulting room was under a bush lean-to attached to one of the smaller storage huts. Already there were two patients lined up waiting, an elderly man with a tropical ulcer that she'd been dressing, and a child who was undernourished. She'd just sat down when she heard a commotion on the hill. A quick glance told her by the warlike stances of the men lined up on the top that it was something serious. It had better not be another fight over pigs. She was sick of patching these guys up.

In the distance, she spotted three people coming up the trail. Her eyes widened—they were too tall to be Hulis. Her heart leaped into her mouth. Two were white—a man and a woman. The other was a Papuan, and as he neared, she recognized his face. Isaac. Relief and joy shot through her. She gave him a smile, careful not to be too exuberant. The chief wouldn't be too happy if they wanted to take her away. She didn't want to give him an excuse to fire their arrows.

After Isaac gave the traditional greeting, he pointed to the white man, "Him Ross," and then at Merritt. "Meri."

Merritt blinked. What the hell did Meri mean? She twigged soon enough when Ross, a solid man in his early forties, strode up to her and took her arm. "Meri."

Okay, so they were married. She immediately moved closer until she felt the warmth of his body. "Masta belong mi," she said, staring the Huli in the eye.

The chief puffed out his chest and said something she roughly translated as, "Her witchdoctor. Worth many pigs."

The wily old bastard! She scowled but shut her mouth quickly when she caught the tall woman behind Ross give a quick shake of her head. Then Isaac, his legs braced widely apart, rattled off something in the Huli dialect. The chief nodded and signaled to his warriors to let them through. Merritt flashed a look at Isaac who nodded encouragingly. They filed into the village to the circle of stones where the tribe conducted their business. Isaac and Ross sat cross-legged opposite the Wigmen, while to view the proceedings, Merritt and the woman had to sit behind the stones without speaking

Merritt glowered but remained silent. *Men's freaking business!* Talk about male chauvinist pigs.

They bartered all afternoon. It was excruciating to watch. The chief still was reluctant to give her up even when the price rose to thirty pigs, far more than the dowry for a wife. Finally, frustrated, Merritt had had enough. Her freedom was slipping away. It was time to break the deadlock. She marched into the circle and with her haughtiest expression, pointed to the goggles. "Tell him I'll give him the goggles as well," she said to Isaac.

Even before Isaac said the words, Merritt knew she had him. The Huli's eyes widened in triumph. He put out his hand. Feigning reluctance, she dragged them off her head and handed them over. He bobbed his head and flashed his red teeth at her. "Masta take now."

And just like that the business was concluded.

With their traditional ceremony, the visitors were welcomed into the village and a feast prepared. It was only then did the white woman turn to her with a smile, "Hello, Merritt. I'm Vivian Andrews. I'm very pleased to meet you."

Merritt shook the offered hand enthusiastically. "Not half as much as I am to see you."

A twinkle appeared in Vivian's eye. "I must admit I didn't expect to find you fitting so well into village life."

Merritt leaned forward and whispered, "They think I'm a witch, or some sort of god." She pointed to the night goggles, which now hung around the chieftain's neck. His face painted brightly for the occasion, he looked regal and smug. "It was the goggles."

"I think you're selling yourself short. These are simple people who value guts and determination. It's a hard life up here. Weaklings don't last long."

"The women particularly are very resilient," Merritt agreed. She pointed to the newest mother of the clan. "Mia over there, had a baby and went back to work the same day."

Vivian eyed her curiously. "You like them, don't you?"

"I do. The men prance around with their wigs and fight, but the women keep everything going. They're shy and gentle, totally without guile." Merritt studied her. Vivian looked like she belonged in the jungle. And after watching her interact with Ross, there was no mistaking she was the boss. "Did my father employ you to find me?"

"No. Austen Farleigh did."

Merritt drew in a sharp breath. "Austen?"

"She was very concerned about you. Your father got the Australian government to send in the special forces, but after three days they hadn't found any trace of you. We specialize in finding missing persons."

"Are you a government organization?"

"Very private." Vivian shrugged. "We're not in the yellow pages."

"Then how did Austen find out about you?"

"Your friend, Terry, came up with our name."

"That'd be her," said Merritt proudly. "She's an organizational wizard. Um…how is Austen? I'm guessing you're in contact with her."

Vivian let out a gurgle. "She's been hounding Claire for news every day." A touch of fondness entered her voice. "Claire is our point of contact in Canberra. She's also my wife."

A warm feeling spread through Merritt. "Austen hasn't given up on me," she whispered.

Vivian looked at her thoughtfully, "She cares about you very much, Merritt. She's a really good woman."

"I love her. It's what's kept me sane here." She brushed away the moisture in her eyes. "How did you find me? This place is so isolated that I doubt it would be on the map. Nor would satellites pick up anything—the mountains are perpetually shrouded in cloud."

Vivian accepted a bowl of pork from one of the cooks and then continued. "It was difficult. For the first week, there was nothing. You had simply vanished into thin air. And being in a disaster area made it infinitely worse. There were so many people displaced and missing it was nearly impossible to track one white woman. The roads were damaged and there were landslides all over the Tari Basin. We employed Isaac to help us. He was keen to, blaming himself for letting you go off into the bushes alone."

"He's a tough customer," said Merritt. "A good man to have with you. The way he drives on these atrocious roads…"

"He's been a definite asset. All we could do was hang around, trying to find leads. Then we had a stroke of luck. We were well into the second week when one of Isaac's contacts heard a new witchdoctor had taken up residence in the mountains. Word was, *she* was very good at fixing up people."

"I've had quite a few patients not from this tribe," interrupted Merritt with a laugh.

"Lucky for us one turned up in Tari. Isaac tracked him down for a description. And bingo! We'd found you." She looked over at the dark rainforest. "We'll be leaving first light. The Huli men will accompany us to collect their pigs. The chief drove a hard bargain."

"Huh! Greedy old coot."

Vivian grinned. "I think he fancies you."

"Not likely," said Merritt, aghast. Apart from the fact he was obnoxious, she towered over the man, even with the hat on. "He's in love with the goggles." Then she was silent and sad for a moment as she swept her eyes over the village compound. The women were going about their business, cooking, laughing, and every now and then, smiling shyly across at Merritt. "I'm going to miss them," she whispered.

"I know," said Vivian, placing her hand over hers. "Let's eat and get some sleep. We have a big day in front of us tomorrow."

CHAPTER TWENTY-NINE

Grabbing her backpack, Merritt exited the cab and walked to the front door. Her mother had it open before she could press the bell, and immediately embraced her. As they swayed together, she put a gentle hand on Merritt's head and stroked her hair softly. Letting out a shaky breath, Merritt bit back a sob. She sank into the soft body, completely at peace for the first time since she'd boarded the army plane for Port Moresby.

Gloria kissed her daughter's forehead tenderly. "It's wonderful to have you back."

"I know, Mom. I'm sorry you had to go through that."

"A mother's job is to worry, dear, though I don't think I want to face something like it ever again." After one last press of her lips, she stepped back to survey her keenly. "You're thinner, but you look very fit."

Merritt patted her stomach. "It wasn't exactly an exciting diet where I was. It's amazing how many ways sweet potato can be cooked. As for being in good condition, I should be... I got plenty of exercise." She searched her mother's face. "How are things with you and Father?"

Gloria's lips tightened. "Put your pack inside the door and take a walk around the gardens with me. It's a lovely day, much too nice to be indoors, and we've lots to discuss. Firstly, I want you to tell me all about Papua New Guinea. I don't know the full story."

The last of the tension in Merritt's body eased as she related everything. She didn't leave anything out, nor did she sugarcoat it. Her mother's expression was incredulous. "What an extraordinary story. Were you very frightened?"

"When I was first kidnapped, I was petrified. Then the fear gradually faded as I realized they weren't going to hurt me. After I got to know the people, I liked them, especially the women. They were simple souls, living what we would consider a very primitive existence, yet they were perfectly happy. I think some of our friends could take a leaf out of their book." Merritt pulled her phone out of her pocket and brought up the photo of herself in the grass skirt. "Especially when it comes to clothes. Hardly Sax Fifth Avenue, but very comfortable."

This drew a smile from her mother. "Very chic! My word, you did go native!"

Merritt grinned, scrolling through a few photos of the Huli women with bare sagging breasts. "I kept my top on."

"I should say so. Have you been in contact with Austen today?"

"I texted her from the airport. She'll be getting ready for tonight's performance. She said she came to see you."

"She's been a tower of strength. She even put off her trip to see her parents to help you, and to support me. A wonderful woman."

Merritt felt a flush of pride. "Austen's become very special to me."

"I know," said Gloria, "And she thinks the world of you."

"Um…how did Father take her coming here?"

"He tried to browbeat her, of course. She stood up to him, which he didn't like." A tic in her cheek was the only outward sign of her next words. "I want to talk to you about him."

Merritt chewed the inside of her lip, hoping she wasn't going to have to be the one to divulge her father's infidelity. "Oh?"

"This may come as a surprise."

Hardly! "Go on."

"I'm flying back home tomorrow with you. I'm leaving him."

"'Bout time," grunted Merritt, then immediately felt guilty. It was a momentous decision for her mother to make and she needed her daughter's support. "Sorry…that was tactless. I just meant he doesn't deserve your love or loyalty."

"As I found out. Apparently, John's long-term mistress is over here." Gloria went on after a slight pause, "When Austen told me she was taking you home from the party, I knew something had happened. And that it was serious. John was very subdued when he came back into the room, and I assumed you and he had a falling out. Originally, I thought it was about your dating Austen, but I've heard since there was another woman involved. One he'd been seeing back home."

"Did you ask Austen what happened that night?"

"She said it wasn't her place to say anything."

"She's discreet," said Merritt, watching her mother carefully as she spoke. She seemed to be in a good place, much better than Merritt would have thought considering Gloria's life was going to be turned upside down. Maybe she was just waiting for something like this to happen to have an excuse to leave him. He had made both their lives hell with his controlling ways. Merritt wondered who the third party was that spilled the beans to her mother. Then it occurred to her it had most probably come from Katie.

Hell hath no fury like a woman scorned.

She would have realized that the only way to ensure the promised divorce was to let her mother into the secret. Easy enough to spread anything that scandalous on the rumor mill. A word in the ear of one of her father's staff—like any closed communities, embassies were a hotbed for gossip.

Merritt looped their arms together. "So, you're coming home with me tomorrow. How is Father taking that?"

"I have no idea. We had a gigantic fight and after that, he rarely comes home. When he does, it's only to go to his study. He's ceased asking anyone to dinner." She smiled at Merritt. "Finding you was the catalyst I needed to make the final break. When I received the call that you had been found safe and sound, it was as if I'd been given a second chance for happiness. I intend to make the most of my life from now on."

"Good for you, Mom," Merritt responded with a happy laugh. "It's about time you thought about yourself for a change."

"Come on and I'll help you pack," said Gloria as they headed to the house, arm-in-arm. "And we're flying first class, booked to your father's private credit card."

"He's going to hate that."

"Oh, yes."

* * *

Terry was waiting at Washington Dulles International Airport. When Merritt caught sight of her familiar dusty-blond hair in the crowd, she'd hadn't realized until this moment just how much she'd missed her friend. Blinking away an errant tear, she hurried over and threw her arms around her.

"I missed you too, best friend," said Terry, giving her a misty smile, followed by a dig in her ribs. "Next time you're off into the wilderness, wait for me."

"I wished you'd been there," Merritt replied, overwhelmed by a sudden flood of tenderness. Damn, she'd better get control of herself. Unlike the aftermath of Peru, it was not so much fear of her personal safety that had been affected. It was her emotions that were left raw and exposed.

"Can't wait to hear all about it," Terry said with a catch in her voice as well.

"Come on you two," said Gloria, tucking her arms through theirs. "Let's get our suitcases and go home."

"I have my car," Terry said as they headed for the baggage carousel. "I'll drive it to the pick-up area while you get your luggage."

Once they packed everything in the trunk and were on the road, for the first time Merritt felt she was finally home.

"I've picked up groceries from the supermarket," said Terry, "so we can go straight to your place."

It was a two-bedroom apartment on the second floor of a condo in the Washington DC suburbs. Merritt had decorated it in a modern, uncluttered style to suit her busy lifestyle, and in the last years, her frequent absences. It was a peaceful part of the city, with the small back balcony overlooking parkland—a perfect place to call home. Though whether she would keep it now would depend on what she did next. And on her burgeoning romance with Austen.

"I'll put you in there, Mom," Merritt said, pointing to the first room, "and Terry and I will share the other."

"Thank you, dear," Gloria replied, her eyelids drooping with fatigue. "I'm going to take a nap. That long flight was tiring, and jet lag gets me every time. I'll see you girls later."

"C'mon," Terry said to Merritt after they dumped their bags. "Let's get a drink. And you can tell me all about your life as Jane of the Jungle." She examined Merritt critically. "You're looking remarkably good considering what you went through."

Merritt couldn't help preening. She flexed her now well-muscled arms. "Lots of exercise." She patted her flat stomach. "Sweet potato diet."

"Shit. I hope you're not going to cook me up that dish."

"God, no. I hope I never see one of them again."

Terry looked at her curiously. "I must admit I expected to find you a mess, but you...well...seem more at peace with yourself than I've ever seen you. Not like after Peru."

With a deep sigh, Merritt leaned back into the cushions. "New Guinea was different. Very scary at first, but I was able to cope better. Perhaps it was because I'd been to hell and back in the Andes and survived. And living with the tribe made me realize the things that were important and the value of what I had." She waved her hand at the room. "Not all this material stuff. It's window dressing. But the people who mean something to me, practicing medicine, our way of life."

Terry looked pensive. "I really hated that I was on that hike and couldn't go with you. You and me, we're a team. I felt I let you down."

"I know. I missed you. How is your sister?"

"Alice is great. She says to say hi."

"And Jordan?"

"We had a great time, but we both knew it was only ever going to be a holiday romance. Geographically impossible to keep it up." She gave a half-hearted shrug. "We called it quits when she went back to Australia."

Merritt reached over and squeezed her arm. "I'm sorry. I know you were keen on her." She turned to stare out the window. "There's something I want to tell you."

"Am I going to like it?"

"Probably not. I intend to resign from DWB tomorrow and I'm not going back to finish my contract." She brought her gaze back to Terry and surveyed her sadly. "I hate to let you down, but I can't do it anymore. Enough is enough."

Terry made a wry face. "No one will blame you. I guess I knew this was coming. It would be selfish for me to ask you to continue just because I'm not ready to move on."

"I've been thinking about it even before Peru. I had decided to resign back in Canberra but meant to finish out the three years. Getting abducted was the last straw." She idly traced the embroidered pattern on the cushion, thinking how free those words made her feel. "I'm not like you, fun-loving and adventurous. I've had enough wandering around the globe. All I want now is a quiet life."

Terry raised an eyebrow. "And you're going to get that with Austen?"

Merritt opened her mouth, and then closed it again as she felt herself blush. "I can always hope."

Gales of laughter burst from Terry. "Fuck me, Merritt, who are you trying to kid?"

"I...we...haven't had a chance to talk about the future," Merritt murmured, feeling exposed. "I don't know what she wants."

"God, sometimes you can be as thick as a brick. She's crazy about you. When you went missing, she was nearly out of her mind. She didn't hesitate when I gave her Claire and Vivian's number."

Merritt couldn't help a huge, stupid grin plastering her face. "She's pretty amazing. Vivian thinks she's great and that's saying something. That woman is the most unflappable person I've ever met."

"Okay. Now gimme the lowdown on everything that happened. And don't leave out any of the gory details."

"We'd better top up our glasses…this may take a while."

When she finished, Terry gazed at her, bemused. "They thought you were a god or a witch or something?"

"Basically, yes. They're very superstitious."

"I wonder what the chief is doing with the goggles now?"

Merritt sniggered. "Parading around with them under that enormous wig. Ew…gross." She rubbed her rumbling stomach. "What time is it? I'm famished."

Terry glanced at her watch. "Time we ate. How about I order some Chinese takeaway?"

"Super. The Bamboo Room up the road delivers. I'll wake Mom," Merritt said, rising to her feet.

"Before you do," Terry said, pulling her back down in the chair. "I want to ask you something. When do you intend seeing Austen?"

Merritt tipped her head back and closed her eyes. As much as she wanted to see her, she had responsibilities. It was killing her. "After I take Mom home and settle her in. I can't desert her…she's going to need my support."

"Where is Austen?"

"Montreal. She has a concert tonight and tomorrow night. That's why she couldn't meet me."

They both sat quietly for a moment before Terry replied. "If you'd like, I can drive your mother home and stay with her. I have five days before I fly to Africa."

Merritt looked over at her with a frown. "This isn't a guilt trip for not being available for PNG, is it?"

Terry flashed a wide smile. "Yeah. Maybe a little. But also, because after that shit-awful time you had, you must be desperate to get laid."

Merritt rolled her eyes. Wonderful. Girl-talk about her love life. "Really?" she said haughtily, but then smiled reluctantly as her libido jerked to life at the words. "You're right...I'm dying to see her. I haven't thought about anything else for days. Weeks."

"Then get up there tomorrow. Seize the day."

Merritt broke into a delighted laugh. "You bet I will. Thank you."

CHAPTER THIRTY

After lunch the next afternoon, Merritt's plane touched down in Montreal. Though it was a bright sunny day, after the heat of New Guinea the place felt cold and bleak. Barely able to contain her excitement, she caught a taxi to the city. It was only when the cabbie pulled up outside the front door of the Ritz-Carlton that it really sank in she was actually going to see Austen. She pushed back the hood of her coat, shaking her head to clear her thoughts for the night ahead. It was going to be one to remember—she was going to make sure of that.

First things first, though. There were preparations to be made.

She was pleased to see the candles, flowers, and the portable CD player on the table, and the bottle of champagne in the fridge. Then she went to work and took a few quiet moments to admire her handiwork. She slipped the CD into the player, and satisfied everything was perfect, adjourned to shower.

After shaving her legs and under her arms, she slipped on her new silken underwear. She smiled. If that didn't get Austen excited, nothing would. It felt fabulous on her skin. Next, she pulled on the white dress, added the chunky blue necklace, and eased into her black ankle boots. After applying a touch of makeup, she arranged her hair into a messy bun, a style she hadn't worn for years. She studied her reflection critically in the mirror.

Geez, she looked twenty again. Lastly, she shrugged into the old black leather jacket. Thankfully, she'd kept it as a memento of her student days. It still fit. She went back to the mirror, noting that though the leather was shiny from wear, the coat had kept its shape.

At half past three, Merritt made her way to the room in the Bell Centre where Austen's signing was in progress. It was buzzing with noise. Fans formed two lines—one for purchasing, the other for signing. She had to curb her impatience as she inched her way to the counter where two staff were taking orders. The stacks of CDs were dwindling so fast that Merritt regretted she hadn't come earlier. Since they didn't seem to be replenishing the supply, she presumed when these were sold the signing session would be over. Thankfully, she snagged one before they were gone.

The CD clutched in her hand, she joined the other line. As one by one the fans moved to the table, Merritt strained her head to catch sight of Austen through a gap between the people in front and the crowds milling about to watch. She was so beautiful it made her ache. As Austen flirted outrageously with her fans, the ache in Merritt's chest intensified. By the time it was her turn, she was struggling to breathe. She pushed the CD across the table without a word and Austen looked up expectantly to greet her.

Her eyes widened and her mouth formed into an O. Then she tilted her head to the side, gazing at Merritt with those impossibly pretty eyes. Austen's gaze swept over her body, lingering on her breasts and her face broke into a brilliant smile. "Well hello, gorgeous."

Merritt nonchalantly flicked back a stray wisp of hair that had escaped from the bun. "Hi, Austen. Would you sign my CD please?"

"And you would be?"

"Merritt."

Her eyes gleaming, Austen leaned closer with a grin. "That's a pretty name. What do you do for kicks, Merritt?"

Merritt closed the gap and whispered in her ear. "Why don't you join me in my room tonight and find out, lover girl?" She pushed over a piece of paper with the address. "Room two-three-four. Don't be late."

Austen quickly scrawled her signature on the plastic cover, then pulled a ticket out of her pocket. She slid it across with the CD. "Front row seat for the concert. If you wait, I've a few minutes after this before I have to go backstage."

"Nope. When I say hello, I intend to do it properly. I'll see you after the show," Merritt said with a saucy wink. Conscious Austen would be staring at her butt as she walked away, she gave an extra sway of her hips.

* * *

Her libido through the roof, Merritt left for the hotel as soon as the concert finished. Seeing Austen onstage had been stimulating to the point of painful. Tingles had run riot across her skin all night, and she had to fight the overwhelming desire to leap up onto the stage like some of the young fans in the audience were trying to do. By the time she let herself into the room, she was a hormonal mess. She pressed her palms firmly on the arms of the couch and took deep breaths. Christ, if she didn't calm down, she'd jump Austen as soon as she came through the door and wreck all her carefully made plans.

She knew she wouldn't be far behind—she'd sent enough smoldering looks from the stage throughout the night to light up a bonfire. Merritt quickly stripped down to her silk underwear, then went into the bedroom to light the candles. Lastly, she tossed the packet of rose petals over the bed before turning on the music. Haunting and beautiful, the love song softly shimmered in the air. Once she'd slipped on the lace negligée over her underwear, she took a seat in a lounge chair.

She didn't have long to wait.

A knock came a few minutes later. Austen was standing outside, still in her stage outfit and wearing a lopsided grin. With a long hum, Merritt threw her arms around her neck. "Hey, there."

"Hi, babe. I missed you." Her voice was rough with emotion, acute need resonating in her words.

Tamping down her arousal, Merritt brushed her lips gently over her mouth. "Come inside. We'll talk later…I really need to show you how much I've ached for you." She took Austen's hand and led her straight into the bedroom, deciding the champagne could wait. It had been too long since she'd touched her to delay a minute longer.

Austen's exclamation of delight when they entered the room made her heart skip a beat.

Merritt gently pushed her onto the edge of the bed. "Sit down," she murmured. "I'd like to give you a present." Standing with legs slightly apart in front of her, Merritt carefully spread open the negligée.

Austen stared up into her face for a moment, then ran her hands over the curves of her breasts and down the length of her stomach. "Beautiful," she whispered. She spread her hands over her bottom, pulled her closer and buried her face between her breasts. Then the bra was off and her thumbs stroking the nipples. Merritt moaned as a surge of arousal spread through her body.

With a supreme effort she stepped back, ignoring the heated protests from Austen. "Not yet, honey." She slipped off the robe and panties, standing proudly for Austen to peruse her bare body. Normally shy about nudity, she suffered no embarrassment now. She couldn't, not with the obvious admiration shining in Austen's eyes.

"You're lovely," whispered Austen, reaching over to fondle a breast.

"Umm…stop that. I'm turned on enough as it is. I'm going to undress you and then we're going to go to bed. It's going to be slow tonight. I want to show you just how much you mean to me. Now lie back and I'll take off your boots first."

Item by item she took off Austen's clothing, thoroughly caressing each newly bare part of her body. When she was finally naked, Merritt pointed to the top of the bed. "Now, up on the pillows and I'm going to give you some lovin'."

As she tenderly and thoroughly brought Austen to her climax, Merritt's emotions spilled over in a rush. She had no more reservations, no more doubts. This woman was her life. When Austen flopped back against her chest, spent, Merritt tightened her arms around her. "I love you, Austen. With my whole heart and soul. You're the best thing that's ever happened to me. I would never have survived the last weeks without the thought that you were home waiting for me."

Austen twisted in her arms until she was facing her. She ghosted her lips down her neck and across her collarbone. "I love you too, babe. I didn't know how much until you disappeared. You'd wormed your way so far into me it was if my skin had been ripped off inch by inch when they couldn't find you. I don't know why you want me, but I'm so fucking happy you do. I love being in your bed, just being with you."

Merritt idly ran her finger over her stomach. "I resigned this morning, and as of now I'm unemployed."

"What do you intend doing?" Austen asked quietly and seriously.

Merritt wasn't sure how to respond. She wanted to be in the same city as Austen, to be near her permanently to allow their romance to blossom into full bloom. But was that even possible? Austen spent most of her life on tour, and Merritt wasn't prepared to be casual. If they lived their life like ships passing in the night, it was inevitable they'd end up growing apart. Love and commitment meant a life together. She toyed with the sheet, wondering how she would phrase her reply. It was important to get her message across without forcing Austen to make a choice.

"I want to be somewhere near you, but only if you want it too."

"Of course, I do, babe. I thought I made that very clear. After this tour and the Las Vegas stint, I won't be going away much.

I've already had a talk with the boys, and they agree. Mick's the only one not in a relationship, and I know he wants to spend some time back in Ireland with his folks."

"I just want to be near you," Merritt said, brushing her hand across Austen's cheek. "I don't care where."

"Then live with me. I don't care where either."

Caught off guard, Merritt's mouth sagged open. "You mean it?"

Austen grinned. "I figure I'm getting the best end of the bargain. I'm gaining a cook as well as a hot lover."

"New York it is then."

Austen rolled over on top her with a whoop. "Is that a yes?"

Merritt smiled up at her. "That's a big fat Y.E.S."

"Good," said Austen, peppering her neck with kisses. "Now that's out of the way, I believe I have something to attend to. And I won't be stopping until you've screamed out my name at least five times."

Merritt lay back on the bed, her body readying for the wonderful onslaught.

Life with Austen was going to be a rollercoaster ride. And she was going to hang on for dear life and enjoy every minute of it.

Bella Books, Inc.

Women. Books. Even Better Together.

P.O. Box 10543
Tallahassee, FL 32302

Phone: 800-729-4992
www.bellabooks.com